ONE WEEK
IN A LIFETIME
OF LONDON

By

Gary Johnston Smith

Copyright © Gary Johnston Smith 2023
This book is sold subject to the condition that it shall not, by way of trade or otherwise, be lent, resold, hired out, or otherwise circulated without the publisher's prior consent in any form of binding or cover other than that in which it is published and without a similar condition including this condition being imposed on the subsequent publisher.
The moral right of Gary Johnston Smith has been asserted.

This is a work of creative nonfiction. While all the stories in this book are true, some names and identifying details have been changed to protect the privacy of the people involved.

*I would like to dedicate this book to my father, Ian John Wilson Smith,
who gave me some great advice over the years.
I just wish I'd acted on it earlier.*

CONTENTS

CHAPTER 1 *Seasoned Travellers*.. *1*
CHAPTER 2 *Work Hard, Play Hard* *9*
CHAPTER 3 *Weekends in London* *23*
CHAPTER 4 *Towers and Seesaws, Social Highs and Lows*........................ *37*
CHAPTER 5 *Fond Farewells*.. *51*
CHAPTER 6 *All Systems Going Reliably to Fuerte*.................................... *68*
CHAPTER 7 *Lift a pebble off the beach and change the face of the world* *73*
CHAPTER 8 *Happy Daze* *79*
CHAPTER 9 *All planned up and ready to go*.. *87*
CHAPTER 10 *Two tickets going 2,000 miles north, please* *92*
CHAPTER 11 *Happily arriving back in time* *100*
CHAPTER 12 *For we have dined on honeydew*.. *109*
CHAPTER 13 *Le Meridien (now the Dilly)*.. *116*
CHAPTER 14 *Big Thursday* *123*
CHAPTER 15 *Hampstead, here we come* *137*
CHAPTER 16 *Quickly travelling the long road home* *156*
CHAPTER 17 *Theatre Nights*.. *164*
CHAPTER 18 *Shopaholics' Paradise* *171*
CHAPTER 19 *Welcome to the BBC* *180*
CHAPTER 20 *Dilly-dallying on a sunny day* *188*
CHAPTER 21 *Camden Market Revisited*... *202*
CHAPTER 22 *Fine Dining and Epicureanism* *207*
CHAPTER 23 *Leaving on a Jet Plane* *224*
ABOUT THE AUTHOR *228*

CHAPTER 1

SEASONED TRAVELLERS

Okay, where do I start? Now it's not as if there's been things written or said about London that you've never heard before. This still-growing vast metropolis that has something like over fifteen million inhabitants, is a collection of little villages that have all joined together and grown up to become the largest city in England. At its busiest it fires into a fast-moving, vibrant place with people charging from A to B with no time to spare. Of course, not all of London is like that, it does have some quiet leafy enclaves hidden around in some of its more affluent areas, which allow the wealthy people to float around at a more leisurely pace. These are places where England's green and pleasant lands have been protected for posterity, not an easy task where money-fuelled investors grab up all they can for their expansive developments. So where am I going with this, you now begin to ask? Well, let me get started and I'll try to explain what I'm talking about.

I've been living and working for nearly twenty-five years on a beautiful island called Fuerteventura. This gorgeous place is situated only sixty miles from the coast of Africa, a very dry, rocky, mountainous place yet along the surrounding coastline we have some of the most beautiful beaches in the world.

Leading a simple life as a madcap lively entertainer, my job was to communicate with and entertain lots of happy holidaying guests seeking fun or just maybe relaxation. A task made much easier by the sun and warmth that would greet these people on a daily basis. Our hotel was a popular destination, very basic but we were lucky enough to build up a good number of repeat guests who would visit every year, almost treating it like a second home, which gave the hotel a very friendly and happy, infectious atmosphere. With the same faces coming through the door on a regular basis many friendships would develop between our long-serving members of staff and our loyal guests, who'd now fallen in love with this wonderful island of ours. Eventually it would become one big happy family and a fantastic environment to work in.

Most of our guests would arrive from the UK, which made life much easier as my capability for learning and picking up new languages was embarrassingly bad. My memory retention was terrible, not helped by my lack of focus. Oh, don't get me wrong, I could talk the back legs off a donkey, but it was listening that seemed to be the difficult part. On the upside, throw me into a big group of people and it all seemed to balance out. I was luckily well suited for my job.

Now there were a lot of repeat guests who would travel to our hotel from London, which was great, as I always loved talking about London. In fact I'd become super excited just being able to talk about London. You see, from 2009 to 2015 Nicky, my wonderful partner, and I would spend a no-expense-spared week there, living it up, eating in the finest of restaurants and always making sure we booked the best seats in the house when going to some of London's fabulous theatres, and most importantly making sure we stayed in a hotel that was in the perfect location.

Yes, these holidays were just the best, so once I got started talking about it, I'd almost explode with excitement trying to relive every moment. Now for the guests standing in front of me this was probably not as interesting to them as it was to me, and even though my impassioned stories were coming out thick and fast I could see that distance beginning grow in their eyes. That's the problem with my ADHD, once I was off and running, I just couldn't stop myself even though I was very aware that I was doing it. At times it allowed me to talk about five different subjects all at once while holding separate conversations with twenty different people, invariably leading to people saying things like, "Geez, where do you get your energy from? I wouldn't mind some of what you've been taking!"

As I rampaged through my stories at pace the recipients at first seemed impressed with my knowledge of London, especially as I knew where all the great landmarks were with almost A-to-Z precision, but again I could see it in their eyes, they would be thinking, *Is he being serious?* They knew I was one for instigating incredible wind-ups and their defences would slowly go up. I understood from their point of view also that people who live and work in London often struggle to work up the excitement of living there. Yes, there are the theatres that they might occasionally visit, the landmarks they pass by hurriedly whilst rushing to get where they need to be, and let's not forget the international tourists who float around aimlessly, clogging up the streets and getting in the way of people who are busily going about their business.

Living and working in London is certainly not for the faint hearted. How did I know this? Because I had been there. I, too, had been part of the mad rat race, rushing from place to place, working in the heart of London. I don't mean to make it sound harsh, but the reality is that people don't have much time for others when they're on that human conveyor belt they call rush hour. Everyone jostling on and off buses, using your elbows to dig your way in and out of packed tubes, that stone-cold look on everyone's faces while inside lies a burning determination not to lose time as you battle your way to your destination.

I'm reminded of one time in particular; I was working in the advertising department of a computer publication on Gray's Inn Road. One of the girls who was always very punctual with her timekeeping hadn't turned up one morning. Me and the other members of staff were asking each other if we knew the whereabouts of our colleague as it was unusual that she hadn't arrived at her desk. Some speculated she may have had a late evening the night before, or had possibly been visiting a client or agency this morning… when suddenly, she came bursting into the office, slightly dishevelled and not looking very happy. In fact she was obviously quite angry and not in her usually chirpy mood. Before anyone could ask her what was wrong, she slammed her briefcase hard down onto her desk and sternly said in a rasping voice through clenched teeth, "Some selfish bastard decided to throw themselves onto the tube line this morning!"

Some of the people in close proximity laughed at her strange entrance and expletives, then one of the other girls stepped in to try and calm the situation down by assuring her, "Not to worry, you're here now." And just to make her feel a little better after her horrendous ordeal, the girl then asked her, "Would you like a coffee!?"

"Yes please," she replied, and that was it, not another word said.

I quite liked that girl. She was always smiling, very pleasant and I couldn't imagine there was a bad bone in her body. But for the rest of that day I'd glance over, wondering how wrongly I'd possibly judged her. No words of pity for this poor person who'd been so low they'd thrown themselves to certain death.

Now this might all sound rather harsh but that's rush-hour London, and everyone gets sucked into this way of travelling. Imagine they made it law that you must say good morning to everyone you pass on your way to work, it would be fantastic. Could you imagine the humdrum of noise it would cause? Okay, admittedly that's probably a ridiculous idea. But, again, while travelling on the tube its very noticeable that no one ever acknowledges anyone as they sit possibly fidgeting with their poorly printed rail line ticket, doing their best to not look anyone in the eye. I mean, God forbid you might. Whenever their eyes do meet, they quickly avert them to the tube map directly above their heads or start reading the passenger warning signs, or even the cleverly placed adverts, the same ones you've probably read a hundred times every journey. Of course there are the more seasoned travellers who have been using these lines for years; some of them have even managed to fold their broadsheet newspapers in such a way that it doesn't take up too much space, or keep a small book in their pocket that can be pulled out at any time, giving added security, knowing they'll never have to worry about making the dreaded eye contact with a fellow passenger.

There's another type of tube traveller out there called the speed merchant; nothing gets in their way as they glide through these stations with the greatest of ease, no matter how busy the journey is. They know when getting into that tube they must not move into the carriage. They always make sure they stay close to the door. It's also important for them to make sure they get on the right carriage, so when the train stops, they're getting out at the closest point to the stairwells. Whereas the less seasoned traveller is only just pulling himself from his seat as the speed merchant is already sprinting athletically up the fast lane on the escalator. The slow coaches who are left in their wake have no chance of getting anywhere fast, as they're relegated to leaving from the middle of the carriage and left to jostle through the oncoming travellers as they want to quickly grab your freshly warm vacated seat.

I'm not meaning to make this sound like hell on earth, I'm only trying to enlighten people to the skills you may need to learn if you're about become a frequent traveller in the great city of London, and might have to endure the madness of rush hour. Another important point to make is that I wasn't some innocent bystander, someone there just to observe the life and times of a tube traveller, nope, I was right in the thick of it. I, too, would jump between casual traveller and an expert-level speed merchant.

My realisation of this was made quite apparent to me while travelling on a tube during my day off one Saturday morning. My first accommodation in London was a shared house in a street named

Gladsmuir Road just north of Archway. This was a lovely street, which in fact wasn't too far away from the beautiful residential area of Highgate. The houses on Gladsmuir Road were large, three-storey, red-brick buildings just far enough away from the A1, which could get very busy at times with heavy traffic, but the streets were lined with lovely old oak trees that I'm sure helped suck up the noise from the nearby dual carriageway. Being only five miles from the centre of London we would always use the Archway tube station. In those days back in the very late 80s we would have our weekly ticket, which we showed to the ticket inspectors just before making our way down the escalator. This was a fairly lengthy downward journey into the bowels of the Northern Line, the deepest of all the tube lines. As you made your way down the escalator not only would you hear the loud rumbling noise of the tubes pulling in and out of the platforms, but you would feel the drafts almost like a wind being pushed through the station and up the escalators, always slightly warm, which could be a bonus if it had been really cold outside on street level.

Anyway, like I said, it was Saturday morning and I was a casual traveller this day. I was able to grab a seat in the middle of the carriage. I remember feeling relaxed and happy and looking forward to my day down in central London. Noticeably it wasn't too busy, and for a change there were plenty of places to sit. It made a nice change looking up and down the train seeing so much space; you could even smell the dry, dusty odour that probably came from the well-used seats. The floors and seats had that well-worn look about them; these things were never noticeable at peak hour as everything was hidden or covered up by the many commuters filling trains on a regular basis.

With less passengers than usual the noises from the train seemed to eerily howl and scream around the old creaking carriages, and as the pace picked up, it felt like we were racing through the very dark tunnels and I could feel the old, empty carriages rocking from side to side as the noise inside grew even louder. It felt like some out-of-control ghost train with its heavy steel wheels shunting across the tracks. Still faster and faster, with new screeching sounds adding to the din, it felt like we could be getting up to speeds of a hundred miles an hour. I was thinking, would this old train even hold together as we were hurtling into the bowels of hell…? Then things began to slow down, the well-lit station of Tufnell Park appeared outside the windows and the noise, the speed dissipated, and I could see more customers preparing to board. Realistically in those days the carriages were rather old and noisy but on average most tubes only travel at about twenty miles an hour, and the fastest they even get on the Northern Line is about forty-five, but for that moment, it was fun letting my imagination run away with itself.

As we passed through the many stations, we began to pick up more customers, though again being a Saturday, things did seem to be a bit more relaxed, people were certainly getting on and off in a more laid-back fashion. Me, I was heading to Leicester Square, so I still had to pass through Kentish Town, Camden, Mornington Crescent, Euston, King's Cross, Warren Street, and Goodge Street. Once we got to King's Cross I noticed we had picked up quite a lot of passengers on the way. But what really grabbed my attention were the two couples who had obviously come down from Scotland, and going by their accents I could tell they were certainly from the Edinburgh area. They sounded happy as they cracked silly jokes, probably just excited. From what I and the rest of the carriage could hear they were down for the weekend. Although louder than your usual daily traveller they sounded nice enough, probably not really noticing that everything they were talking about could be heard by everyone on the carriage. It wasn't till they started to look up and down the now-busier carriages that they could see there were lots of people slightly crammed up together, no one smiling, and certainly none of them communicating. They began to wonder why everyone looked so stern faced.

One of the girls jokingly remarked, "Maybe the Queen's died or something." They all laughed out loud.

"Naww, I would have seen it in the paper this morning."

His friend quickly jumped in with, "Ha, great, you can read now!"

Again they all started to laugh. I was sitting looking at all these stern faces thinking, *Brilliant, you tell them. I'm glad I'm not the only one that's noticed this.* And then just at that, the penny dropped. Wait a minute, I was one of them! Although inside I was bursting with joy at my fellow Scots revealing to everyone in the carriage that we were acting like inanimate zombies, it finally dawned on me that I was doing exactly the same thing. Not an ounce of emotion on my face as I listened intently, but stared up to that well-read tube map. What had happened to me?

CHAPTER 2

WORK HARD, PLAY HARD

Okay, so I may have been less than cordial about myself and all my previous tube-travelling companions. I'd even gone as far as to call everyone stern-faced, inanimate zombies. This was obviously not true, maybe I was being a little cruel, and remember, in my defence it was only an observation. Of course, they were human beings, so I knew that underneath the cold, hard-looking exterior, they were caring, warm-hearted souls, probably very conscientious and hard-working. These were people from all different backgrounds, people from not just all over the UK but all over the world, a mixture of all different age groups with different professions, such as expensive-suited financiers, models, investment bankers, designers, advertising executives, actors on their way to one of the many theatres, local government officials, civil servants, project managers, computer programmers, hairdressers, hoteliers, artists, graphic designers, curators, dancers, architects, lots of people who worked in many of the big-name retail stores in places like Oxford Street, and I've probably missed out lots more. These people were all just trying to get on with their lives, people whose only mission while travelling was to get to their preferred destination without any hindrance. All thrown together in this fast-paced city of London, all cramped together in this oversized tin can, trundling along deep underground. This was something they had to do out of necessity, and being crammed up together, the last thing on their minds was to strike up a conversation with a complete stranger.

Yes, everyone was aware of everyone else, but experienced tube travellers know there's an unwritten code. Do not acknowledge anyone at all on your journey at any time, these are the rules. Oh, they can spot a first-time tube traveller or someone who doesn't travel by tube very often quite easily. This is made obvious by their dithering between platforms, looking around aimlessly, lost. That helpless look in their eyes, just hoping someone will pointing them in the right direction. But sadly, no, it's not going to happen. Everyone knows you've got to learn the hard way, and quick. Okay, if they were sitting on the tube making a plea out loud, hoping someone might take kindly to their predicament, and if it was all being done in a pleasant manner with that sound of desperation in their voice, someone might take pity and quietly point them in the right direction.

It's just the way it's got to be. Everyone must keep moving, there's no room for sentimentality or dilly-dallying. The underground plays such an important role in the transportation of people in and out of London and everyone that uses it regularly plays their part. Again, once you get used to using the tube and begin to understand the unwritten rules of the system, it becomes easier jumping from tube to tube, crossing all the different platforms and escalators till eventually you become a qualified exponent of the rat race. And just to give you something else to think about, Mondays to Fridays they can have as many as two million people using the tube lines daily. That's a hell of a lot of people and a very big job indeed for London Transport, who just to run these services seven days a week employ nearly 8,000 people.

As you get to street level and start to leave the tube station the first thing that hits you is the change of air and depending on where you are, even the change of smells. The noises of the traffic, the sounds of impatience as drivers frantically push their horns, even the traffic crossings with their continual repetitive beeps letting people know when to cross the road. The speed merchants become a bit more noticeable here; they show no regard to the lights as they cross when they see fit, dodging through the traffic and crowds in their unstoppable fashion. The roads are full of buses, taxis, vans, cars, larger freight lorries loaded with deliveries for the department stores, and the self-proclaimed kings of the roads, the bike couriers. Whether it be motorbikes or cycles they practically live for this, every day a challenge that fills them with excitement, the modern-day urban cowboys just like the great pony express before them who would race across the dusty Wild West. Even people who are just commuting back and forth from work get sucked into this great race, but like the speed merchants travelling on foot, nothing gets in the way of the courier kings.

In the 80s and 90s they played such a crucial part in making sure copy could get from graphic designer to printers, printed documents were quickly delivered to publishers, and last-minute negotiations by high-powered advertising agents would see copy needing to be rushed through as deadlines had to be met. This would create a flurry of activity. That all-important phone call would be made to the heroes of the day, the bike courier. Like the well-trained and knowledgeable taxi drivers they, too, knew the streets of London, but these fearless bikers could steal time by taking advantage of the small streets and alleyways that these old black taxis couldn't. I always remember thinking back in those days, when you heard that familiar sound of the police siren echoing in the distance, *Oh, dear. I bet it's one of those bike couriers come a cropper*, but it's actually quite surprising how rare accidents involving couriers were. Sadly, of course, it did happen, but the numbers are surprisingly low considering the number of dangerous journeys they made on a daily basis, and I'm sure it wasn't for great amounts of money either.

Now as I'm waxing lyrically here and showing great admiration for these legends of the road, not everyone felt the same. The bus drivers, taxi drivers and other regular users of the busy roads of central London had a completely different opinion and could often be heard screaming out of their windows as they suffered a heart-stopping moment. These daredevil riders would cut across their line of travel, heads down and cycling like maniacs. Just as the drivers adjusted their feet to the clutch and brakes in a frantic moment of panic, their two-wheeled adversary would be gone, they would just see the back of the rider cutting in between the traffic ahead of them. The drivers could only hope that the last-ditch scream out of the window might at least prick the conscience of that daredevil on wheels. Oh, I'm sure the courier could hear them, but it was head down, there was a job to be done, they couldn't let their regular trusting clients down and anyway, the screaming drivers were all part and parcel of the rigours of life on the road.

Maybe the frustrated motorists of these London streets would have the last laugh as technological improvements regarding email and printing techniques severely reduced the number of couriers needed. Although still around to this day their numbers have dwindled. Again, like their fellow riders from the pony express, their history and past is now a thing of folklore.

Okay, I must admit I used to cycle through the streets of London myself during the very late 80s. Yup, all the way from Archway down to my job at Tower Records in Piccadilly, so I can sympathise and relate to all those brave cyclists. It wasn't just the couriers who would fly along the roads, heads down, pushing hard on the pedals, no. London had another 50,000 regular cyclists travelling backwards and forwards to work in those days. It was certainly okay in the lovely long summer days but far more challenging once the cold winds and wet winters kicked into play, and as you can imagine it made the journey far more precarious.

When you first start to try and cycle the streets of London, I would certainly advise getting used to some of the quiet streets, then slowly begin to dip your toe into the busier traffic. In honesty, if you're confident enough to consider progressing into the madness of rush hour you'll be fine. It won't take long before you'll be shifting along at pace with the flow of the traffic. Before you know it, you'll be checking your watch and setting yourself little challenges and exchanging little nods with some of the other daredevils out there.

Being someone who'd grown up with pushbikes, it didn't take me long before I was racing through the traffic. I was young, carefree, and enjoyed my daily adventures charging up and down the busy streets. There were even times I would hold on to the passing traffic and let it pull me along. Looking back, I realise how foolishly dangerous this was, but it seemed really easy back in the day. There were still the old London buses, so I'd grab a lift by holding on to the well-placed bar at the entrance, well, at least until I was chased off by the conductor. Yup, getting on and off the old buses was so much easier, as the entrance was much wider. No waiting to pay the driver, just quickly try to grab a seat and wait on the conductor or conductress coming to you. The young and the smokers would always make their way upstairs, as some of the more elderly would feel safer downstairs, but there was always that bar that could be grabbed hold of as you were getting on and off. It was just in an ideal position. I'd grab hold of it and let the bus pull me along through the traffic. Looking back, I'm so glad I didn't end up as another traffic accident statistic.

The busy streets of the West End are full of different types of people from all walks of life. Of course the West End has a vibrancy that is fuelled by theatres and the luxurious five-star hotels with their well-dressed doormen. Adding to this is an array of different restaurants serving up cuisine from all over world, and lots of small offices tucked away hidden around Soho filled with publishers, agencies, artists, dance studios, sex shops, and high-end retailers. And of course, last but not least, the many tourists who tend to float around at a much more relaxed pace. They can be seen standing on the corners of the busy streets, maps in hand, looking left and right but never sure which direction to go in.

Of course, not all of London is the same; the atmosphere can be completely different depending on which part of the city you're in. For instance, I remember travelling on the tube from King's Cross to Liverpool Street. It was during rush hour – the carriages were mostly full of men wearing expensive suits. Most were quite happy to stand, it was different from the other tube lines. A lot of people were in groups; they all seemed to know each other, chatting, laughing, even shouting a little, a mixture of young to middle aged, but mostly men. They all seemed very sure of themselves, you could tell by the way they stood, chests out, sometimes stretching their arms out so their jackets would pull out of the way and they could check their top-of-the-range watches. Sometimes even revealing the shiny cuff links inscribed with some motif like a badge of honour. Yes, you could tell most of these guys were city boys. The girls would not be outdone either, confidently laughing along with them and not shy at cracking their own little in-house jokes.

These were all ABC1s. Well, I'm sure that's how the NRS (National Readership Survey) would socially grade them, especially when a lot of them carried newspapers such as the *Financial Times*. Their outgoing demeanour would suggest they had been traders or stockbrokers readying themselves for another day in the bear pit of the fast-moving financial services industry. And although their pre-match bravado appeared a bit ostentatious, maybe they could be forgiven, as it certainly wasn't a place for the faint hearted, so there was a need for these warriors to show that they were strong willed and ready to do battle. You could see the older, more experienced guys sitting back and just watching with that knowing smile. They'd been here before, they were obviously quietly confident in their own abilities so they'd leave the young cubs to carry on with the frivolities. This was all character building and this new, assured confidence would give them the strength to go out and do well, and let's be honest, their success was putting a great deal of money in their bosses' pockets. Not only did they look the part, but they were full to the brim with positive mental attitude and sales adages to fend off any unnecessary doubts. Although they all knew in the back of their minds that in these jobs every day was possibly the biggest of their lives. This might sound a little overdramatic, but in that dog-eat-dog environment there is a very fine line between being on top of the world and that poor lost soul that throws themselves onto the tube line.

Now of course there's lots of positions in the city that are a bit slower burning and not so fast paced, but companies were dealing with extremely large investments and targets had to be met, so everyone would feel some sort of pressure, just some more than others. It's difficult to talk about how much money and commodities are traded on a daily basis but it's worth remembering that London contributes something like just over 20% to the total of the UK's GDP, so these people running the city can't be taken lightly. I always felt it was like some big gambling house, an extremely large bookies where all these people were in there betting with lots of other people's money; the addictive highs and lows of winning and losing. It makes you wonder if there are medical practitioners or psychologists having to deal with all these people who might actually have a serious gambling addiction.

Yes, once you came out of Liverpool Street Station there would be a lesser number of tourists on the streets here. The ones you did see were possibly walking from the worldly famous Saint Paul's Cathedral to the architecturally beautiful, mosaicked Leadenhall Market. This part of London is steeped in history and the location at Leadenhall has been a marketplace ever since the 14th century. But generally, most of the people you see around the financial district are centred around one thing – the financial services. The city is home to most of the largest banks in the world, even the coffee shops and restaurants would be full of eagle-eyed investors celebrating or deliberating the day's acquisitions. It's not a friendly place, it can feel slightly cold and aggressive, you can almost smell and feel the tension or maybe even the testosterone that fills the air, as people hustle and bustle back and forth juggling with their coffees, newspapers, and briefcases. Some of these busy people might stop off to make use of the few shoeshines dotted around, things you might have felt had been left back in a bygone age.

Again, I must point out that these people are driven by targets; it's their job to maximise profit at every turn. In some cases things move so fast they don't even get time to realise the pressure they're under. So as soon as the day is done it's quite normal to release all that tension by going to their regular pub or wine bar and in any case, it's always an excuse to miss the rush hour. This is easier for the young and single, they have less responsibilities, but hey, if it's been a good day there's no way anyone should miss out on a little celebration.

Whenever anyone made plans to do something on an evening in London it was always straight after work, whether meeting up with friends to go and see a show or going for a meal, even just meeting up for a drink, it was always straight from work. Nobody had the time to fight through the busy crowds in rush hour, possibly two tubes, then walk back to your house or accommodation, get showered then back down into London, there just wasn't the time. People would always just go straight from work, even people playing sport or going to the gym after work would have a sports bag with them; it was just the way, it was the London lifestyle.

I had experienced this myself while working in display advertising for *The Observer* on Chelsea Bridge Road. Most nights it would be a case of finish work, then a brisk walk across the Chelsea Bridge then up to the Rose and Crown pub not far from Sloane Square. Of course, we didn't have the pressures of these financial wizards in the city, but still, we had deadlines to meet so it was good to get things across the finish line. In those days most of us smoked which at the time was still allowed inside in the pubs. So, we'd laugh and giggle our way through the evening.

The hardcore group of us were there most nights, about five guys and two girls, and at that time most of us were drinking Guinness. As soon as all the frivolities were finished it was just a short dash to the Sloane Square tube station. The first tube would just be a few bumpy stops along to the embankment and then an escalator a little deeper down to get me onto the Northern Line, and from there all the way up to Archway.

Now at that time of evening after a long day chasing up business down the phone and maybe a little worse for wear after drinking a few pints of Guinness, you had to be very careful not to nod off during the journey. I was lucky it never actually happened to me, although at that time of night there were always lots of people like me in the same predicament. You would see these weary travellers slumped in their seats, and of course with it being London, you'd never dare wake someone up, it just wasn't the done thing. Every now and again you'd see your fellow traveller awaken from their slumbers, they'd look around in that dazed fashion, give themselves a shake, then try to work out where they were. They'd do the usual and have a quick glance up to the tube line map, which really didn't mean anything till it pulled into the next station, then they could begin to work out where the hell they were. If they'd missed their stop, as soon as the tube stopped, they would usually frantically pull themselves together and make an incoherent mad dash out onto the platform, then hurriedly cross to the other platform and get themselves going in the right direction again. At the same time, you would nonchalantly sit there like you hadn't noticed your fellow traveller's plight, still trying to keep that well-practised tube line poker face, pondering the question to yourself, *Should I have tried to awaken him earlier...?* No, rules were rules, no physical or eye contact with any fellow passengers at any time.

As the tube reached my stop, which was Archway, I'd be out of my seat and off the train, onto that long escalator up to the station entrance where that cool air hit you as you made your way out onto the street. It was still another five minutes' walk before I would finally make it to my digs. Thankfully, it was a really nice street I lived on at the time, so I always felt safe travelling home at night. In fact, to be honest, in those days, I don't know if it was just because I was young and gallus, but I always felt safe wherever I was in London.

After getting back to the bedsit there was a feeling of relief. Now it was a case of taking every last shortcut you could to finally get yourself into that bed, because you were feeling so knackered your jaw would literally be hanging from the rest of your head as you threw clothes off in no uncertain fashion. There was no time for folding things properly and putting them neatly away, nope. The good thing about dropping everything as you took it off, it made things so much easier to find in the mornings. Okay maybe when I was wearing suits, I'd always make the point of hanging them up, but in general most of my belongings could be found somewhere on the floor.

Once you managed to climb, or more realistically collapse into bed, you would let out a massive sigh of relief and that was it, out like a light. No time to lie back and think about the day, all these thoughts disappear into your neocortex as the rest of the brain decides to switch the lights out…

Ping, all of a sudden, it's morning again. The light is shining in the window.

Sometimes you may find that your brain managed to switch the lights out in your head, but not always in the room. Yup, it wouldn't be the first time the light was still on from the night before. This was the least of your problems, as you were in a mad rush to try and do everything at once; get washed, get dressed, brush your teeth, and possibly quickly iron a shirt for work. Okay, I'm not proud of this, but has anyone else ever found themselves standing in the shower brushing their teeth, then realising the first thing you did was put a shirt on?

Anyway, the point I'm trying to make here is that more times than not, a night's sleep just seemed to disappear and there was no time to ask myself where it had gone. And when time wasn't really on your side, sometimes decisions had to be made as to whether the shirt really needed ironing or not. Sometimes I'd take one look at the shirt and say to myself, "Ah well, as long as I keep my jacket on nobody will notice as long as it's clean."

Now I don't mean to embarrass anyone here but I'm sure there will be a few people reading this thinking, *Wow, I used to do the same thing*, and as my other friends who were maybe not so good with ironing will remember, once you have the shirt on your warm body for a while the creases begin to drop out.

This, for me, was living in London's fast lane; a normal day very regularly was just non-stop, from the minute you got up till the moment your head hit the pillow. Now I was a single guy at the time, so my responsibilities were far and few between, there was only me I had to look after or think about. But it can be a little tougher for someone trying to hold down a relationship and even harder for the many people who have the responsibility of trying to bring up a family. From the minute you wake up it's just one mad dash, and even if you're travelling straight home after work, by the time you eventually get to your front door the evening's already nearly over. Let's not forget, working and travelling in London every day is energy sapping in itself, never mind having to get home and fulfil all your parental duties. It's not like you can just put your feet up and switch the box on.

Just to drop another little fact in here, a lot of TV presenters and soap stars are less well known in London than they are in the rest of the UK, all because there's so many people still travelling during peak TV hours.

Living close to central London was something that could only be afforded by the very rich. Even renting was a costly business, never mind thinking about buying property, as the prices were astronomical. To live in London comfortably you had to be in a very high wage bracket, so the vast majority of people had no other option, they just had to make that very crowded journey and become part of the rat race, or a kinder way of putting it would be the vast commuter exodus in and out of central London.

Another good point here is that most of the people (and I suppose this could be said of many places) would spend more time with their work colleagues than they did with members of their own families. It could even be said you could talk about things freely that you might never talk about with your own partners. There's no commitments demanded from these friendships. It was easy to see how in these busy cities people could grow apart. They could have nothing to relate to, their conversations were limited to a few hours late in the evening when everyone was shattered after a busy day. And let's not forget this was before everyone had the latest up-to-date mobile phones where people can video chat and declare love for each other at the press of a button.

Now I apologise once again if I'm painting some terrible dystopian picture of London, which I suppose is a little unfair. Of course lots of people enjoyed themselves and I'm sure the saying 'work hard, play hard' was probably invented in England's capital city. And there was certainly no shortage of places to go if it was your desire to 'play hard'.

Personally, I wasn't a sort of clubby person. I was young, lively, always jumping around, but in those days, I didn't mind noisy pubs or going to see bands I liked. I think that was the rub. Even though I had short hair and was dressed in a suit my mind would still hark back to the days of loud music, denims and long hair, although I did have my moments. Any time we did end up in clubs was usually a last-minute decision, so our entourage and I had probably had a few beers and if I remember rightly, I think I was just going with flow. Thinking back, most of the clubs' names I can't remember, or the locations, just the loud music, and dancing around with flashing lights to songs I was very unfamiliar with. Every now and again I would escape to the bar and guzzle more very expensive beer. Then when it eventually was time to leave the club, I probably looked like I had been dragged through a hedge backwards.

If you were lucky and you hadn't been separated from all your cash, you could possibly hail a taxi. But failing that it would be a mad dash to get to the top of Trafalgar Square where around 2 o'clock you could catch the night bus with all the other late-night revellers. My faded memories are of people leaning against things that might help them stay upright. The rest who were more awake would be gathered in small groups still giggling or laughing and possibly finishing off some late takeaway food.

Thankfully the night bus wasn't something you did every night. I mean, going out until the early hours of the morning then working all day would just be impossible, but it's something we would do every now and again.

Being on your own on the night bus was a dangerous thing. I mean, you were quite safe but there was always the risk you might fall asleep. On your own there's no one to talk to, which can help keep you aware and awake, and yes, I did it once. I remember being wakened by the driver who said to me, something along the lines of, "Right, that's as far as I go."

I vaguely remember not knowing where the hell I was as I squinted and peered through the windows. I quickly replied to the driver in a mild panic, "How far are we from Archway?"

But as he shuffled away from me, he replied, "I'm sorry, we passed that a little while back."

I wasn't happy as I dragged myself off my seat and made my way off the bus. I think I was in North Finchley. It was cold and I was extremely tired; all I could do was get my head down and get on with marching down the road in a rather disgruntled fashion. I was only five minutes into my journey when I spotted the same bus and driver going in my direction and he just drove right past me. I couldn't believe it; he heard me ask how far I was from Archway and I'm sure the bus depot there would be his final destination. I thought he might have taken pity on me and said, "Ahh, just stay where you are, I'm going back in that direction," but no, not him. I was fuming in a sort of still drunk, half asleep sort of way, as I stumbled angrily in the direction of home.

I would eventually get home to find I had even less time to grab some sleep before the whole process of getting up and rushing to work started all over again. Impetuous youth had a lot to answer for. These sporadic bouts of poor decision making late at night really didn't help make my daytimes any easier. If only in the pub I could've stopped and said, "What, going to a club now? Sorry, but I think I've had enough to drink and I've got another busy day tomorrow so if you don't mind, I'll just catch the late tube and go straight home." But I was too weak willed and stupid to say something as sensible as that. There's an old saying back home. You shouldn't drink on an empty head.

CHAPTER 3

WEEKENDS IN LONDON

Yes, having late nights and a busy job to go to in the morning was not a unique experience. Lots of people were doing it. And let's be honest, it's called living. The important thing was to find a balance, some way of recharging the batteries.

One club visitation I'll never forget was organised by my good friend Ian Myles. When he first told me about it, I was rather hesitant. It sounded way out of my comfort zone. I'll be honest and I'm not proud of it, but if you caught sight of me on a dance floor it was usually alcohol fuelled. The fires of this bravado were lit by the consumption of a little Dutch courage. As I may have pointed out earlier, I was certainly a lively character but wasn't inspired to dance to the latest tunes. It just wasn't my thing, as they say. So, when Ian came a-calling with his great idea of visiting this fantastic place, you can understand my apprehension.

Ian was a very happy, positive person. A very 'the glass is half full' kind of guy. Ian was a successful, hard-working industrial designer but like me, he liked to enjoy himself. He was of sharp wit and had a cracking sense of humour. I remember one time there were a few of us having a pint in a small pub called the Tottenham on the end of Oxford Street, just on the corner of Tottenham Court Road. The streets were very narrow in those days and as you can imagine, it got very busy, especially when rush hour began to pick up. It wasn't just the busy traffic that was starting to build up, there were obviously lots of people flowing down into the Tottenham Court tube station. For the amount of people out on the street, the pub was surprisingly quiet inside, so it was a fairly comfortable situation for us all. Most of us had travelled from our work to rendezvous at this one little pub. Now, we were certainly not there because of the décor, or the very friendly service, it was just a handy location, based right next to the tube station where once the night was finished it was an easy journey home. That suited all of us.

On this occasion Ian had cycled there and managed to lock his bike to a fence out on the busy street. At the time I was still working down at *The Observer*, which was then based down at Chelsea Bridge Road. I had caught a tube from Sloane Square to the Embankment then straight up to Tottenham Court Station, so it certainly suited me come the end of the evening. It was a fairly straightforward journey all the way up to Archway.

If my memory serves me well, about four of us had managed to gather first, with Ian arriving last which made it five. It didn't take long for the evening to get going with everyone laughing and cracking jokes, so everyone was in their usual high spirits when Ian decided to call it a day. Most of us were disappointed he was going, as Ian would be central to most of the joke cracking or nonsensical behaviour. But quite sensibly Ian knew he still had another five miles to cycle before he got home, and it wasn't as if he was travelling through quiet leafy streets, he was right in the heart of London.

As we bid our farewells and the last shouts of where and with whom we would be meeting up again faded, the rest of us settled down to discuss whose round it was next. All of a sudden Ian came bursting back through the door again, shouting, "Okay, get me another pint!" He stopped, looked around the pub, held his bike seat aloft and shouted, "Is there anyone wants to buy a bike seat?" We all immediately burst out laughing, as did most of the other people that had managed to grasp why he'd shouted out to everyone in the pub. Yup, sadly his bike had been stolen. He had secured it with a D-lock and brought the seat in with him as it had a small bag which was fixed to the post, but he was realistic enough to know that by the time he'd filled out a police report the bike would be long gone. Talking about it later after all the hilarity had died down, Ian was philosophical enough to understand that people would've seen it being stolen and were probably thinking to themselves, *Oh my goodness, look at that, people stealing a bike in broad daylight.* But that's it, nobody would intervene; I mean, why would you? So, it was just a shrug of the shoulders and on with evening, that's the kind of guy Ian was. It wasn't the end of the world, he'd say.

So, when he was enthusiastically telling me about this club called the Metropolitan, I knew there must be something special about it. His exact words were, "Trust me, you'll love it." I didn't really need much convincing especially as 'no' was never a regular word in my vocabulary. It wasn't the easiest place to get to and it certainly wasn't in the prettiest of places. The streets were dark and dingy. But as we got closer to the club, we could see lots of people gathered and lots more queuing outside this old building. It looked like it had been an old factory in its heyday; nothing about it said it was a club. Mind you, lots of places were like that in London. Strange old buildings with small doors, then once you got inside they were like the Tardis from Doctor Who. On the outside they seemed small and lifeless, but once you got in the door they took on new dimensions. Light, sound, darkness, and lots of very lively people. This is very much what it was like on getting into the Metropolitan.

I felt wrongly dressed for the place when I first got in. My suit was a grainy, light bluey grey in colour and to top that off, I was wearing a sort of black pork pie hat that had seen better days. Regardless of my ill-fitting attire, it didn't take me long to settle in. The place was very earthy, urban even, although I don't think that term or description was used in those days, and it was bloody massive. The place took over three floors. Two of the floors were loud and played Afro-Caribbean music while the other was Latin, South American salsa.

The atmosphere was just fantastic, it was full of energy and fire. Yes, we were literally jumping between floors. I found the Latin salsa bar a little easier for slight feeling of relaxation if you were wanting to enjoy your drink.

Now for someone who wasn't big on dancing, never mind actually dancing to Afro-Caribbean music, I was enjoying it so much that I spent ages on the dance floor. The music was loud and fast, lots of bass and heavy drums but still lively, rhythmic and upbeat. It seemed to have everything your body needed to dance.

As we left the club we were exhilarated, really excited after a great night's fun. While in there, we hardly even spoke to each other, so we had lots of things to talk about. Mind you, God knows what I looked like at the end of it all. My only regret was that I'd never gone back there, that I'd actually only gone the once. Even on the Saturday morning, although my legs were a bit sore, and my ears were still buzzing, I had that very satisfied feeling. I'd had a great night.

While I was working as an advertising salesperson at *The Observer* it was always good to know you had the whole weekend off. Although my short time in London I spent as a single person, I don't think I ever felt really lonely. Though, thinking back, it would have been nice to have someone there to share my time with. I wasn't a shy person so I'm sure if I desperately needed company, I could've found it. But I suppose it's not that simple for a lot of people, especially if they are of a sensitive nature. Going out on your own to meet people can be an awkward and emotionally challenging task, and the more they think about it the more difficult it can become.

If you come from a small town or village, it can be difficult to express yourself or even have people understand your feelings on certain issues. So, to escape to a city like London with all its diversities, you can really come out of your shell and be whoever you want to be. Although this was never an issue for me, I was a lively Jack in the box wherever you put me. But lots of people move to London due to work commitments, or even in some cases move there with a partner and things maybe don't work out the way they'd hoped, and with unforeseen circumstances things begin to fall apart. So, although London is a city full of millions of people, sadly there were a lot of people who probably felt very lonely and stuck in a rut, as they struggled to become socially mobile. And of course, there was the cost of going out and meeting friends. Some people were forced to live on a very strict budget and felt constricted by their lack of funds.

In the summer this wasn't as much of a problem. With London having more greenery and parks than any other of the more contemporary cities around the world, there was always lots going on for you to go and see. Me personally, if there was too much month left at the end of the wage, I would take to getting out and about on my old trusty bicycle. This had been obtained through an advert through what was known in those days as the LOOT, which was a free paper full of advertisements. This came out every Monday to Friday; each paper would be a specific colour to represent the day. This paper was so handy and extremely helpful. With no internet to talk of in those days, it really helped. Much the same could be said of *The Evening Standard*, which back in 1989 was still printing three different issues in one day. Regardless of your opinions of its editorial, it was really handy for finding out what was going on. In fact, that's where my attention was drawn to a recruitment agency advertisement which eventually led me to getting my job at *The Observer* in the first place. The classified columns in both aforementioned papers played such an important role in informing and helping to bring lots of people together. Whether it be dancing classes, clubs to go to, shows, concerts, or even the wide and varied self-interest groups that existed. The importance of these classified columns has now been lost due to the expansion of the internet and smartphones.

With me living in the north of London I was very fortunate to be able to cycle up to the beautiful and opulent Highgate, and just a little further to Hampstead. These were wonderful places and although I'd always cycle far and wide around London, I would magnetically be drawn back to Highgate and my most favourite place at the time, Hampstead Heath.

I could cycle the whole perimeter of the park at least two or three times a day in the summer. When the weather was sunny and warm Hampstead was like London had gone on holiday, people lounging around and basking in the sun. Whether it be down by the swimming ponds or watching young people running up Parliament Hill to capture that spectacular view of London, and even to the west of the park you could escape into the quieter woodlands. The sounds were fantastic. The breeze brushing through the heavy foliage, dogs happily running around with that excited bark, never straying too far from their owners. Lots of well-to-do families who always looked like they lived close by, strolling through the park at a nonchalant pace. The fit and healthy running with that very serious look of determination on their faces. Then there were the elderly people who might be eccentrically dressed, sitting on the benches, sometimes looking a bit perturbed when the young caught them by surprise as they noisily ran past, laughingly chasing each other.

I used to find myself staring, or what you would call people watching, wondering where they all came from, wondering about their backgrounds. Slowly feelings of melancholy would come over me as I watched in silence, and my mind would begin to wander. I'd be thinking back to my own childhood, being with my two younger brothers running around places like Tentsmuir Forest in Fife, my mum and dad shouting in the background, warning us to be careful. I strangely would never get tired of running through a forest, it was something I could do all day. And even watching the older people my mind would drift back to my grandparents, the way they'd fuss over you, always making sure you were fed well.

Looking back now, maybe I was a little lonely and just couldn't see it. I was just a wee lost soul looking for someone to play with.

It was maybe then, watching an elderly person travelling slowly through the park on their own, it began to dawn on me that of course they were young once. They probably had lots of friends; they'd probably led a really fulfilled life but now it was all beginning to fade away.

I must admit when I was young, I used to think elderly people came from another planet; the way they dressed, their attitudes towards everything, I just felt they had no knowledge of youth at all. But now, although a bit slow on the uptake, it was beginning to dawn on me that getting older was a reality.

These feelings of melancholy would soon pass once myself and the bike became mobile again, but these were moments I'd never forget; they would stick with me forever. Again, I do remember feeling that it would've been nice to have someone there to share the experience of these beautiful days cycling around the Heath.

Another place in the park I was always drawn to would be Kenwood House. It stands proudly at the top of the Heath, a very elegant palace surrounded by very quaint landscaped gardens, a great place to just sit and enjoy the tranquillity. People always seemed to give it the gentrified respect that it quietly demanded. I was certainly no snob, but I just loved the dreamy atmosphere that accompanied every occasional visit. A few times I was fortunate to be there when just below the green grassy slopes, there was another pond and on the opposite side was a stage, where musical concerts would be performed. Everyone would sit around on the grass or maybe even on deckchairs, eating food from their picnic baskets. It was just so quintessentially English.

People were friendly, happily drinking wine as their children were further back happily playing. It was just a place of sheer beauty. As I would sit and gaze around in wonderment, I'd see a lot of people close to the front. These people were mostly elderly and exclusively there just to enjoy the music. The stage across the pond and the surrounding areas were encased by beautiful woodland and again, at the top of the grassy hill stood the magnificent Kenwood House. The music wasn't my usual taste, but seemed to carry through the summer evening beautifully, and it was something I only ever experienced the once, but thinking back, it must have been something the locals looked forward to every year.

Another place not far from my doorstep was Camden. I say not far from the doorstep, it was actually a couple of tube stations away, and even on a Sunday the tube line to Camden was extremely busy, but the people would be a bit more relaxed. Even though there were people flowing in from all over London, you didn't get as many tourists back in the late 80s and early 90s. Camden was still very rough around the edges; litter would gather around the fronts of the old empty shops, but as you got closer to the market at Camden Lock, you'd begin to smell the fried onions from the hamburger stalls. Or the warm, mouth-watering smells from fish and chips as people passed by chomping away with their fingers drenched in either vinegar or tomato and brown sauce. This may not appeal to everyone's taste, but like a ravenous wild dog I was always hungry when I was young, and visiting Camden Market when you didn't have loads of cash could leave you yearning for things you couldn't have, especially the food.

Camden Market always had its own kind of style, with lots of second-hand stalls intermingled with all the latest fashions, or trends even. Out by the old arches you could pick up lots of old furniture and of course not forgetting the fruit and veg stalls, which were still frequented by the older locals. And even if people were not buying, there were still lots of people mulling around socialising or generally just hanging out. And last but not least the many music stalls covering all different genres, and each of these stalls would play their favourite tunes, which was another added layer to that special Camden atmosphere.

Camden, of course, has a long history of places to go, especially if you enjoy the arts or in particular music. They've had very iconic venues, from Dingwalls, The Electric Ballroom, KOKO, to the unique Roundhouse.

But there's one place I'll never forget. It was only my first weekend in London, so I was feeling like a very small fish in an extremely large pond. Not to worry, on Saturday afternoon Ian was going to take me to some pub in Camden that played live music. This is where I would meet lots of people and in his words, "You'll have a great time."

I was still feeling slightly apprehensive. I thought, *Oh, a few pints and some live music, I'm sure it'll be fine.*

Most of Ian's friends were designers, or young people like himself just on the cusp of an up-and-coming career in some sort of high-end profession. So, I thought, it's bound to be quite laid back and with some background live music it should be an easy afternoon.

As we made our way to Archway Tube Station it was very noticeable that Ian was in great spirits. There seemed to be a real spring in his step as he started telling me about some of the guys and girls I would be meeting on my day's adventure. Well, I suppose it was Saturday and it was just the beginning of the weekend so what was there not to be happy about?

Eventually leaving the steep escalator at Camden, you could already feel the hustle and bustle of the busy street, when suddenly two of Ian's friends jumped on him from nowhere. "All right, Myles?" said the first guy in a very distinctive Australian accent.

The other guy laughingly introduced himself to me straight away. "All right, mate?" This lad was called Dougie and like Ian and myself he was Scottish and originated from the lovely city of Edinburgh. The big Aussie lad who worked with Dougie was called Brett. They both worked as traders in the city. They also seemed very excitable and looking forward to their Saturday afternoon. I could tell straight away they all got on like a house on fire. I felt like I was in good company and their fun-loving, excitable behaviour was infectious, so I knew I was in good hands.

As we made our way through the busy streets of Camden, I could tell by the way they were talking that they were still planning on meeting quite a few other people. Eventually we ended up in a corner pub called the Camden Head and although it was still early it was quite busy and vibrant. The first tables we came across seemed to be the rest of the entourage. It was a mixture of girls and guys; most of the girls were Australian, very bubbly and like everyone else looking forward to the day's antics. In honesty this pub was great, so I felt really comfortable. We only had time for the one drink, but it gave me a chance to be introduced to the rest of the crowd.

So, before I knew it, we were off to the main event which was another pub called the Caernarfon Castle. The band had already started so we had to push our way into this very busy place with rhythm 'n' blues playing loudly in the background. People were already dancing and singing along while still holding on to their beers with cigarettes wedged tightly between their fingers. It didn't take very long for everyone to get carried along with this lively, happy atmosphere. In fact as the afternoon wore on, I wasn't completely sure who was a regular visitor to the pub, or part of the original entourage I came in with. But it didn't seem to matter as everyone was happy and joyously bouncing around to the music. The lead singer had everyone in raptures as he whipped the crowd into a frenzy with his mouth organ.

After a good few hours, I began to look around, trying to take in what was happening around me. It was like some tribal furore, fuelled with pints of snakebite and what we were affectionately calling laughing brew (snakebite, if you didn't know, is a mixture of lager and cider, and laughing brew is Lowenbrau).

I remember as it all came to an end with my ears still ringing from the noise, I shouted to Ian, "What a brilliant night!"

He quickly looked at his watch and cheekily shouted back, "What do you mean 'what a great night'? It's just going on half past five."

It took me slightly by surprise. I'd forgotten it had just been an afternoon gig, a very lively one at that. So, when we made our way back out onto the street it was still daylight, people walking around getting on with their usual daily business. And here was us, like we'd just spilled out of the greatest party ever. It wasn't so much that we were really drunk and staggering, it was more to do with us still laughing loudly, and our bodies were going through some dance fatigue syndrome, obviously aided by the alcohol consumption. Obviously, it didn't all end there as the leaders of the pack were now planning our next move, which wasn't part of my decision making, I was once again just going with the flow. One thing that did grab my attention was the number of Aussies with us, but again, all very friendly and in extremely high spirits.

It'll come as no surprise that the rest of the evening became a bit of a blur. In fact my next date with reality came around to meet me early on the Sunday morning. As I woke I lifted my head very heavily from a pillow only to find I was on a hard floor, not on a comfortable bed. Well, a carpeted floor. As I looked around, I seemed to be one of many. I shook off the one blanket that had been afforded to me and got myself onto my feet. I desperately needed a drink of water. Looking around me, I could see there were another seven or eight bodies. Some of the faces I thought I recognised from the night before as my mind started to try and piece together all that had happened.

I spotted the kitchen and made my way to the sink. It felt like life or death, my body needed that drink of water. Just as I gulped it down a young Australian girl came bounding into the kitchen and shouted, "Blinding night last night, Smithy!"

Well, she obviously knew who I was. That was certainly a bonus as I didn't have a clue where I was. So, I replied as best I could with, "Yeah, brilliant night, really enjoyed it."

She then offered to make me a cup of tea which I declined. I told her I had better get going. She then said, "Do you want me to phone a taxi?"

I quickly replied, "No, I'll be fine; I wouldn't mind getting some fresh air."

So we said our goodbyes and agreed it would all have to be done again sometime. As I left the house, I felt slightly embarrassed that I couldn't remember her name as she seemed really pleasant. Then as I walked to the end of the garden path and out onto the narrow street, it dawned on me that I didn't have the foggiest as to where I was. The fresh air was certainly helping to clear my head, but it was also awakening me to the realities of not knowing how I was going to find my way home. After checking my pockets, I had just under a fiver. *If I can find a tube station, I can work my way home from there.* Now knowing I had a plan, my slight panic was beginning to dissipate and if I was to be honest, I was feeling rather peckish.

Turning out of the small lane I could see I had come out onto Golders Green High Street; this was made more obvious by all the shop signs and adverts dotted around the street. It was nearly midday, so it was very sunny, and the main street was quite busy. It didn't take long for my nose to latch on to the fabulous-smelling bakers. That was it, decision made, I would fill the tank (my stomach) and a good walk home would do me the world of good, and on a more positive note I'd be able to take in the sights on the way. It felt like I'd hit the jackpot. I managed to get two gorgeously filled bagels and a hot drink. Sunday just got a lot better. *That should last till I find my way home*, I thought to myself.

It only took me another five minutes to find the tube station so feeling energised after my Sunday feast, it didn't take me long to work out my direction home. On the tube map it said from Golders Green it was on to Hampstead, Belize Park, Chalk Farm then on to Camden. That was it easy, and from there I could walk from Camden up to Archway. I was feeling pleased with myself that I'd managed to find the route home. I was literally just following the tube map.

With quickened steps I began to make my way out of Golders Green and as I walked up the side of a busy road, it eventually brought me out onto a large roundabout. To the left of me was a place called Jack Straw's Castle and across from it looked a bit more like countryside, but fortunately I could see the signs pointing me in the right direction for Hampstead.

As I made my way down the hill into Hampstead, I noticed that either side of me I was surrounded by beautiful large houses. It was all very green and leafy, and the traffic seemed to be made up of very expensive cars filled with what I imagined to be very wealthy people out for a Sunday drive. Seeing all this reminded me of my childhood, when my two brothers and I would be sat in the back of the car with a small Shizu dog running backwards and forwards across our laps, each time jumping to look out of a window. My mother would be in the front as my father drove. I loved when we made our way up to places like Pitlochry of Aberfeldy; the only downside was that my mother smoked so I suffered badly from car sickness.

Breaking from my bout of nostalgia and realising I'd been walking for half an hour, I eventually came to Hampstead Tube Station. *Brilliant*, I thought to myself. *My plan is working.* And so far, everything was downhill. The walk was enjoyable, but I began to realise there was more distance between the tube stations than I had imagined. It seemed a long time before I eventually came across Belize Park, then even longer to Chalk Farm. My filled bagels seemed like a distant memory. My hunger was coming back, and I was beginning to feel tired. Thankfully it wasn't long after that I realised I was heading into Camden and my spirits began to lift.

Once I reached Camden Station, I knew exactly the direction I had to go in. Obviously there was still a bit of distance to cover but I knew I was on the last leg of the journey. I still had to pass Tufnell Park and Kentish Town before I finally reached Archway.

After getting back into the house on Gladsmuir Road I finally caught up with Ian. He was interested to find out where I'd been for most of the day. So, I told him of my predicament, of how I wasn't even sure where I had been staying and how I cleverly planned my journey home on foot. I proudly waited for a pat on the back after showing I could be the great adventurer who always finds his way home. But sadly, I was greeted with howls of laughter. Ian told me, had I taken a left at Jack Straw's Castle I would've passed Hampstead Heath, then after a short walk through Highgate I would've been down into Archway. I'd added about 10 miles to my journey and would've saved a few hours to boot.

A few other pieces of the previous evening's jigsaw puzzle came to light. First of all, the band we saw at the Caernarfon Castle was a rhythm and blues band called Wolfie Witcher, and secondly, I'd got into the wrong taxi at the end of the night, although Ian remembered someone shouting out of the taxi, "Don't worry, we will look after him!"

As I made my way up the stairs looking forward to getting my feet up and having a well-deserved rest, I could still hear Ian laughing in the background. Mind you, it had been a great night.

CHAPTER 4

TOWERS AND SEESAWS, SOCIAL HIGHS AND LOWS

Monday mornings must be the same the world over, mostly people apathetically pulling themselves from their beds just to face a new weekly onslaught of the drudgery of life. For me, I was rushing towards Archway Tube Station so I could head down that escalator in a robotic fashion to join the legions of lost souls. You could see the little glimmers of life in their eyes, as they were possibly pondering over their weekend, little moments of relaxation and happiness that they may have been lucky enough to experience. But now these thoughts would soon be extinguished by the oncoming calamity of the workplace. The noticeable suits that have become a ubiquitous part of London's city culture were very much on show. The quality and cut enhanced by the popular half Windsor knotted tie, which leaves a feeling of being in uniform, but one with class, and it certainly left them looking the part. Here I was, sitting amongst them all as we gently rocked backwards and forwards to the motion of the tube carriage.

The majority of people were not reading anything, just looking around quietly but still making sure not to catch anyone's eye. For someone like me who is a loquacious character at the best of times, it always felt kind of strange being amongst so many people but nobody talking. It was like this every day, but Monday mornings it always irked me. *Not to worry*, I'd think to myself. *I'll soon be with my colleagues at work where I can boast about my fabulous weekend.* But like everyone knows, five minutes into work these conversations evaporate very quickly. Yup, deadlines must be met and usually you were trying to recap where you had left off on the Friday. Then it hits you, there's still another five full days to go before it's the weekend again. *I've just got to do my best to survive.*

Once a month I would head back up to Scotland and either travel back to London by train on the Sunday, or fly down early on the Monday morning. The train journey was always the hardest. First of all, a lot of Sunday would be wasted travelling, and I would always grab a window seat looking out, watching people mull around the station. I could see the people who lived in Edinburgh walking from the Waverley station up the road and back up towards Princess Street. Then I would get this mad rush of emotions. I didn't want to go, I'd rather stay there. There were so many times I nearly got up and walked off the train, even as it was slowly pulling out of the station. I'd think to myself, *It's not going too fast. I could still get off the train…* Yup, I used to get very homesick for my home town of Kinghorn and I loved Edinburgh, with so many wonderful childhood memories of the place.

Even as a young adult myself and friends would travel from Kinghorn to Edinburgh, always departing the train at Waverley and charging through the hustle and bustle with that feeling of excitement. Whether it was just to spend the day enjoying all the different pubs or going to watch the rugby, which was always a fantastic day in itself, or maybe going to see some of my favourite bands. These memories flashed through my mind as I sat in the carriage quietly, waiting to be dragged down to London. My eyes would be fixed, staring out of the window looking at all the old pillars of the station and thinking, *No one can force them to travel.* Inside I was screaming, *Should I just make a break for it? London would certainly survive without me.* Thankfully once the train got moving that yearning for home would start to dissipate and my emotions would settle down.

Flying down on a Monday morning was always a bit of a rush,

having to get up early to get all the way to Edinburgh Airport, and although I was never a great fan of flying the journey always gave me a feeling of wellbeing. It left me feeling quite the young professional, all suited and booted, to eventually arrive late at *The Observer* on Chelsea Bridge Road. The least enjoyable part of the journey was always as the plane was beginning to land at Heathrow. The views were fantastic, as you flew down only a few thousand feet above the Thames with all of London's glory on show. But the plane would always sway back and forth in a turbulent fashion, made worse if I didn't have a window seat. It didn't seem to matter if it was sunny or cloudy outside, it was always the same – a long, turbulent landing.

One other method of travelling back from Edinburgh to London was the night bus. This gave me most of the Sunday at home or with friends, then late into the evening I'd catch the bus at the St James' Centre not far from St Andrew's Square. It was still sad leaving, though, as the bus would travel along George Street with all its wonderful Victorian architecture. My priority would be to get as comfortable as possible so I could catch some sleep. In those days I would be going straight to my work at Tower Records in Piccadilly, so I knew it was going to be a long day, feeling grubby from travelling all night.

I remember one night, it was a cold Sunday in February, the surrounding streets were all very quiet, there wasn't even much traffic on the roads. I could hear the chilling clatter of the road signs rattling gently in the cold wind. Oh, how I wished at that moment things could be different and was imagining that all I had to do was leave my place at the bus stop and maybe go home to my comfortable flat in Edinburgh. Just at that, I remember the bus pulling into the station with London on the front of it. Although the bus was early, I noticed that there weren't many people waiting. With it being quiet there was no hanging about and as soon as the door opened, I rushed upstairs and managed to get to the front seats. It wasn't long until this nearly empty bus was pulling out of the station, and I had the four front seats all to myself. This was fantastic as it gave me panoramic views of the city as we left Edinburgh. Once out of the bright lights I settled in for the long night's journey. But as I hunkered down and tried to get some sleep, I'd wake up feeling so cold. It took me a good couple of hours before I finally realised that being in front of those large glass windows was the reason. As soon as I made my way further back into the bus, I found it much warmer and eventually got myself more comfortable.

The next time I woke properly I could see we were beginning to enter London and feeling a bit warmer, I decided to move back to the front seats. Being February, it was still a little dark and daylight was just beginning to befall London as we headed down Edgware Road. My spirits would really lift as the bus hurriedly made its way past Marble Arch and on down Park Lane. To the left of me were all these iconic five-star hotels such as The Grosvenor, The Dorchester, and the tallest of them all, the 28-floor Hilton. Just as the bus drew nearer to Hyde Park Corner, was the Continental Hotel. Yes, these were places that belonged to the rich and famous, of which I was neither. It seemed a nice thought, though, wakening up in a five-star hotel looking over Hyde Park. The closest I'd ever been to this was sleeping in Hyde Park on the Sunday night after spending the weekend at Knebworth Park.

It was August 1979. We were there watching the mighty Led Zeppelin. The coach wasn't picking us up until the Monday morning so myself and three other friends grabbed four deckchairs and slept under a tree not far from the band stand. It was me, Eric Pattie, Ian Myles and Ian Fisher, all of us still very young and very green behind the ears. Even then I had a soft spot for Hyde Park and its salubrious surroundings. I'd memories of visiting there with my Uncle John away back in 1974.

Once the bus passed Hyde Park Corner, I knew we weren't far

from Victoria Bus Station, but my mind still delved back into the past, remembering that night many years before in Hyde Park, 1979. We hardly slept as we were too busy talking and laughing our way through the evening. A great adventure at the time, especially as we were so young. Unfortunately, it was tinged with sadness as Eric had not long died from a massive heart attack while out living in the Philippines. My little world was left with a big hole in it after that; it was just so unfair that one of your best friends should die at only 26. The pain was still fresh in my mind.

It wasn't long before we pulled into that diesel-fumed bus station and I was spritely making my way down the bus stairs. The first thing that immediately grabbed my attention was that London definitely seemed a bit warmer. I wasn't sure if it was due to all the fumes coming from the now busy bus station, or just London being further south and not getting those cruel north winds coming off the sea.

As I left the bus station, I quickly crossed the road and made my way towards Victoria Train Station, through the shopping arcade, down the elevator then quickly to the tube station. It was still only 07:30 and I had plenty of time. It wouldn't take me long to grab a tube to Green Park then jump on another to Piccadilly. I'd still be at my place of work, which at that time was Tower Records. The entrance of this fantastic record shop faced the centre of Piccadilly and was wedged nicely between Green Park and Regent Street. There were two entrances to the shop. The first, or the main entrance looked directly over towards that very famous statue of Eros, and the other could be accessed from the Piccadilly tube station.

I'd easily made it before 8 o'clock. Still feeling tired and groggy, I tried to bring myself back to life with a quick coffee, just before attempting to prepare some boxes for sending off music to our American shops. I worked in a small area with four others in what was called the Exports Department. I was usually surrounded by piles of CD singles and lots of sheets of printed paper. I was just about to get stuck in separating this deluge of music and paper into their allocated store, when Herve, my boss, walked in. We had a brief chat about our weekends, and I told him I'd literally just come straight from the Victoria bus station and wasn't feeling my best. I noticed he was looking at me rather strangely. He then said in his very soft French accent, "Did you know a bomb has just gone off in Victoria Train Station!?" I had to be honest and say I knew nothing about it, but I said I'd passed through the station and hadn't seen or heard anything. Herve then went into a little bit more detail, with first reports coming in stating that there had been many injuries. Herve and I were both now staring at each other. You could tell what was going through our minds. He was looking at me as if to say, 'Did you really pass through that station!?' while I was looking back at him thinking, *A bomb, seriously?*

As it turns out I'd missed the explosion by minutes. My tube must have been pulling out of the station as it happened. We were able to find more information on these terrible events after grabbing a first edition of *The Evening Standard*. Sadly one person had died, with another 53 injured. Poor, innocent people just trying to get to work and getting caught up in something not of their making.

London had a way of picking itself up and quickly dusting itself down after these terrible events, but there must be a lot of people very close to these situations, who would have to live with the physical and mental scars for the rest of their lives.

Tower Records wasn't just a job, it was a lifestyle. I'd joined a new community of small groups of people who were almost tribal in the music that they followed. Yes, Tower was my second stint in London and a far cry from my suited and booted days from before. This time (within reason) you could wear a uniform of your own choosing, which meant it was back to wearing jeans and a t-shirt emblazoned with a band you loved on the front. My humble beginnings saw me working between the receiving department and front of shop working on the tills. No deadlines, no pressure, just a happy, friendly environment to work in. The money was obviously considerably less than what I was used to but there were other benefits. I was reconnecting and had access to all my favourite music.

To be honest, my love of music and seeing bands was sucked away from me in my previous jobs in London. Only because you were mixing with different people with different attitudes. These people, although lovely in their own way aspired to all the riches in life, the big cars, houses and holidays in far-off places. By rule they'd have to buy their clothes from only the best and most reputable of stores. I must admit once suited and booted, like everyone else, I certainly looked the part, but again to be honest I wasn't entirely comfortable in that attire.

I'll never forget the time a small group of us had been on a night out, I'm sure I'd been working for a computer publication called PC Business World at the time. Just as we're laughing and jovially making our way through Covent Garden, I heard one of the stall holders talking to his friend as he sneeringly remarked, "Look, bunch of bloody yuppies."

This stopped me in my tracks. I felt really insulted and before I knew it, I shouted back in a deep Scottish accent, pointing my finger, "I'm no fucking yuppie, pal," which seemed to take them by surprise. It wasn't just the stall holders that looked shocked, the rest of the entourage looked quite taken aback as well. Just for a moment I stood between them all feeling like I'd just disassociated myself from my friends. Sharp as a knife, I quickly looked at my friends with a big smile and replied, "I bet they were not expecting that."

Thankfully they all started laughing again as one of the lads shouted, "You tell 'em, Jock."

It was most definitely an overreaction on my part. Although I felt quite comfortable wearing a suit there was something underlying that

I wasn't the complete package.

So, the relaxed dress sense at Tower left me feeling far more comfortable in my own skin and of course in that shop environment, wearing your favourite bands across your chest allowed shoppers to approach you as they appreciated that you may have the knowledge about music they required. I certainly wasn't an aficionado on all things music but there was certainly plenty of people around that were. Every department had their self-trained experts completely qualified by the love of their own particular music. They knew what was coming out and when, if it was good or if it was bad, and hey, if you liked that you might like this. A lot of these people were or had been in bands themselves and would almost certainly have lots of friends who were in a similar situation. These people were far more than just regular shop assistants who came in to do an eight-hour shift, these folks lived and breathed music 24 hours a day.

Working in the receiving department alone was an education in itself. Again it was all run and marshalled by a tribe of guys who all loved their music; it was all long hair, nodding heads, guys that walked with a swagger, a mixture of punk, underground and heavy rock always playing in the background. At the time my tastes were considered very much middle of the road, and that's me being kind to myself. Their opinions of my music were far more scathing. But it didn't take long for me to catch up. I was really enjoying a lot of this music they were playing; it seemed to strike a chord with me very quickly, so it didn't take long for me to finally be accepted into their tribe.

For some reason Mondays were always new release day, meaning that was the day all the new releases would hit the shelves. There were always lots of people from all the different Tower departments coming in and out, like drug addicts looking for their fix. They'd all be excited as their hands were tightly clasped on the music they'd been waiting on for weeks. The few disgruntled moans when certain things hadn't been delivered, that wouldn't stop them revisiting the receiving department two or three times a day, nervously waiting on their music turning up like their lives depended on it. Once it eventually arrived you could see the excitement and relief on their faces, with that wide eyed smile as this musical gold was delivered into their hands.

It certainly didn't take me long to get into the swing of it. I was going to see lots of new bands I'd never heard of and our association with Tower got us great discounts and, in some cases, would see us getting into events for nothing. The gigs were always extremely loud, smoky and all washed down with whatever beer was on sale. It was great. Every band I saw was fantastic. Whether it be band members or just your usual gig-goers, they all seemed to mix well together and no surprise that most of them seemed to know each other from previous gigs.

Going in and out you were always handed flyers. It wasn't like you were standing on the high street being handed another leaflet from someone obviously just doing it for the little money they were being paid, offering carpets or another big sale at some Flash Harry store. You'd sometimes accept those out of courtesy then quietly drop it in the nearest bin. No, these flyers were something else, these were informative guides to the promised land, these were how the bands communicated; they helped keep everyone informed as to who was playing next and where. And it wasn't a case of someone being paid a pittance to do it, these were passed around the followers by the band's musical disciples. No need for fancy advertising budgets, this was delivering the message right into the heart of the bands' many followers, which they proudly called the underground scene. This is all made a bit more significant when you realise that way back in those days there was no readily available internet that everyone now seems to take for granted, these flyers played an important part in keeping people informed. Even the process of making them was made a little more difficult as people were still using basic printing technology.

Sometimes it got quite hectic as you could be seeing two or three bands a week, again falling into that trap of getting home to fall instantly into bed, only finding yourself getting up to start all over again, with nothing in between.

As much as it was fun, the late nights and long hours would really catch up with you at times, and it wasn't just the fast living. Your diet would suffer also, through either not eating or when you did it was fast food, which in itself is a contradiction of terms as it was usually hot, greasy, gloopy mush covered in some sort of sauce, eaten using your bare hands as you plucked and pulled it from its low-quality paper wrappings. I think it's important here I should quickly add that I think a majority of people would say a fish supper always smells better when it's been wrapped up in old newspaper.

Yes, I was beginning to look the part. Not that I was following some sort of fashion, but it was the lifestyle that was determining my look. My hair was getting longer and although I had lots of band t-shirts most of them were black. My eyes had permanent dark bags under them, highlighted by my very white skin as I wasn't seeing a lot of daylight, and add to that my thinning frame from not eating very much. Again, I must stress I was enjoying myself, but London had still been leaving me with too much week left at the end of the wage.

On reflection, and again just pointing out, so many people walk the same streets in London, yet the way they lead their lives, they are worlds apart. I was now sampling and understanding this from first-hand experience. It didn't seem that long ago I was wearing a suit and leading a completely different lifestyle. The people from the advertising world seemed more connected with family; they had an outlook on life that would eventually take them on to, hopefully in their eyes, better things. Climbing the metaphorical ladder into increased wealth, eventually investing in property, while still keeping a lookout for improved employment prospects but not ruling out the idea of branching out and formulating some business of their own.

Whereas the majority of people I was meeting at Tower were doing the opposite, completely shunning that lifestyle. Their ambitions were more about maintaining a foothold in the world of music, free from what they'd call the mundane rigours of life. Yes, of course they'd enjoy wealthy living, but it certainly wasn't something they were going to prioritise. They were hooked on their art and chasing their next musical fix. There's no way I'd have been accepted into the tribe had I been short haired, wearing a suit and discussing the latest advertising trends. They would've been disgusted at my shallow appearance and what would seem to be a lack of any real imagination. They'd see me as if I was just another faceless money-chasing suit and, in their defence, they'd have a valid point.

But when I consider what my former colleagues in the advertising world would think, they'd have the same feeling of disdain. With my Tower dress code, they wouldn't even give me a second look; in their minds they wouldn't have to. I'd obviously have the appearance of someone who's not even trying to fit in. I don't have a proper career with prospects, which would probably suggest, along with my lack of ambition regarding money, a complete lack of understanding of the real world. In fact their cognitive dissonance would probably stop them from bothering to waste any time thinking about the whole subject. Me or my like didn't have anything to offer or to do with their upwardly mobile plan. But even with such a divide in individual perspectives, I'd always imagine certain people within the advertising world, Tower, and even friends from back home, if they could only meet, would get on well. Remember that old saying, 'ach, we're all Jock Tamson's bairns at the end of the day.'

I remember travelling back to Scotland for Christmas and New Year and was so glad to get home. It was great to see family, not to mention eating properly as well. I always missed home and came so very close to not returning. Yeah, I'd miss some of what London had been offering me, but I missed home more. I reluctantly travelled back down anyway. I'd been offered another job in Tower to go and work with Herve in the Exports Department. I think this is what swung it for me; the idea of getting a new job in Tower just managed to keep me seated on the train at Waverley. It was moving into another environment, a little bit more laid back from the hustle and bustle of the Receiving Department and anyhow, I was still going to be hanging out with the same guys most of the time.

The Exports Department was all based around selling CD singles to all Tower Records shops across the length and breadth of America. This proved to be massively successful from Tower in Piccadilly's point of view. And the real driving force behind this success came down to one man, Herve. This mild-mannered Frenchman just had a knack of finding the right music at the right price and was able to keep the costs of delivering this music to the bare minimum. At one point he was even cheekily ordering music from the USA and still making a profit from sending it all the way back to the Tower stores back in the States.

It was generally a four-man team. Herve from France; Seamus, a massive Prince fan from Ireland; a young lad called Patrick, from Japan; and of course last but not least, me, the latest member of the team. There was one other lad called Richard, a talented musician and artist who would come in to help on the odd occasion when were really snowed under. Like me, Richard was from Scotland. I'd always enjoy when he came in to help; he always seemed so positive about things and was one of life's great philosophers. For someone like me who's probably spent most of his life using his mouth more than his ears, it made a change for me to just sit back and listen. Now if only my memory was better, I might have been able to elaborate.

In the Exports Department there was always something to do, whether it was boxing up music to send off to the allocated stores or going back through to the Receiving Department chasing up music for outstanding orders. But there was always a real excitement that would start round about two o'clock in the afternoon, when our fax machine would burst into life. Herve's eyes would always light up as he'd excitedly gather up the faxes to see if his cleverly put-together catalogues had garnered much success. Yup, we never seemed to get finished. Just as you were beginning to think the decks were being cleared of orders, that clicking sound of the fax machine burst into life again.

After a hard day's graft Herve and I would head to a pub called the Glassblower. This wasn't far from Tower, just on the edge of Soho and close to Regent Street. A remarkable building and steeped in history, originally it had been a workhouse but spent the last few hundred years as a pub. The downstairs was always very vibrant, so we'd usually head upstairs where we'd be more or less guaranteed a seat, as it was always a little quieter. Usually, we would grab a window seat looking down onto Glasshouse Street. Once we finished a few drinks Herve always remembered he'd left something at work, so we would quickly make our way back to Tower. I'm sure this was all just part of his plan to see what other faxes had come in from America. Sure enough, before we knew it, we'd be going through faxes and looking around to see if we had said music that the American stores had requested. I didn't mind, I'd easily get caught up in Herve's excitement, but little did we realise the time would fly by and it would get close to the shop's closing time.

Tower opened at 9am then closed at 12 o'clock in the evening, which is incredible to think the pubs shut at 11pm. This made for some interesting times for the poor security guards. As you can imagine, a few people would leave the pub and come into what must have looked like a sweetie shop in their sometimes more than obvious drunken stupor. All these fantastic records, t-shirts, CDs, magazines and different types of musical accessories. Suddenly what seemed like a bit of mischievous drunken tomfoolery would hit home as the security guys were right on their phones calling the police. As the tears streamed down their heartbroken faces some of them would get off with a caution. You've never heard people being so thankful. On the other hand, due to people being worse for wear, it could also lead to music lovers getting rather overexcited, all caution thrown to the wind as they galivanted around the shop carefree, gathering up as much music as their arms could hold, probably to wake up in the morning to find a rather large financial dent in their credit cards.

Tower was such a vibrant place all day, every day, what with the many in-stores, meaning either bands playing a few acoustic numbers to promote their music or just sitting down to sign their latest records. With most of the shop's staff being music lovers themselves, there was no shortage of people willing to help and advise when needed. So many young people would come into the shop just to hang out, as the music was all hand-picked by members of the staff. Out of the great music chains around the world I'm sure Tower was the best. If not, it was certainly the coolest!!

CHAPTER 5

FOND FAREWELLS

One other little benefit I wish I had taken more advantage of, was that just at the Piccadilly tube station entrance, there was a little office where people would book or pick up tickets for shows at theatres, tickets to see bands, and the many cinemas. The West End was certainly not short of these, but this was a small kiosk tucked right in the corner at the tube station entrance. Normally as I left or entered, I'd stop and chat to an Australian lad called Matt. He was a few years younger than myself but always had time for me. One day while chatting he was telling me that it was about time for closing, and he was amazed at the number of booked tickets that had not been picked up. He had a real bundle of tickets, all for different shows.

"Will they all manage to get a refund?" I enquired.

"Nope," said Matt.

"That's a lot of empty seats this evening. Such a waste of money."

"Do you want to have a look through and see if there's anything you fancy going to see!?" he asked me.

I could not believe it, some of them were great seats for shows such as Les Misérables, Blood Brothers, Cats, Starlight Express, and Miss Saigon. At the time it wasn't really something that inspired me and anyhow, this particular evening some of us were off to see a couple of bands playing at the Astoria on Charing Cross Road. I thanked Matt for the offer and said I really appreciated the gesture but did tell him, "Look, keep me informed if anything else crops up in the future." Looking back, I now wish I'd taken up the many offers Matt put before me on countless occasions.

The one time I did take him up on it I managed to get hold of six tickets for a Scottish band called the Soup Dragons; they were playing at the Marquee Club. So off three of us trotted from Tower. The other two lads both worked in the Receiving Department and were more interested in heavier, punk-sounding music but were quite happy to go along especially as there was nothing to lose since it was free. I had planned to sell the other three tickets, which would then be used to pay for our beers, but as it turned out, as we were sitting in a pub not too far from the venue we got chatting to another group of people. They were just in the pub with their friends socialising, with nothing else planned. I happened to mention we were going to see the Soup Dragons shortly. It was then I decided to ask them if they fancied coming along. Hesitantly they declined as they were quite happy just sitting chatting, but thanked me for the kind invite. When I produced the three tickets and said, "Hey, they're yours if you want them, it won't cost you anything!" all of a sudden their eyes lit up and they looked at each other excitedly.

One of their company, a lad called Paul, asked, "Seriously!?"

I said, "Yeah, of course, and it's only round the corner from where we are."

The three of them laughed and agreed that it might not be a bad idea. The lads said okay, but insisted they buy us another drink before we left for the Marquee.

"Deal!!!" I shouted as we all laughed, and enjoyed our free beer.

The three guys had been friends for a long time and had actually just met up for a quiet pint, but were now excited that their evening had taken an unexpected turn for the better. I also felt good that I'd done something nice and contributed to giving some people a good night out, so we all introduced ourselves a bit better, with some of the lads finding out they had quite a bit in common, with music and a love of motorcycles. I don't think anyone had a Soup Dragons record in their collection, but we were all agreed we'd make the most of it.

What was supposed to be an exploratory evening out to see an unfamiliar band just for something to do, turned out to be an absolute cracking night with our newly found friends. We stayed in the pub for one last round as we were all enjoying each other's company, with jokes and funny stories coming from all quarters. By the time we all eventually swaggered into the Marquee the band had already started and of course we made our way straight to the bar.

Getting home that evening was no problem for me as it wasn't too far from Tottenham Court Road Station. Thankfully the next day I felt quite refreshed, which was a bonus. Astonishingly as I was going through my pockets in the morning I found I still had the six Soup Dragon tickets in my pocket. Somehow, we must have managed to get into the Marquee without even producing the tickets, although I do remember one of the Tower lads, Andy, speaking to someone he knew at the door just before we went in.

That was another fantastic thing about Tower. It didn't matter what venue you went to, if you were in a large group somebody always knew someone that was involved with bands or the venue. Without a shadow of a doubt, it was such great fun meeting lots of like-minded people, always greeting them with a smile. Everyone with that special glint in their eyes knowing we were on the same wavelength, that feeling of being permanently submerged in a twenty-four-hour world of music.

Another great pastime that seemed to become very popular in London was playing softball in Regent's Park. This I was introduced to by my good friend Ian Myles. It was a mixture of work colleagues and friends who would travel straight from work to the park. These warm summer nights would have Regent's Park buzzing with all sorts of activities. All very vibrant and happy with people playing football, softball, and the many runners going through their paces. The lucky people who lived close by would be out and about walking their dogs and yes, there were times when some excitable mutt would call a halt to a game, running around joyously with a softball in their mouth, teasing the people chasing them as they tried to retrieve the ball.

As the evenings drew to a close, many might head into Camden for a last drink. Ian's group in particular would always head to the Edinboro Castle. It had a lovely beer garden, which in those lovely evenings was always busy. The conversations were light-hearted as most people sat around with flushed faces from their exertions, and let's not forget these were long days as everyone there had travelled straight from their place of work.

Again, these people would mostly travel home in the evenings using the trusted public transport systems to finally get in the door, eventually getting to their beds where they would automatically fall asleep. Not even time to dream, their heads would hit the pillow like they'd been knocked out, only to open their eyes to find out it was morning, and it started all over again.

On many mornings travelling down to work I'd say to myself, "That's it, no going out for me tonight, straight home," but it never seemed to work out that way. There was always something going on. Even if only a last-minute invitation to some gig or event, you knew it was sacrilege to say no, and any excuses were shot down in flames. I suppose being young at the time it was always easier to drum up that energy needed for another eventful night. Everyone knew there was nothing worse than missing out and having to listen to people next day saying, "You should have been there, it was a brilliant night," and usually they were right enough. These were great times. People would jokingly say, "Oh, c'mon. You'll get plenty sleep when you're dead."

The great thing about Tower was that they had so many deals with so many venues; a lot of the time you were never really having to put your hand in your pocket. To see a lot of these great up-and-coming bands, most of the time you only had to concern yourself with making sure you mustered up enough money for beers. This was always backed up by the many sweet-smelling cigarettes being passed around.

Life at Tower definitely felt like one big party, which was fine but personally I had nothing else in my life. I was still finding there was too much week left at the end of the wage, and it was all beginning to wear me down. Some evenings I'd find myself walking from Piccadilly all the way up to Archway, which must have been just over five miles. It didn't take too long, and I would take in all the sights on the way. I'd enviously watch all the people sitting in the many restaurants and bars, eating and drinking, and wonder who they were and what they'd possibly do for a living. They always seemed happy and relaxed. Often these moments would make me think of the little town of Kinghorn in Fife, going home to a cooked meal and being amongst family and friends. It all seemed so far away, like a distant memory.

A lot of people, when you say you live and work in London, they think you have this expensive lifestyle. Of course it's where Buckingham Palace is, London Bridge, Oxford Street, the beautiful Hyde Park and Park Lane. They probably think all Londoners like to lounge around in the very touristy Covent Garden. Of course some people do spend time around these wonderful places, but the vast majority don't. Even if they are travelling above ground, most of this iconic architecture doesn't get a second look, it means nothing to the daily traveller. They're most likely to be glancing at their watches, focused on getting to their next destination. And let's not forget the many people underground battling through the argy-bargy of the very crowded tube carriages, all bound together on what was aptly named the rat race, myopically racing to their next destination. Maybe the resentment shown towards pesky tourists who only ever seemed to get in people's way was a feeling of envy. These people were free, not shackled to the rat race.

Again, this was a dichotomy between me and other people's situations, so it's unfair to be so disparaging towards the many happy Londoners who love and enjoy living in this wonderful metropolis. London is arguably one of the greatest cities in the world with all it has to offer, which attracts tourists from all over. And the same must be said of the many people I knew at Tower, most of them very well adjusted and in complete control of their lives. Sometimes their positions in Tower were a sideshow to some other ambitious projects they were putting together.

Sadly, the same could not be said of myself. I wasn't laying down any roots, there was no great plan, I was just bundling along in my haphazard way, living from hand to mouth.

It finally dawned on me it was time for a change. I'd been riding my luck for too long. I must start planning to go home to Scotland. As soon as I'd made my mind up, I was going, I started to feel very positive that this was the right decision. No fuss, no song and dance, I would just slip away, cut my losses and go. There was light at the end of the tunnel.

Still being young, my planning was more impetuous than meticulous. I'd finished work around 5 o'clock on that Friday and was planning to use the underground to get to Victoria Bus Station but just at the last minute, I decided I would walk. I knew if I did it at a brisk pace it wouldn't take me too long. The only nagging doubt I had was eventually getting to the station and finding the last ticket for the Saturday morning bus to Scotland had just been sold. But it was a chance I was willing to take. It was late into the summer, and it was such a beautiful evening, I really fancied a last walk through some of the loveliest parts of London.

So, that evening I chose to leave through the front door which faced out, looking towards Eros, that lovely iconic statuette that sat proudly right in the heart of Piccadilly. London was moving into rush hour and the throngs of people were already rushing down the steps leading to Piccadilly Tube Station, so I took a right and headed along Green Park, passing the south side of Tower Records and Air Street. As I looked up this small street, I could see the roller doors leading to the Tower Records Receiving Department were still open. They must have been expecting a late delivery. I was tempted to go up for a last look in but decided against it.

Directly across from the Tower Records loading bay was a small sandwich shop we frequented. I could see they were now preparing to close. I felt a slight sadness. Would that be the last time I'd cast my eyes up that small street? I wasn't too sad, in fact I was excited. I realised my journey home was beginning now.

Green Park was busy with people on both sides of the street. The traffic was slow moving as the roads were becoming congested, all clamouring to find a way out of the rush hour. The buses, too, were all very busy with people moving out of the West End, more than likely taking them out to suburbs, bodies packed together looking out of the windows, their minds lost in thought. It's what people regularly did as they were travelling out of the city.

I passed the Meridien Hotel, always with their smartly dressed doorman. One guy I would regularly pass was a large, stout guy who was always smiling. I'd said hello to him on a few occasions. This time as I was passing I just managed to catch his eye as I shouted, "See you later!" With his inimitable smile he waved back and said goodbye. I wasn't sure if he actually recognised me or was just being his usual polite self. You always got that feeling he was a really nice guy, happy with his lot, probably had a nice home with a loving wife who obviously made sure he was well fed. I sort of nodded my head and gave him a knowing one-finger salute. I managed to hold his stare for that moment; maybe he did recognise me after all.

I was now rushing across the entrance to Sackville Street and then passing the iconic Royal Academy of Arts, then past the Burlington Arcade filled with little shops only the wealthy could afford. There was no doubt about it, Green Park was certainly not the sort of place I could afford to hang around in, but I certainly admired its luxurious beauty with Fortnum & Mason regally standing on the other side of the road. Although I must admit I'd spent plenty time on my knees just along from there in Waterstones, scouring through their books, usually looking through Scottish history. This would be done during my lunch break at Tower.

It hadn't slipped my attention that I was very aware of everything around me. Not only that, but I had a nice spring in my step. Usually after a long day at Tower your feet are sore and uncomfortable, your energy drained from a long day at work, probably still fighting the aftereffects of the night before. Usually as you're making you way home your head's down and you're just going through the motions of getting yourself onto the tube, cattle herded back to your destination. But not tonight. I felt quite fresh. I was dressed in a t-shirt, a grey bomber jacket, jeans, and training shoes. With a little money and keys in pocket I was flying along at pace. I knew in the back of my mind this might be last time I'd make this journey.

The street was still busy, some hurriedly trying to make their way home as others were still browsing some of the more fashionable shops. It wasn't long before I was passing the Ritz Hotel with Berkeley Square to my right. It all looked fabulously grandiose; this area was a renowned hangout for the rich and famous, with its high-end restaurants and member-only clubs. Again, I think it's important just to repeat this, but when you tell friends you work and live in London people's imaginations always jump to these iconic locations. They probably think of Buckingham Palace, the Houses of Parliament, London Bridge, theatres on Shaftesbury Avenue, shopping on Oxford Street, or the very touristy Covent Garden. They think, *Wow, you're part of all that?* which couldn't be further from the truth. You have little or no relationship with these places at all. A lot of the monuments, you don't give them a second glance. When you do take notice of them you may look down at your watch as you're just using them as a marker in the timing of your journey. In fact, many Londoners probably try to avoid these places, as they do become very congested with camera-laden tourists.

I was now taking a left turn down the Queen's Walk in Green Park. It was a little quieter than the busy streets. Through the trees I could see the Queen Victoria monument and to the left of that the magnificent, stately Buckingham Palace. By the time I got down to the Mall I could see the Royal Standard flying, so made my way to the crossing at Constitution Hill. *Wow,* I thought to myself. *Imagine seeing the Queen on your last night in London.* (Just in case any of you didn't know, the Royal Standard only flies above the palace when the Queen is in residence.)

As I made my way past the front of the palace, there were still plenty of tourists mulling around eagerly watching for a possible glimpse of the Queen. Looking down at my watch I could see it was nearly 6 o'clock as I, too, stared into the palace forecourt. I thought to myself, *There's no chance of seeing the Queen. She'll be settling down to watch the 6 o'clock news, feet up watching telly. Perhaps someone will bring her evening meal on a tray.* My mind was wandering and again thinking about eating. Something that should now seem very apparent, is that most of the time I was in London, I was hungry. As I travelled past the palace I wondered what was really going on behind those doors. After tea would she take the dogs for a run around in that expansive walled garden at the back of the palace!? Imagine having a house that big right in the centre of London's West End. Gee, some people are really lucky in life. If I did catch a glimpse of the Queen, I'd probably shout over to her, "That's me off now, I'm going back to my hometown of Kinghorn in the morning."

All of a sudden, my mind came rushing back to the task at hand, a realisation that this touristic jaunt of mine might cost me a place on the bus home in the morning. I feared I'd get to Victoria Bus Station and someone at the ticket office would say, "Oh, sorry, we just sold the last ticket half an hour ago." Surely not, I hoped. But that's the way life works, sometimes the littlest of decisions can affect the rest of your life. There's an old saying: 'lift a pebble off the beach and change the face of the world', again meaning the smallest of things can create the greatest of changes. This little spark of an idea to walk to the bus station, possibly missing out on my ticket home, could see me postponing my journey for another week. Worse still, something might happen and I'd not do it the following week. There might be another tremendous gig that I'd have to see, leading to another chain of events that saw me never leaving London, ever. *That's it*, I thought to myself. *No more pebble lifting, let's get straight to the bus station and hope nobody's taken that last ticket.*

Eventually arriving at Victoria Bus Station, I could see things were hectic, in fact I'd never seen it so busy. People heavily laden with bags, quite a few backpackers carrying camping equipment, I'd never seen so many buses coming and going. The warm summer's air was tinged with that familiar smell of diesel and the constant sound of the bus engines was almost deafening. But very much on the downside was the ticket office; it was mobbed. I had to join a very large queue. Okay, I knew I wasn't the greatest guy in the world but when it came to timing, I used to think I was pretty good, but it certainly looked like I'd got it wrong this time. Looking into the ticket office, you could see the staff were really up against it. They were very focused and working as fast as they could. A lot of the people in the queue were agitated and probably minutes away from missing their bus. Then it dawned on me, most of these people were queuing for tickets for this evening. There was still hope I'd not missed my chance for a ticket for the following morning.

Eventually I was at the desk. I could see the three people in the ticket office were really stressed. I thought I'd try and lighten the mood. I started by remarking, "Wow, you guys are really busy," foolishly thinking that by being nice I'd have more chance of attaining my ticket.

The young lad serving me, still shuffling through schedules, replied, "You could say that. Now what can I help you with!?" He was trying to be patient with me as he gave a tired-looking smile.

"Hi, I'd like a ticket for the early Edinburgh bus for tomorrow morning?"

He didn't directly answer me, but I could see him checking a schedule, then before I knew it, he was organising my ticket. Bingo, yes, I was going. I was bursting with excitement. I tried to calmly say to him, "Oh, I take it I've been lucky to get a ticket so late on," but it wasn't the case. He told me there were quite a few seats left, but he did think it strange himself; usually at this time of year these buses were packed to the rafters.

I paid my money for the ticket, thanked him and about turned out of the station, again bursting with excitement. *It's really happening*, I thought. *Tomorrow at this time I'll be in Edinburgh or if I'm lucky, I might be home in the small town of Kinghorn.* I decided on not wasting any more time. I headed straight across the road, through the shopping arcade and down into the Victoria train station. I had no time to waste. I had to get back to my digs and start packing.

My first tube journey was quite busy, from Victoria along to the Embankment then down deeper to the Northern Line to get all the way back up to Archway. Noticeably the human traffic had lessened; it was obviously moving out of rush hour. There were still lots of people filling the carriages, but they were somewhat different. There were seats still available; not everyone was fighting to grab these for their homeward journey. More people were relaxed, happy even. Some were well dressed, either going to shows or possibly a meal booked in one of the West End's swanky restaurants. Usually, my head would be parked tightly between my shoulders, taking the odd glance at the tube map to check the progress of my journey, but not tonight, not this Friday. I was happy to take it all in. Still, inside me I had the burning excitement that I was finally homeward-bound in the morning.

But seeing all those people laughing and happy and alighting the tube at London's most central stations brought on a realisation that maybe I'd missed out on a few things, notably the couples happy in each other's company looking forward to whatever plans they had for their evening's entertainment. Yup, I wish I'd had someone closer with me to share some of the other delights London had to offer. I thought of Sigrun, my German girlfriend. I say girlfriend, but our relationship began to fall apart as we had different interests and aspirations. This was certainly brought more into focus when I moved out of my suit and into my more relaxed Tower Records attire. I loved my loud music and more raucous lifestyle, although saying that, we did have our moments. We always stayed in touch, and would always meet up, especially visiting her in the house she rented with some other girls. It really was something special, and more so to me than it was for her. Sigrun was roughly six years younger than me and wasn't really a big fan of music, let's say, especially my kind of music. The house was in Highgate and used to be home to most of the original Pink Floyd members many years before. I couldn't believe it when she first told me. Obviously, I couldn't wait to visit.

The house was on the upper part of Stanhope Gardens and beset with leafy foliage as you climbed a few steps to the front door. Inside was fabulous; strangely shaped rooms with Victorian-style windows, with really heavy curtains that reached all the way down to the floor. I was blown away by it, but Sigrun seemed to just take it in her stride, like she was entitled to live in a house of such luxurious style. I had to hand it to her though, she'd really managed to find the nicest of houses to live in. I felt she was really showing off to me, sending me a message that she was right all along, and that my thinking was rather skewed. I could see it, she was right, but I just couldn't change so I chose to ignore her lessons in morality.

Sigrun and I still got on well and she could see I was mesmerised by this magical palace. If only she could sense how massive Pink Floyd were. I was always looking around for some relics (pardon the pun) that may have been left lying around by the band members. When we were young and first started listening to Pink Floyd, we knew nothing about the band, we could only make judgements from the very heavy-sounding music. From the album covers the band seemed dark and moody, people from an underworld that was dangerous and intimidating, and they produced music from a place only they could reach. It was another world, not accessible to normal human beings like us. In reality they were all actually very intelligent, well-educated and came from very middle-class backgrounds, although I suppose the once band leader and frontman Syd Barrett may have been somewhat different from the rest.

The landlord was an old guy called Mike Leonard; he could always be seen pottering around doing any little restoration jobs needed around the house or gardens. You can imagine my surprise when Sigrun finally told me that at one time he had been a tutor for some of the Pink Floyd members when they were at university. Mike had always lived in the left-hand-side of the house whereas the other part (which Sigrun and the girls lived in) was the part frequented by the band. Again, the house inside was fantastic, really old with lots of strange mirrors in places that made the house seem even bigger. Had I been a bit older at the time and surer of myself, I would probably have been endlessly asking Mike questions. He was always quite chatty and had a way of asking you more than you could ever ask him. In fact before I knew it, he'd have me helping him clear garden debris or ferry boxes full of old bits and pieces round to an old shed in his side of the garden. Incidentally the band were almost called Leonard's Lodgers, eventually settling for the name Pink Floyd. I think it was Syd who came up with name, derived from two blues singers called Pink Anderson and Floyd Council.

One final note on this house I'll never forget, was Sigrun's bedroom, which was on the second floor and had a lovely double glass door leading over a little bridge into the garden. It was serene on a summer's evening, and we spent hours just chatting away till we fell asleep only to be woken by the birds singing in the morning.

Sigrun eventually left London before me and headed back to her home, which was Frankfurt in Germany. We said our teary goodbyes one afternoon at Victoria Station. From there she would travel on to the airport.

So, my tube journey was nearly at an end. I was so surprised how quiet the carriages were for this time of night. There were plenty of available seats as the train pulled out of Camden Station. The noise coming from the near empty carriages became thunderous as they were free to jostle and rattle at will with no heavy passengers to hold them in place. I wondered how many people this old carriage had carried over the many years it had been in service. The dusty, old-looking seats and well-worn floors were now very much in evidence as we rattled along at pace. Only two more stops and then I would arrive at Archway Tube Station.

Racing up the escalator, I decided to visit 7-11. I was hungry. I thought, *A quick snack will see me through to the morning.* I knew I still had to get back to my digs and start packing, the problem was, what was I taking and what would I leave? With only two arms I still had to get to Victoria early in the morning.

Eventually getting to my digs, I didn't hang about. Everything was sorted within an hour. I was amazed how quickly I had got through it all. There was a stack of miscellaneous nonsense that would need to be thrown out but rightly or wrongly, that job would be left for the new occupier. On the upside there was a very healthy collection of music magazines and other bits of memorabilia that may have some worth. Without further ado I climbed into bed, thinking that with all the excitement I would never sleep. The last thing I wanted to do was miss my bus home, but before I knew it, I was being woken by a radio alarm. Luckily, I'd slept like a baby.

There was certainly no difficulty in getting out of bed on this morning. It was almost like I was electrically charged. I quickly showered then changed into the clothes I'd left prepared the night before. A few last bits and pieces packed into the bags and a last look around the room just to double check I hadn't forgotten anything important. (In honesty, I never really owned anything so important that I could forget.) That was it, I was off. Not forgetting to leave the key in the door, down the stairs I went. Both bags were slightly heavy, but my mixture of excitement and adrenaline made it a little easier.

With no time to waste myself and the bags quickly shuffled down to the tube station. It was early Saturday morning, and the streets were deadly quiet. I crossed the A1, which was usually teeming with traffic. This road would lead eventually north and out of London. Ironically, I was having to make a five-mile journey south to Victoria Bus Station first. It wasn't long before I found carrying the two bags really hard work. I could feel the sweat running down my back and managed to put them down on the escalator as it slowly took me down to the deep Northern Line.

The station was quiet, just a number of people obviously travelling to their place of work in central London. Still excited, I knew I couldn't settle till I stepped onto that bus at Victoria Station. Thankfully as the tube arrived there were plenty of seats, as it was just after 6:30 in the morning. Now it was a case of waiting till we arrived at the Embankment station. I thought this last journey might have been a bit more like the evening before, where I'd look around the carriages and reflect on my time in London, but no, there was a nervousness about me. I was solely focused on getting to my destination. And if I was to be honest, travelling between tube lines and having these really heavy bags with me was a complete workout.

Changing trains at the Embankment wasn't too difficult – I had to board the next tube for Victoria. I passed the stops for Westminster, St James and then alighted at Victoria. Still sweating and very excited, I made my way across the concourse at Victoria Rail Station. It was a lot busier now, with lots of people making their way out of London, albeit most of them going in a different direction to me, rushing towards the train lines going either southeast or southwest, and not forgetting the very handy Gatwick Express. But I was heading for an escalator at the far right of the station, which would lead me up and through the shopping arcade. With one last look across the station I turned left off the escalator and headed for the sliding doors that would lead me onto the main street.

The traffic was a little busier here now with buses, taxis and lorries heading in all directions. I eventually crossed the road and entered the bus station. I was early, in fact really early; it was only just after 7 o'clock. As far as I could tell my bus wasn't yet available. Not to worry, the main thing was that I was there and ready.

It wasn't long before the time dwindled away, and the bus finally turned up. I was even more relieved to find there weren't too many people there for my bus so choosing a seat was quite easy. My bags were loaded into the bottom of the bus so upstairs I went, getting a double seat to myself on the left-hand side relatively close to the front. It was nice to get sat down and feel a lot more relaxed and comfortable. Also waiting in the station can be very noisy, with constant strong fumes of diesel filling the air. The buses that frequently travel in and out of the station actually move at quite a pace, probably experienced drivers who are skilled at making these journeys regularly through the busy streets of London.

Just as I was settling into my seat, I realised I was feeling quite tired. I'd been up very early and dragging the heavy bags around had obviously taken a lot out of me. I felt the bus engine start up, so I quickly sat up and looked around. It was more than half empty. I smiled to myself, remembering all the worry I'd put myself through the day before wondering if I'd get a ticket or not.

I was sitting straight up again. The bus had started to move. This was really it, I was leaving London, I'd done it. To me it was a great achievement to organise this massive journey. Ridiculous, I know, it was a bus journey from London to Edinburgh, but in my overexcited mind this was another pebble lifted, another dramatic change in my life.

Suddenly we were travelling round Hyde Park Corner and heading up through Park Lane. From my window seat I could see through the trees and into the park; to the right of me the hotels, the Hilton, the Dorchester and then the Grosvenor Hotel. I felt like I was leaving in style with these fantastic views. Soon it was off round Marble Arch and along Edgeware Road. Again, I felt happy knowing it was really happening, with a slight tinge of sadness as I'd had some great times in London that I'd never forget. One thing was for sure, I was equipped with so many great little stories I'd be able to tell all my friends when I got back home to Kinghorn.

Now sinking back into my seat, I began to feel weary and could afford myself a little sleep. My last thoughts before I dropped off were, *That's it, no more big ideas, no more picking up life's little pebbles. This time I was going to settle in Scotland.* Kinghorn was where I belonged. Slowly, I drifted off, probably with a contented smile on my face…

Ironically, a few years later I'd be heading 2,000 miles in the other direction. What did I say about life's little pebbles!!

CHAPTER 6
ALL SYSTEMS GOING RELIABLY TO FUERTE

Being back in Kinghorn was a great feeling, and I couldn't wait to get out and chase up all my old friends. I had to catch up and find out what I'd been missing these last years and of course I had a catalogue of stories to tell of my adventures in London. Like most small towns nothing much had happened. Yup, it was the same old faces, just some of them were looking older and in their defence probably a lot wiser. The main high street was much the same; a few of the old family shops had disappeared and a few new ones in their place. The population had grown also, with newer houses built around the edges of the town. Slowly but surely, Kinghorn was becoming a commuter town for people who would travel back and forth to Edinburgh. Property prices were on the way up and the demographic of the town was changing. New, young, upwardly mobile families were the order of the day as the old faces were slowly disappearing. It dawned on me very quickly that I wasn't that young anymore. How could I have been so naive to think that I would be returning to good old Kinghorn where nothing changes?

I was reminded of my dad shouting down at me as I lay sprawled on the couch watching total rubbish on TV. "Christ, life's passing you by and you don't even bloody realise it." Dare I say it, but I think he may have had a point.

At the time I probably just shrugged my shoulders and rolled my eyes and thought to myself, *Geez, what's he in a bad mood about this time?*

while ignoring his words of wisdom.

Although now heading towards my thirties, my attitude towards life hadn't changed much. I was still very much of the mind that I was going to live for ever so there wasn't much call for me to take life too seriously. It would be made very apparent to me much later in life that I had ADHD, so procrastination was something that hampered me all the way through my formative years. For example, if I was to have my very own motto it would probably go something like: 'why do something today that can easily be put off until tomorrow?' Don't get me wrong, I wasn't a lazy person. I probably just spent lots of my abundant energies on less than productive activities, but I lacked the common sense to prioritise things that were more important. Paradoxically, I could be a very thoughtful guy and had what you would call a big heart, and was always willing to please although, again, symptomatic of my ADHD.

Thankfully when I first arrived back in Scotland, I picked up work helping some of the local builders. In fact one of the guys called Kevin Meldrum was a friend from school, and he had his own joinery business. Now in fairness I'm sure Kevin didn't desperately need an extra pair of hands but was going out of his way to help me, so I should really be eternally grateful that he would do this. Saying that, I have some horrific memories of trying to put roof joists up on a late afternoon in Perth during the winter, as we watched the snow clouds moving in our direction assisted by a cold, strong wind that felt like it was cutting you in half.

One Christmas, while there were lots of visitors at our family home in Kinghorn, I managed to strike up a conversation with my Uncle Robert, who was sales director at my dad's company called Systems Reliability. Robert knew that I had a little bit of experience when it came to advertising sales and suggested I come along and try my hand at computer sales. I was quite honest with Robert and said, "Look, I wouldn't know a good computer if it hit me on my head."

Robert said not to worry. "Computers are just boxes with different names on them." He made it sound so simple. So, before I knew it, I was back in a suit and travelling along to Systems Reliability in Dunfermline, but this was far bigger than just having a new job. I was now working for my dad. The people in this place of work knew I was the boss's son. Myself and my dad were like chalk and cheese. What would they be expecting? I mean, the pressure was really on, I just couldn't afford to slip up. I knew this time I'd really have to focus. Mess this up and I wouldn't just be letting myself down, this would come back directly to my dad.

I really hit the ground running and with the inspiration coming from my determination to make this work, I pulled my sleeves up and got stuck in. Cold calling was something I was used to and to make it easier for myself, I was finding the heads of these companies and sending out some of our well put-together catalogues. As soon as I knew the catalogues were sitting on their desks, I would call them up. It didn't take long for me to start bringing in orders. I'd have two phones on my desk – one for talking to the clients and one for calling any of our engineers whenever I felt I was getting out of my depth. I mean, in the beginning I didn't know the difference between a floppy disc and a floppy hat. Okay, I wasn't that bad but being flung into a world of computers when your life depended on it was quite overwhelming.

I may be blowing my own trumpet a little here, but I was eventually outselling the other four girls my Uncle Robert had employed and more, so things were going swimmingly. Then I had a little altercation with one of our young receptionists. I was only politely asking her to stay on the reception so she could take any important calls we might have been expecting. But she decided to reply to me by telling me where to go. This, as you can imagine, didn't go down too well with me, so honour dictated only one course of action. I reciprocated in likewise fashion.

Later in the day my Uncle Robert picked me up on said incident, was extremely annoyed with me and gave me a real dressing down regarding the subject. I was shocked. Not only was my Uncle Robert there but also one of the other guys who worked with him. I felt ambushed. Before I knew it, I kicked off and stormed away from Robert, and walked out in calamitous fashion. It was an unmitigated disaster. I couldn't believe what had just happened. Everything had crashed around me, just as everything was going so well.

I've played that scenario over in my head a million times. I still feel sick thinking about it now. But whatever happened, I should never have reacted the way I did; it was inexcusable. I'm sure Robert was misinformed and had not been told the truth about the incident. I should've explained my side of the story; I even had a witness to verify what exactly happened. So just one moment of madness and my life took the most dreadful turn for the worse. I'll never forget walking away from Systems Reliability that day, my heart exploding in my chest as I asked myself, "What the hell just happened?"

It all felt so unjust. Even to go as far as to use my ADHD to help people reading this understand things a bit better: One of the problems with people who have ADHD is their need to people please, so to react the way I did was so out of character with the person I really am. So again, what had happened left me with massive anxiety. Throw in a feeling of hyperfocus as I was overthinking every detail of my predicament and how I'd let everyone in my family down. I had just metaphorically burned all my bridges and left myself marooned in a quagmire of shit. Dazed and confused, I took the one road I always had open to me. Yup, getting drunk and stoned, a nice little world I could lose myself in.

Just for the record, I didn't talk with my dad for a good year after that. I mean, how could I? It was a no-brainer. I was going to have to avoid him as best I could.

So, it was back to helping out builders every now and again, on a pathless journey, just stumbling over rough ground that was nothing more than an existence. It didn't take me long to heal and I was back to my happy-go-lucky self with still no real plans or ideas of what the future held for me. That was until one morning, the phone rang. It was early, and I wasn't really expecting to hear from anyone in particular. It was a friend called Barry phoning from Fuerteventura. Barry and his wife Sarah had moved out to Fuerteventura a few months earlier and settled in fairly quickly. I told him I was glad to hear things were going well for them both and jokingly said, "If you hear of any jobs going give me a shout and I'll pop over."

As the phone call finished, I thought, *I can tell the lads later that I heard from Barry*, and then didn't think much more about it.

That evening I didn't leave the house, so I never did manage to pass on the message that Barry sent his best regards. It wasn't till next morning that the phone rang again. It was Barry. Before I could apologise to him and say, 'Sorry, I didn't see anyone last night as I stayed in,' he was too busy trying to shout down the phone, "Get yourself out here, there's a job, if you want it?"

I didn't really have a chance to think about it. The day before had just been a throwaway comment, but here I was, in another predicament. "Eh, yup, okay, I'll come out."

That was it. Just like that, another proverbial pebble had been lifted. I was now hurriedly scraping together what was left of my life (which wasn't much) and preparing to head south, a whole 2,000 miles south, in fact.

CHAPTER 7
LIFT A PEBBLE OFF THE BEACH AND CHANGE THE FACE OF THE WORLD

It's funny, the twists and turns life can take. One day kicking around the streets of your hometown, not knowing what tomorrow brings, then all of a sudden, you're sitting on an aeroplane and heading for the beautiful island of Lanzarote. Oh yeah, I forgot to mention, away back in 1995 we didn't really have internet available and let's just say, my geography wasn't as good as it is now. I foolishly thought Fuerteventura actually was in Lanzarote. Yup, even to this day I get reminded of this cock-up. It wasn't too disastrous as I got a taxi to the harbour in Puerto del Carmen and was lucky to catch the then-hydrofoil boat over to Fuerteventura. I'm sure with the islands being so much more popular now, that defunct boat would be much busier.

One other good point to make here is that the hydrofoil, instead of sailing straight towards Corralejo Harbour, actually went around the east board of Lobos and as it turned towards Corralejo you were looking directly at the two big hotels, the Hotel Riu Oliva Beach and the Hotel Riu Palace Tres Islas. Not only that but you could see the beautiful, long white beaches and the fabulous rocky volcanoes in the distance. The sky was also a very light blue with not a cloud in sight, all while sitting in this crystal-clear water. Yup, I suppose you could say it was love at first sight as my view was lit up by very hot, bright sunlight. Okay, I may be slightly biased here but I'm sure the beaches around the island of Fuerteventura are some of the most picturesque in the world.

If you've never been to the island of Fuerteventura before, it's just sixty miles across the sea from Africa. It's not as densely populated as Gran Canaria, Tenerife or Lanzarote, but is the second largest of all the Canary Islands. I think the special thing about Fuerteventura out of all the other islands, is that it has a big bit of everything, including long, gorgeous stretches of uninhabited beautiful beaches with the sort of backdrop that film directors can only dream about. In fact, on that subject, there have been quite a few blockbuster movies filmed on the island, which means we've had some of the biggest-named A-listers in Fuerteventura as well. And for people who enjoy hiking there are some fantastic walks to be done, with incredible views from the tops of our many volcanoes.

The sea during the summer months is warmer than our swimming pools and is a sight to behold when we get some of the biggest waves in the world crashing onto our shoreline. These regular humungous waves attract some of the best surfers from around the world. The sport is more prevalent during the winter months when we always get the large swells. The name Fuerteventura directly translates as 'strong winds', associated with the trade winds, which means we are also a popular destination with all the biggest names in wind and kite surfing. The world championships are held every July down by an area called Sotavento, near the south part of the island on the east coast.

Jandia, Morro Jable, which is just a little further south of Sotavento, seems to be much busier with German tourists. It's fantastic if you want to just get away from everything, being a place of great beauty, especially if you want to put your feet up and do nothing. My good friend Trefor and I have been down there quite a lot, walking. Actually that makes it sound too easy, it's more of a hike/climb when you're trying to clamber to the top of Pico de la Zarza, which is one of the highest volcanoes on the island. But on a clear day the views are probably some of the best I've seen in my life. From the top you look down onto Cofete Beach and the very infamous Villa Winter, and from the very southern tip of the island, you can sometimes see Gran Canaria.

But it's Corralejo on the very northern tip of the island that would eventually become my home. Not fulfilling a lifetime's dream, or part of an organised plan to complete my list of places to visit, just because of a few phone calls. Yes, I had been extremely lucky to say the least. I'd managed to cut out a life for myself in a little corner of the world that resembled something close to paradise.

I'd start my new life working in a hotel called Dunas Caleta. Little did I know then that I would eventually spend twenty years of my life there. Everything just seemed to fall into place. I started off working on the bar within the hotel, which fit like a pair of your favourite shoes. Further down the line I reluctantly crossed over from the bar and took on the position of the hotel's entertainer. This, again, was something that just seemed to work for me. I always enjoyed other people's company and with my ADHD-charged energy it was another perfect fit. I didn't fully realise it at the time, it's something I only became aware of after having time to reflect over the years.

Even though there's a terrible downside to having ADHD, the job of entertaining lots of people was probably made so much easier because of it. For instance, I had boundless energy, I could talk to twenty different people on twenty different subjects all at once, my creativity was always on fire as situations would force me to think on my feet. And because of my ADHD I never took myself too seriously, even when people sang my praises, deep down I always felt I was an underachiever, which left me feeling a little insecure. Oh, don't get me wrong, these feelings were always well masked and hidden from daylight, so when people said I was doing a good job I'd shrug my shoulders and tell them I was just being me. I was lucky that I was in an environment where everyone wanted to be happy and enjoy themselves. Another ADHD trait is a desperate need to people please, so once again the job was the perfect match for my personality.

Yup, this was certainly the best pebble I had picked up; it changed the face of my world. Now obviously I'm not the only one who has had these strange, small, but life-changing events, there must be millions of people out there with their own little stories to tell. I don't know who came up with the saying 'lift a pebble from the beach and change the face of the world' but it's my favourite.

Another great story I have is about a nice guy called Jason, who now happily lives in Corralejo with his Italian wife and two lovely teenage kids. Twenty years ago, Jason was sitting in his house in London flicking through the channels on the telly one evening, getting rather frustrated that there was just nothing to watch. He was comfortable, he didn't want to move, was it too much to ask that maybe something he liked might come on the box? There was only one thing for it. He knew his friends were meeting down at the pub for a celebratory drink as they were all heading to Fuerteventura the next day for a stag do. He wasn't really dying to go down and join them as he would just end up feeling left out. They would all be joking around and looking forward to the week ahead of sun, sea, sangria, and no doubt girls. One last scour through the channel to no avail; there was still nothing on. So, with that, he grabbed his jacket and wallet and headed to the pub.

Not really in the mood, Jason promised himself he'd probably only stay for a couple at the most. Just as he got close to the pub door, he could hear the familiar sounds of his friends laughing in that pre-holiday fashion. His heart sank. He wasn't really in the mood for this. As he pushed the pub door open, he saw his group of friends positioned around the bar, laughing and smiling like Cheshire cats. He could tell they'd already had a few as in their excitement they hadn't even noticed Jason joining their company.

Eventually one of his friends turned round and noticed him. "Jace, that was good timing, mate."

Jason automatically thought they were going to tell him to get the next round in. But it wasn't what he was expecting. Suddenly the group of friends gathered round him. Simon, who he was very close to, said, "Jace, mate, Bill's had to pull out, why don't you take his ticket?"

Jason shook his head in a dismissive manner and said, "No way." He didn't think they were being entirely serious. Mind you as he looked around, he could see that Bill wasn't there.

One of the other lads shouted, "C'mon, Jace, it'll be a laugh. Anyway it would be a waste of a ticket."

Other voices were now joining in. "C'mon, Jace, we will chip in so you've got some cash. You can pay us back later."

Jason didn't really know what to say. As it always is with a group of mates when they are all on your back at once, it's very difficult to say no. Jason was working with his brother at the time so he knew in the back of his mind that missing work at short notice wouldn't be too much of a problem. So, as the clamour of voices reached fever pitch, with them haranguing him to go, he gritted his teeth and smiled and spoke. "Yeah, alright."

The rest of the lads gave out an almighty cheer. Before he could say any more, he was handed a pint as shouts of, "Well done, Jace!" filled the night air.

I was working on the bar when I first got to meet them, on the evening of the day they arrived. Straight away you could tell they were a good group of lads, all from Canvey Island in England. Four days into their holiday I was working a day shift when in the morning a few of Jason's entourage came in looking for breakfast. One of the lads, sadly I can't remember his name, came up to the bar and said, "I think our Jason got fixed up with one of your barmaids last night." In his defence I remember straight away noticing that Jason was one of the quieter lads in the group, but I remembered him chatting a way with one of our barmaids called Manuella a few nights earlier. She was a lovely girl, very pleasant and very good looking as well. I didn't really know her that well but was good friends with her sister, who used to live very close to me.

It wasn't till one of the other lads said, "I think she went back to Jason's apartment with him last night." Just at that one of the other group members came walking in, this was Paul the guy who was actually sharing an apartment with Jason.

One of the guys asked him, "Was Jason up in the apartment?"

"Yeah, he's up there conked out with that girl Manuella that works here."

That was it, music to my ears. I got the lads together and with a group of people I knew who had already been sitting on their sunbeds, we headed off to Jason's apartment. We already knew the door was open so with a total of about twenty people we all sneaked into Jason's bedroom. They had all been primed and informed of what we were going to do on the way up. Once we were all gathered round Jason's bed, we could see both himself and Manuella were out for the count. When I gave the word, we started shouting and bawling at the top of our voices. Needless to say our two lovers nearly hit the roof with fright, with everyone cheering and shouting at their now very embarrassing predicament.

Thankfully, it was all taken in good humour and was a great talking point for the rest of the guy's holiday. A bit more embarrassing for Manuella. But all is well that ends well, as only a matter of two weeks later and Jason was back out again to visit her. For the next two weeks they were inseparable so it came as no surprise to any of us that Jason would move out to Fuerteventura permanently. Even to this day Jason and Manuella are still very happily married with two lovely kids. Jason is now fluent in Italian and has visited Manuella's parents many times in Italy. And Jason's family are now regular visitors to the island, at least once a year as they, too, have fallen in love with the place. Imagine that, a whole string of events and changes all because one evening back in Canvey, Jason couldn't find anything decent to watch on the telly.

CHAPTER 8

HAPPY DAZE

As the years went on, my past was slipping to the furthest reaches of my mind. Not that I was doing this intentionally, just that working split shifts six days a week didn't give you much time to think about anything else. Again, it's very far from what people might term a normal job. The minute you walk into the hotel to the minute you walk out, you are permanently on show. It doesn't matter what kind of day you've had or whether you're not feeling well, you still must smile and keep those energy levels up. Now I would again suggest that any normal person looking at it would see a very demanding position. But for someone who has ADHD, it helps. It's not what you would call therapeutic or relaxing, it's more like going through life on a trampoline, jumping up and down, talking a lot, laughing, dancing and permanently running around. Being chemically wired to seek to increase my levels of the neurotransmitter dopamine, this demanding job was just perfect. And again, I think it's important to reiterate that at the time I hadn't even considered that I might have ADHD, so incredibly I was already self-medicating for a problem I didn't even know I had.

Stepping away from my ADHD for just a moment to discuss some of the more integral points of my job and lifestyle, I was certainly getting to meet thousands of people from all over the UK, from all walks of life. This was made more apparent while doing my regular volcano hike once a week. It was five miles in distance and a thousand feet high, which gave us panoramic views right around the very north of the island. After I had given out loads of information about the views and everything we could see, I'd then give a bit more about the history of the island. But after that was all done and dusted, as soon as we were making the long trek back, I'd really enjoy listening to some of the other people talking. Okay, not all of them but I must admit I learned a lot over the years.

This gave me a great insight into how other people lived back in the UK. I'd learn a lot about people's attitudes towards things and some of the different places they came from. Again, lots of people from different professional backgrounds, whether they be doctors, nurses, bus drivers, railway workers, police, engineers, social workers, lots of young people with great aspirations for the future, with many of them still studying at university. Some of my favourites were people who had been in the forces for a number of years and travelled most of the world. I was always taken aback by their knowledge of all the places they had been stationed, and some of the more horrific situations they'd been in. I was blown away by how philosophical they were about it all. I found the longer they had served, the more understanding they seemed to be. I was always very honest with them as I'm not a huge fan of conflict and can be very sceptical of some of the reasons we enter certain situations. So, I was most surprised when many of them were of the same point of view.

One of the sillier moments that always sticks in my mind was one time I was chatting away with a guy about a worldly situation. We seemed to be in total agreement over everything, which was great. As the conversation drew to a close, I decided to ask him what he did for a living. As he told me, I literally fell over; I jumped back like I'd had an electric shock and landed on my backside. And what caused this sudden rush of excitement, I hear you ask? Well, he just casually told me he was a dentist. Yes, you guessed it, I have a massive fear of dentistry as a whole, so I was caught unawares. I couldn't believe I was striking up a friendship with a dentist. I'm not going to make a big song and dance about this but maybe some of the older people reading will remember the film 'The Marathon Man' with Dustin Hoffman. That's all I'm saying on this subject.

Christmas time would take the job to another level. Not only did you have all the usual demands expected of you, but they were doubled up with all the extra razzamatazz that Christmas brings. I would do my very best to try not to think about it till the first day of December, then the first thing I'd do is work out what days Christmas Day and New Year's Day fell on. For instance, was it a big changeover day when loads of guests were leaving the hotel as new ones were coming in? This was always the worst-case scenario. Yup, what day it fell on mattered. It could have massive consequences regarding planning and organisation. Not only that but if people were arriving late, it was difficult trying to control the atmosphere.

We were lucky because the majority of Christmases we had an incredible number of repeat guests that would visit. That made things so much easier for us all, but if there were new people, it was good to spend a few days with them before the festivities started so we could prime them for the up-and-coming events. And just to throw in a little extra added pressure, my mother and father would visit for a month during the Christmas and New Year period. To be honest I didn't mind. It was nice. After my formative years, my relationship had been a bit strained with my parents for a multitude of reasons, but now things were really good between us all. In fact my dad would even cook a Christmas dinner of sorts when I could eventually get time off during that busy period. Unfortunately, my mother wasn't a hundred percent and after a terrible accident was wheelchair bound, so yes, we did have our moments but in general it was great having them there.

I suppose that was one of the hardest things during that period. There was just no rest, there was no let-up, we were always busy at work and then it was hectic at home. You could never find time to put your feet up and relax. But as hard and as hectic as it all sounds, there were thousands of great moments and laughs all the way through.

My time as an entertainer at Dunas Caleta (now under another name) was all consuming. I literally lived and breathed my job. It became a real challenge for me to make sure everything ran as smoothly as possible. I was also very lucky that my bosses just left me to my own devices. It worked. What's the old saying, 'if it's not broken, don't fix it'? So I knew if the guests were happy, the holiday companies that sent their guests were happy. And if they were all happy, my bosses, too, would be happy. Yup, there's no getting away from it, the magic ingredients were all about being happy.

Again, during that busy period in my life I was having a little personal success, and even though I probably didn't realise it at the time, I was really enjoying myself. The only thing I was having trouble with was taking time off. I was actually allocated forty-eight days off a year and I was only ever using seven of those. One of the problems I had was finding someone to cover me. It wasn't like you could just pull someone off the bar to do it, and offering someone a week's work is not an attractive offer at the best of times. Then there was the hassle of trying to entertain a hotel, which sometimes held up to four hundred guests a week. That in itself is quite a daunting prospect for someone that's not used to that particular environment, especially when you're trying to fill the shoes of an ADHD-fuelled madman. When I did eventually find someone to cover me, I would usually fly back to my hometown of Kinghorn in Fife, Scotland. Yup, even though I was beginning to notch up lots of happy years in Corralejo in Fuerteventura I was still calling Kinghorn home.

Another symptom of my ADHD is that my hopes and emotions can become somewhat misplaced. Sometimes you don't recognise a good thing in front of you till it's gone. Too busy spending my energies running around thinking on my feet and not taking time to settle down and think things through, but again, I couldn't grumble, I was having a good life.

Eventually in 2005 my partner Nicky would start joining me on my travels back to Kinghorn. She could see the attraction; it was a small town, well positioned on the Fife coastline with fantastic views across the River Forth to Scotland's capital city, Edinburgh. Kinghorn was also blessed with beautiful beaches but obviously not as nice as Fuerteventura's, and obviously not as warm. But still, Kinghorn was a nice place to get out and about in. For a small town it certainly played a big part in Scotland's long and turbulent history. Yes, the last of the Celtic kings, Alexander III tragically fell from his horse while late one evening during a storm he was trying to return to his castle in Kinghorn to see his young wife, Yolanda. Not only did I find it really weird that the King of Scotland made that journey on his own, but to fall from a very obvious cliff seems very strange. Trying to find historic reports from the twelfth century is certainly not easy but you only have to look at the events that took place after his death. Do I think Edward the first had a hand in it…? Yes!! Do I have any evidence…? No!!

It wasn't just Kinghorn that Nicky enjoyed on our visits to Scotland. We very much enjoyed getting the train over to Edinburgh; it's a fantastic journey as the train travels mostly along the coastline and eventually takes you over the very iconic Forth Rail Bridge. When I was younger, I used to love going to Edinburgh; it was always a really great place to go. We only ever seemed to go to Edinburgh to have fun. As a kid, my friends and I would venture over there just to explore the city, then as we got older it would be to see great bands and eventually just to enjoy a great day out amongst all the great pubs.

It wasn't just Nicky and I who were going over, we began to take my brother Kenneth's two kids, James and Amy, with us. This was just brilliant fun. I'm sure I was reliving my own childhood, only now it was a no-holds-barred extravaganza. We would go wherever they wanted and spoil them rotten. We would visit the castle, the National Museum of Scotland, where in honesty James and I would spend more time playing hide and seek from the girls. Saying that, museums are fantastic places to take kids as it really helps open their minds to the ever-evolving world around them.

And on that subject, we would then travel down to the bottom of the Royal Mile and just past the Scottish Parliament we would visit Dynamic Earth, which is a must for everyone, not just kids. It covers the Big Bang right up to the present day while still making you think about the future as it tries to peer out into the cosmos. I just wonder how many kids became interested in astrophysics after visiting.

These places were visited in the first part of the day and we would then make our way to Princess Street so the kids could buy something nice. Once that was done, we would always go for a slap-up meal and no, it didn't stop there, it would be back up the Royal Mile so we could visit Camera Obscura and its world of illusions. It was just the greatest day out.

As you probably suspect by now, I enjoyed it just as much as the kids. Imagine it, you've got a wallet packed with money that can only be used for fun in the capital city of Scotland. No heavy baggage, just the four of us running around the streets of Edinburgh having the best time. I mean, when I was a kid, I just didn't have all that extra cash so hell yeah, I was going to make up for it. It was great going back to Kinghorn to see friends and family and I was over the moon that Nicky enjoyed it also, but there's no shadow of a doubt the best days were when me, Nicky, Amy and James would head to Edinburgh and I'm sure that planted a seed in my mind for my future extravagancies.

As the years went on Nicky and I knew we had to try doing something else. We were already living in a hot climate with some of the nicest beaches in the world, so we needed to go somewhere different. So, one night while enjoying a meal at La Luna's, which is very close to Corralejo Harbour and not far away from my apartment, we got back onto the subject of holidays. I had just ordered a large Macallan's whisky and Nicky a Carlos I brandy. Julie, the girl serving us, was a good friend and had been working at the restaurant for years, so she always made sure our drink measures were more than adequate. It had been a lovely meal and we were both in good spirits as we began to talk about going to Venice, Lake Como in Italy, Switzerland and even considered Paris, and then Nicky suggested London.

"London, really?" I asked.

"Yeah, I'd love to go to London," she replied.

I wasn't sure at first, the idea didn't really excite me, but the more we talked about it the more I began to like the idea. Eventually after another couple of large drinks we decided to make the short journey home, where the subject of possibly going to London was still very much at the forefront of our minds. Back in 2008 I had a computer at the end of my bed so we both started checking out Google Earth and pinpointing London. I'd focused down on Covent Garden, remembering how much I loved that place. I began to tell her about the time my friend Simon came down from Kinghorn to visit me in London, and with some of my friends from the *Observer* and a collection of Ian Myles' friends we had all had a great day at the Punch and Judy bar in Covent Garden. Everyone got on so well and we commandeered the whole balcony upstairs looking over the entertainers on the West Piazza.

We must have spent hours looking at all the different areas around London. I was getting especially excited as each one I'd have a little memory tied to it. We were able to focus in on where I stayed in North London and the one that lifted my heart the most was Hampstead Heath. I told Nicky how I'd spent lots of time cycling through the park on summer days, just people watching and wishing that I had someone there to share the experience. This made me stop and think. This had started off as an idea about going on holiday to London and was now turning into 'let's troop around London reliving Gary's memories'. And wait a minute, if I remember rightly, I couldn't wait to get out of the place.

Nicky just laughed and said, "I'd love to visit Hampstead Heath and all these other places you've mentioned." Well, that was good enough for me.

Next day, reality had kicked in. It was a bit late in the year and if we were going to visit London it was certainly going to take a bit more planning. We would still need someone to babysit our four cats and there was no way I'd be able to find someone to cover work at such short notice. But the seeds were sown. In 2009 we were definitely going to have a holiday in London.

CHAPTER 9
ALL PLANNED UP AND READY TO GO

Two thousand and nine started just like every other year. The weather was great, and we were getting all our regular guests and more. We were lucky, as the island was beginning to struggle a bit with so many cheap flights laid on for places like Egypt and Turkey, but fortunately for us our hotel, the Dunas Caleta, was getting more repeat guests every year. The Dunas Caleta wasn't a five-star hotel and was certainly not a place you would describe as luxurious, but it was a place that was very special in many people's hearts. First off, the hotel was well situated in Corralejo, so it wasn't too far away from the main drag and was very close to the town's beaches. Secondly our poolside was a great sun trap and well protected from the winds. And last but not least, it was super friendly. Most of our staff had worked there for years and having so many repeat guests, everyone got on like a house on fire. We were all just one big happy family.

This year was slightly different, though. I had something new to focus on especially with us planning a holiday in London. As the year went on, every Friday night we would sit by the computer looking at all the different areas around London and possible places we could stay. Nicky, within reason, was quite happy to leave me to make the final judgement on where we would eventually book, only as I had some experience and knowledge of where everything was.

The one thing we wanted to do was find a really nice restaurant, but even though I'd lived there for a few years my knowledge of restaurants was pretty limited. Of course, London was filled with prestigious restaurants, as we were finding out as we searched the internet on these late Friday evenings, but trying to decide on one wasn't easy. Then, during a brief conversation with my dad on the phone, I just happened to tell him that Nicky and I had decided to visit London. I asked him if he was going there, what restaurant would he most like to visit? "Oh, the Gavroche most likely," he replied. He then began to go on about the Roux brothers, which sparked a memory. Of course, my dad used to watch them on TV when we were younger. Well, that was good enough for me. Little did we realise we were dipping our toe into the world of the finest of dining.

It was only through further research that we began to realise the Gavroche was part of the Roux dynasty, and was highly regarded as one of London's iconic restaurants. Not only was it famed for its classic French cuisine, but it was legendary, with a great number of the big-name chefs beginning their careers at this most famous kitchen based in Upper Brook Street. Names such as Gordon Ramsey, Marco Pierre White, Marcus Wareing, Pierre Koffman, Monica Galletti, Jun Tanaka, Bryn Williams, Stephen Terry, Rowley Leigh, Paul Rankin and Bryan Maule all learned their trade from the Roux masters, Albert and Michel. Now to be honest, at the time I wasn't really familiar with any of these names, but I did know about the Roux brothers as they had a show on the telly in the early eighties called 'At Home with the Roux Brothers'. Again, in these days I was still more interested in eating rather than cooking, but it was my dad who was in control of the TV.

After a looking at lots more restaurants we had our hearts set on booking the Gavroche. If we were going to do it, we may as well do the best. I also realised I had better consider buying some decent clothes, as the Gavroche had a dress code to be followed. Living in the sunny climate of Fuerteventura, you spend most of your time in shorts and t-shirts. That may stretch to jeans and a jersey during the cooler months of winter.

This really spurred on the whole idea of holidaying in London. We had now decided on a fantastic restaurant, so we really needed to book somewhere to stay before we could book anything else.

There was no doubt about it, the brief conversation we had with my dad really got the wheels in motion as all our efforts on an evening were spent trying to find the ideal place to stay. One other important thing preying on my mind was that if we were going back, I just had to revisit all the places I'd spent a lot of my time while I'd been there before. Archway, Highgate and one of my favourite places of course, Hampstead Heath. But to get round all those places in a day, I was going to have to look at hiring bikes.

At first, in the planning, I was foolishly full of trepidation. Maybe it was because I almost ran away from the place. I couldn't leave quick enough as I scuttled my way back up to Scotland. But now I was looking at things completely differently. I was really excited to be revisiting after a nearly twenty-year gap and having someone to share the experience with.

It was really good fun on these evenings. We would drink wine as we scoured our way through the internet looking at hotels and maps, trying to pinpoint our perfect location. London being the size it is, there are so many places to choose from, but as you can imagine some of the swankier hotels are just so expensive. It was massively important that we could find a balance; somewhere that was in a good location but wasn't extortionate when it came to price. Eventually, after weeks of searching we came across a fantastic bed and breakfast called the Parkwood Hotel in Stanhope Place. This was just off the Edgeware Road, but more importantly it was just across from Hyde Park, very close to Marble Arch, which meant we were just across from Park Lane and a stone's throw from Oxford Street.

It was still only July, but this was us really excited now, especially as we had sorted a hotel in a fantastic location. It dawned on me that it wasn't just talk, we were really going. It was only for five nights so the next thing we had to do was organise the flights. I say we, but this was a job for Nicky; she was much better at stroking the 'T's and dotting the 'I's. Having such specific dates always makes things a little more challenging, but I knew once Nicky had the bit between her teeth we couldn't go wrong.

Our first night in the hotel was booked for Friday the 18th of September, which meant we would travel back the following Wednesday. The only slight hiccup I could see was that our flight was booked for a late arrival to Gatwick Airport, which would see us landing at around half twelve in the early hours of the morning. This probably meant hanging around the airport till the Gatwick Express started running. I was not going to start worrying about that just yet, as it was still a few months away and there were still other little plans to be made.

I was scouring the internet to find somewhere we could hire bikes. I had a burning desire to retrace my old haunts, especially Archway where I lived, and Highgate, and finally one of my favourite places, Hampstead Heath. My only real concern was taking Nicky out onto the busy roads. We had both been cycling around Corralejo for years, but this was hardly comparable with the busy streets of London. The one bike hire company that kept grabbing my attention was The London Bicycle Company, which was then based down in Gabriel's Wharf, right next to the ITV studios and not far from the NFT, right in between the Waterloo and Blackfriars bridges. But worryingly, in the back of my mind was the possibility of Nicky being overwhelmed at not just the distance but the more obvious hazards, tackling the horrendous amounts of traffic we would encounter on the way. I made a point of reassuring Nicky we would target the quietest of streets on our journey and the idea was to start early on the Saturday morning so there wouldn't be any of that usual weekly rush-hour traffic. Again, I knew I was trying to convince myself, not just Nicky, that we would pick out the perfect route, so for the next few weeks I made a great deal of effort to work out the safest of routes.

It wasn't lost on me that it was nearly twenty years since I had last cycled the streets of London. Youthful bravado had waned ever so slightly over the years so just as a precaution I didn't book anything. I knew we could make our way down there on the Saturday morning and it left the door open just in case we had a change of plans. And it gave me a chance to get to London so we could assess our capabilities once we sampled the traffic for ourselves. So if I was to be honest, I needed to know if I was confident enough to cycle those mean streets myself.

There was only one last thing left to organise, and that was to get myself some decent attire. Don't get me wrong, I had loads of clothes, just that most of them were probably not suitable for London, especially as it was going to be the end of September, just as winter was beginning to stick its chilling nose into the proceedings. Most of my clothes were splashed with motifs such as Quicksilver, Oneill, Billabong and Rip Curl to mention a few. Yes, these were all worldly renowned surfing brands. Okay, I had dabbled in surfing through the years but there was no way I could call myself a surfer. In my defence, though, I spent a lot of time out in some really huge waves, right on the doorstep of my apartment. And at the ripe old age of forty-six there was no way you could be some kind of hip dude, especially as the years were beginning to show on my well-weathered façade. That was one great thing about living in Fuerteventura, you didn't have to get sucked into the latest trends; there were no rules saying you had to grow up and act your age. There was no doubt about it, time and maturity flew past me in that wonderful sunny climate and I didn't have any regrets.

CHAPTER 10
TWO TICKETS GOING 2,000 MILES NORTH, PLEASE

It was the 18th of September 2009; the day had arrived. We were all packed up and ready to go to London on holiday. Nicky's mum, Mandy, was staying with us. She had fortunately agreed to come and babysit our Yorkshire terrier, Harry. It wasn't just our wee dog, we had four cats as well – Scraggy, Alex, Harvey, and Sophie.

The day went quickly. It wasn't long till we were making our way along to the harbour at Corralejo, which was only five minutes from our apartment. As our flight to London was set to leave from Lanzarote at eight o'clock, we had to catch the Fred Olsen ferry at five. It was only a twenty-minute journey and from the harbour at Playa Blanca we would get a taxi to Lanzarote Airport. As usual it was a beautiful, warm, sunny day so we made sure we stood right at the back of the ferry on the top deck. From there we could wave goodbye to Fuerteventura with the sun still blazing down on our faces. There wasn't a cloud in the sky, with very little breeze and not much swell to talk of, so we knew we were in for a smooth journey.

The good thing about the Fred Olsen ferry was that it was only in open water for just under fifteen minutes, so you didn't get much time to feel seasick. In any case my stomach was too full of butterflies and excitement to be worried about the swell. It's a great view from the back of the boat. To the left is the small island of Lobos, which is only a mile from Fuerteventura. Looking down the middle you can see the harbour and beyond that, the beautiful beaches, Grandes Playas, which glow brightly in the late afternoon sun. Just at the back of Corralejo is my volcano, Bayuyo, as it stands proudly keeping a watchful eye over the town. And to the right-hand side is the north shore, with its many dangerous reefs. Only the time-served surfing experts from the island know when and where's best. Even the people that have surfed the north shore for years know to treat it with respect, as many little wooden crosses lay testament to the dangers of being overambitious in these perilous waters. I'd never spent much time in the sea round there, but I knew the place well as I had cycled to the small fishing village of Cotillo many times.

Looking north, you can see Lanzarote getting ever closer as the ferry cuts through the oncoming swell at around twenty-five knots. The slight breeze blowing from the north is still warm but fresh, keeping the top deck nice and cool.

At that time of day on Thursdays, things were quiet so we had no trouble getting a taxi to the airport. There was very little traffic on the roads as we easily skirted our way around the edges of Puerto del Carmen. The airport itself is well set out; we literally got out of the taxi, straight through the front door and practically walked into our Gatwick queue. It all seemed to happen so quickly. Everyone around us was still proudly wearing their holiday attire. Some of them a very dark brown colour, obviously having spent most of their time oiled up, never leaving their sunbeds unless for an emergency, while some of the others look like they've had a flash burn, noses and foreheads still peeling as their bodies glowed as bright as their luminous t-shirts and shorts. You could tell Nicky and I lived in the Canarias, our tans were well blended, our dress sense a little more sober and not screaming out 'Look at us! We've been on holiday!' Little did our fellow travellers know we were actually bursting with excitement at the prospect of landing at Gatwick, whereas it was just the beginning of their holiday blues.

Looking around me, it reminded me of my earlier life where

people who worked in the building trade or had to do hard manual labour would dress up at the weekends, but people who worked in offices or had to always wear suits would always dress down. Then there were the clever ones who wore whatever they wanted, whenever they wanted.

I have never been a fan of flying so I'm always very nervous before a flight, but once we took off and I caught a glimpse of Lanzarote all lit up, it had a very calming effect. I don't fly very often and knowing I'm going to be sat in once place for over four hours, there's no hesitation when it comes to considering booking the extra leg room. Having that little bit of extra space makes such a difference regarding the comfort of the flight and definitely helps you feel a lot better mentally and physically when you arrive at your destination.

Thankfully, I was relaxed enough to grab a few hours' sleep on the flight, so it went a lot quicker than expected. That weird noise from the plane's engines has a calming effect, which if I'm not mistaken is called pink noise. Its hypnotic effect helps drown out any other sounds around you. For a lot of people, the worst part of the flight is when the plane starts to descend, which is usually a hundred and twenty miles from the destination. In aviation terms this is meant to be the riskiest time in a flight, as there's a multitude of things that can go wrong. Obviously, this is all worked out from a law of averages and considering how many aeroplanes land in a day there's not really a lot to worry about. Personally, my spirits really pick up when we start to descend. No one has to tell you as you can usually feel the drop in the thrust, or the biggest give away is your ears starting to pop as the cabin pressure changes.

I had never flown into Gatwick before, so I didn't have a clue what to expect. All I knew was it was going to be late and we would need to find somewhere comfortable to hang out before the first Gatwick Express was available. This was a direct train that would take us from the airport right into Victoria Train Station. I'd been through Victoria Station many times before, so I thought it couldn't have changed too much. Mind you, again, it had been nearly twenty years since I was last there.

As the plane was landing, we could see streetlights and roads with quite a bit of traffic still on them. The airport itself looked massive, all lit up and still very much awake. We landed smoothly. I knew we were in no particular rush so instead of hurriedly getting our things together I just gazed out of the cabin window with Nicky sitting at my side. The airport looked expansive, cold, but still lots of things going on. There were quite a few little vehicles buzzing around us with their flashing lights. Just a little further into the distance we could see lots of other aircraft docked beside the gates leading back to the terminal. Most of them looked like they'd been sitting there for a while as there seemed to be no sign of life around them.

The cabin had sprung to life as everyone stood up, rushing to get their luggage down. Leaving the plane, we could feel the cooler air around us. We were so used to the warm September evenings in Fuerteventura, it was obvious that even the southeast of England was expecting an imminent visit from winter's cooler nights.

Not knowing exactly where we were going, we just followed our fellow passengers through what seemed to be a maze. In fact, maybe even a rabbit warren of corridors and tunnels, lots of little signs asking us if we had anything to declare and to make sure we had our passports ready. It felt like we were walking for ages before we eventually arrived at passport control. The size of the place is quite overwhelming, so I wasn't to surprised when I heard that Gatwick employs over twenty thousand people, and that probably doesn't include flight crews and outside contractors.

As we stood in the queue with our passports at the ready, we could hear some of the people in front of us talking on their phones, letting friends and loved ones know where and when they wanted to be picked up. It was different for Nicky and me, we had hours to wait on that first train to Gatwick. On the upside it would give us time to suss out where we would get the train from. It was something I'd taken into consideration before we even started the journey. I had been concerned that being awake all of Thursday night through till Friday morning would leave us shattered up until the Saturday, which wasn't much use when you consider we were only there for five nights. My only hope was that once we checked into the hotel, we would manage to grab a few hours, so we weren't too tired for the rest of the Friday.

Once we got through passport control it was only a short distance to the luggage area. Again, we were in no rush but as luck would have it our suitcase was one of the first to come out along the conveyor belt.

As we walked out into concourse of the south terminal, things were still open and seemed relatively busy with people rushing back and forth. Nicky had spotted a chemist, whereas my eyes were drawn to the newsagents. I didn't need anything in particular but like I said, we were in no rush, so I decided just to pop in for a browse. When in there, it didn't take me long to find some mountain bike magazines. I hadn't bought one in years, so I grabbed one of the best, which is *MBR magazine*. From a very young age I'd always been fascinated by these two-wheeled machines. One of my very few achievements was learning to ride a bike. It still amazes me to this day the way they defy gravity as inertia and rolling motion work together, all backed up by the energy from a good strong heart. Mountain bikes to me were the greatest invention of them all as they allowed you to cross all different types of terrain, giving you freedom to go wherever you wish. Luckily, I was still deeply in love with my Trek 9.8 elite mountain bike, which I'd had for seven years, so there was no danger of being turned on to a new bike. That was the thing with these magazines, once you read them from cover to cover it could leave you frothing at the mouth dreaming about getting your hands on one of the latest machines. But again, I was only browsing, and it was something to do while the minutes ticked away as we could only patiently wait for the Gatwick Express into Victoria.

Just across from the newsagents was a Marks and Spencer's food hall, which was still open. Nicky and I hadn't really eaten much since we left Corralejo, so this was just perfect to satisfy our appetites. It didn't take us long to get really excited about this; every shelf was packed with the most exotic of selections – filled sandwiches, salads, smoked salmon, prawns, cakes, desserts, and a vast choice of drinks – coffee, smoothies, fruit drinks, milk, and a decent selection of wines. We were almost running around in there like a couple of kids in a sweet shop. This was a far cry from what we were used to in Fuerteventura. It was only a few years earlier that our main supermarket in Corralejo called 'Masymas' was only half the size of this Marks and Spencer's food court, and their selection of foods was far from appetising. I remember one day I had bought a box of muesli and on returning home decided to pour out a large helping with lots of milk. I remember sticking on the telly as I shovelled down a few spoonfuls of the milky mush, then as I was munching away, I looked down into the bowl only to see the whole thing moving. I had already swallowed a generous helping of this bug-infested mush before I noticed it was crawling with weevils. Yup, I'll not forget that day in a hurry. Oh, there was no point in complaining, they would've only wanted to charge me more for the weevils.

It'll probably come as no surprise to hear Nicky and I bought way too much from that food court that evening, and to think, that was even with Nicky trying to restrain me from my over-excitedness. We managed to find a few seats, so we got ourselves comfortable and did our best to scoff as much as possible of all the food we bought, read our magazines, chatted a bit and watched the world go by. Thankfully the time seemed to fly by and it wasn't long till we were making our way up an escalator to the train terminus. The excitement was starting to build again as we bought our tickets. We knew it wasn't going to be long before we arrived in London.

We shuffled our way along the platform and got onto the six-twenty Gatwick Express, which would get us directly into Victoria for dead-on ten to seven. The train was nice and quiet, which made the journey far more relaxing. The idea of being flung straight into the mad rush of London life after leaving the quiet and tranquil peace of Fuerteventura seemed quite daunting. Yup, Nicky, our two rucksacks and suitcase being uncontrollably swept along with throngs of people during rush hour would've been overwhelming to say the least. So, it was nice just sitting looking out of the window of the train with our bags beside us, wondering what lay ahead, both filled with excitement and high expectations of a great holiday bubbling away in the back of our minds.

Though it was early morning we could see it was going to be a cloudless sky by the time we arrived at Victoria. Even the trees were still laden with heavy foliage so we could see London wasn't finished with summer just yet. The excitement began to build even more as we drew closer to our destination. I almost jumped out of my seat as I excitedly pointed out the Marco Polo building to Nicky. "That's where I worked when I was with *The Observer*!" I shouted. Yes, it was living proof. Mind you, I struggled to believe myself sometimes, as I'd tell people standing in surf shorts with long hair. I don't know how many people thought I was just making it up. That was sometimes the problem with me; when you spend so much time winding people up, they begin to not believe anything you say, a little like the boy that cried wolf.

I can't imagine what any prospective employer would think if they read my CV, it would probably leave them exhausted with only enough energy left to scrunch it up and throw it in the bin. Entertainer, barman, labourer, computer salesperson, Tower Records, labourer, advertising executive (now defunct computer publication), labourer, advertising executive (*Scotsman* publication), labourer, display advertising executive (*Sunday Observer magazine*) labourer, Edinburgh Napier University business studies course, Nationwide burglar alarms (defunct) salesperson, labourer, Marconi's storeman, Stahly's butcher/bakers, and two and a half years of wasting Balwearie High School's time in Kirkcaldy. It's here reading this, that someone in the medical profession may recognise by the way I bounced through life in a very unorthodox fashion, that there might be some neurodivergence going on. It wasn't till 2018 that a good friend, who sadly is not with us anymore, was able to make me aware of the possibility that I was very much an ADHD casualty. It's a complicated infliction that covers a very wide and varied spectrum, so I won't spend too much time on this subject as I'm sure as intelligent readers you get the basic premise of it all.

CHAPTER 11

HAPPILY ARRIVING BACK IN TIME

As the train pulled into Victoria we got up and grabbed our large case. Again, there weren't too many people on the train, so we were not expecting a mad rush. As the carriage door opened, we made our way out onto the platform. Straight away we were confronted with the sounds you only hear in a large train station; the echoing roar of other train engines, the tinny sounds of the tannoy system, the screeching and shunting of carriages and the familiar smells of grease and diesel smoke. We didn't get much time to take it all in as everyone around us was moving at pace towards the ticket barriers. The other passengers seemed to glide through these with ease as I struggled to get my ticket round the right way. Thankfully a lady rail guard saw me struggling and helped out by automatically opening the gate, probably out of necessity. The last thing they needed was a confused tourist holding up the morning traffic.

Once we were out in the main concourse I began to relax as I recognised the entrance and shape of the station that had been so familiar to me in the past. Just to buy us some time and to work out our bearings, we went to a small kiosk and ordered a couple of coffees. To the right of the kiosk, I saw the escalator which would take us through an arcade of shops and then out into the busy street. Although we should have been really tired from the lack of sleep, we were feeling very excited as we had to find our way to the hotel. Now Nicky was slightly confused as she didn't have a clue where we were going. Me, on the other hand, I couldn't contain myself; I knew I could get us there. I wasn't exactly sure where we were going but had a rough idea.

As we headed up the escalator, I looked round over the concourse of the station, smiling to myself as I recollect that view from many years before. Of course there'd been a great deal of modernisation, but the shape of the place was generally the same.

As we walked through the arcade all the shops were still shut as it wasn't even eight o'clock yet. There were lots of people heading in the opposite direction to us, rushing to catch their trains. Again, the layout of the arcade hadn't changed, only the shops and their new signs. Looking towards the glass doors at the entrance I could see we were just about to make our way out onto the street. For the time of morning, I was surprised to see how bright and busy the place was. It was like a lovely summer's morning, almost warm. I wasn't sure if it was the busy traffic and fumes creating this warm air, but as we turned to our right, I saw it, just across the other side of the road – Victoria Coach Station. Still as big and bold as ever, it was the last place my feet left London all those years ago.

Without hesitation we made our way to the busy crossing, my eyes still fixated on the bus station. I was thinking to myself, *Will it be the same inside, I wonder?* I didn't even explain to Nicky what I was doing, she just faithfully followed me. Again, without hesitation I headed right through the bus station doors, holding them open for Nicky, then proceeded to walk through the station. Straight away I noticed nothing much has changed; even the smell of diesel and the sound of the coaches as they drove in and out of the station were familiar.

Suddenly, I was hit by a wave of excitement, a complete rush of different emotions. It's difficult to explain but I'll try. It was like one of those platform games, as the character goes through a beam of light and there's a ping as a sparkly sign flashes up that you've just won a hundred points. Well, it was like I, too, had just walked through a beam of light with my nerve endings exploding as they were hit with different emotions and memories. Everything had come rushing back; I felt like my whole being had been elevated. Before I knew it, I had turned to Nicky and was trying to tell her everything at once. There's no doubt I was making no sense at all, I can only hope and imagine that she could see I was happy in my fit of excitement. But from that moment I knew what the holiday was going to be all about. I had so many more of these memories and beams of light we could pick up on the way. I could remember all the places I had been before, when I stood looking, wondering, *Will I ever be here again in the future?* A feeling of melancholy and hope that the future might just be kind to me one day. That I might get a chance to share and talk about my times before with someone who is close to me.

Going to Victoria Coach Station that morning was like I'd just arrived where I'd left off the last time I was in London. Not only could I enjoy reliving my past, but could build new even better memories with someone I loved.

It wasn't till many years later with a great deal of research that I was finally able to discover what this rush of emotions was, this feeling of empowerment, like my body had been electrically charged, this excited clarity that gave me the feeling I had the answers to all the questions I'd struggled with before.

I would eventually discover that I had the wide-spectrum mental disorder called ADHD. All through my life I had been aware there was something wrong, but never knew what it was. My memory retention problems, my executive functioning disorder, my desperate attempts at people pleasing, never completing anything as I was chained to constant procrastination, never being able to focus on one thing for more than five minutes, happy to babble on for hours about anything and everything, loads of energy spent on wasting myself and everyone's time. Another terrible habit is when someone is talking to you and although you're looking directly back at them while nodding your head as you agree with everything they say, you've actually zoned out. Your peripheral vision might have caught something moving, or there's a bird just flown overhead, then you realise after the conversation's over you've not taken in anything at all. It's so frustrating. People can start to get angry with you, as they feel you're not interested in what they have to say. You try and mask it by making unconvincing excuses that only accentuate their feeling that you are completely disinterested. Little do they understand that you're left ruminating on why you're so stupid. You can't understand why your focus is so bad, which can leave you feeling quite depressed.

But as luck would have it, I fell into a way of life that suited my ADHD down to the ground. I became an energetic, people-pleasing entertainer who would talk to anyone and everyone, sometimes all at the same time. On the upside, ADHD can make you very creative, as you think out of the box. Where there's a will, there's a way. It's what they call an ADHD person's superpower. Oh, don't get me wrong, as I've already explained there's a lot of downsides to ADHD, which are a lot less than fun, but managed properly it can all be put to good use.

So, to go back to the explosion of emotions I had in the bus station that fateful day, it was something I had felt at times all through my life, something uniquely called 'hyperfocus euphoria'. The one downside from this is that ADHD sufferers will sometimes run around aimlessly trying to find another fix of the supercharged feeling they get from this. Personally, I always find solace in a sentimental feeling of nostalgia, some sort of trawling through my memories to establish balance for building strength and moving forward.

As we left the bus station my tiredness had left me too. I was still fully charged and now hyper-excited, thinking about this fabulous journey we were on. Nicky seemed to be on board with my excitement also, although I'm not sure if she was just glad that one of us seemed to know where we were in the lively city that was London. I didn't know exactly where I was going but I knew we were heading in the right direction. The previous plan of just jumping in a taxi once we got to the station was now not an option. I'd decided to head due north. I knew that would take us in the direction of Hyde Park and from there it was straight forward when it came to finding the hotel. So instead of making our way down the busier route of Buckingham Palace Road we headed up the quieter Elizabeth Street.

As we walked along Elizabeth Street, it was noticeable that we were moving into an area of extreme wealth. Lots of boutique shops, all very high end and elegantly fashioned for people that could afford them, designer fashion, antique shops, and chic furniture stores. It was dawning on me that it had been a much better idea to walk, as no doubt our hotel room wouldn't have been ready this early anyway, and walking was really helping us to get a feel for the place.

Still very excited and walking with pace, we eventually came across the busier stretch of road at Eaton Square. There were private gardens either side of the busy street, but we had literally come to a crossroads. My excitement dampened here as I realised I wasn't sure where I was, and there were another three directions to choose from. "Not to worry," I said to Nicky and chose to keep heading north. Whether it was luck or intuition, we managed to take a right-hand turn at the end of Lyall Street and this took us directly into Belgravia Square.

Nicky and I were not doing much talking, mesmerised by the grandeur of the buildings and expensive vehicles parked in the vicinity. It was obvious this was a far cry from the sun-parched, dusty streets of Corralejo. Now we could see the international embassies, with colourful flags all blowing slightly in the cool breeze. There were consulates from all over the world and the townhouses they occupied were all very well maintained, there to cater for their wealthy international residents. Strange to think back to the Middle Ages, this area was part of the place known as the Five Fields, more renowned for highwaymen and robberies. Although I do believe it was a swampy grazing area in the daylight, where people would happily hang out. Another amazing fact is that most of this expansive and very wealthy area is leasehold only, and many of these fantastically fabulous townhouses and high-end hotels are still very much owned by the family-operated property company, Grosvenor Group, which is controlled by Hugh Grosvenor, the seventh Duke of Westminster. Nicky was flabbergasted when I tried to explain that to her; she couldn't imagine how anyone could be that rich. I'll be honest, I couldn't get my head around that either. This was a side of life I couldn't relate to.

One thing we picked up on just before we left was the statues in gardens in the centre of Belgravia Square. Two in particular that grabbed our attention were one of Christopher Columbus and the other, Simon Bolivar. I found this incredible. These statues were both made by different artists at different times, but these two guys were completely at opposite ends of the scale to each other. Columbus' history has been tarnished by the revelation that his colonisation of certain South American countries was done in a very brutal and barbarous fashion. In fact it has been said he was directly involved in enslavement and theft of indigenous lands. Simon Bolivar, on the other hand, was more famous for the complete opposite. Born in Venezuela, he would go on to be famously known as the liberator, the man who would free many South American countries from Spanish oppression. I just found it so strange for these two guys to be so close to each other. For me it was like having statues of Hitler and Churchill together and that of course is just unthinkable. Was the two statues being so close together symptomatic of London and its Machiavellian past?

Making our way out of Belgrave Square, I could feel the excitement building inside me again. As I could hear the heavy traffic just ahead of us, I knew we were very close to Hyde Park Corner and was pleased that my automatic pilot of a compass was getting us where we needed to be. Again, Nicky and I were mesmerised as we watched the fast-flowing traffic whizz around Hyde Park Corner. It wasn't just the speed they were moving at, it was the variation in types of vehicles racing past us. Again, a far cry from the quiet streets of Corralejo. Bentleys, an array of sports cars, big red buses, touring coaches, taxis, and delivery trucks, all rushing to get to their destinations, even at this early hour. Last but not least were the helmet-wearing cyclists who seemed to be literally taking their lives in their own hands as they sped round the fringes of the busy roundabout. You could see the determination in their eyes as they did their upmost to keep up with the fast-flowing traffic. I'll be honest, I was hoping Nicky hadn't noticed these daredevil cyclists frantically trying to keep up, as we were planning on hiring bikes at some point and I'm sure if Nicky had spotted this, she would tell me defiantly, "There's no way we are cycling on these roads!!" Thankfully our attention was taken up by the surrounding splendour in every direction we looked. No surprise, really, as Hyde Park Corner is right between Knightsbridge, Belgravia, and the very swanky Mayfair, and all of this just hanging off the largest and most prestigious park in London.

Eventually we safely made our way over to the southeast corner entrance to Hyde Park, the sounds of heavy traffic still very much in earshot. Still buoyed with excitement we made our way up Park Lane. There was a feeling inside to go right into the park, as I had a really strong connection with it, but not right now, I'd get my chance to revisit the park once we had properly settled into the holiday. Something that did grab my attention was the distance between the pavement we were on and the other side of the road. What I mean, is there were three lanes of traffic heading north on the outside and other lanes heading south, just across from us, and that's not including the fairly wide grass verge dividing them both. I couldn't believe how heavy the traffic was both sides, and the speed, it was like a full-on motorway right in the heart of London. Although I've pointed out the three lanes, it's actually classed as a dual carriageway.

Even with so much going on around us, it didn't affect the wonderful views of the park and the incredible buildings on the other side. In fact one thing I always remembered from all those years before was the muffled sound of the traffic. The buildings seemed to coerce the noise of the traffic back under the trees. I'll never forget that sound. If you were to blindfold me and I was unknowingly placed in Hyde Park, I would recognise that sound straight away. Even more incredible is that only a few hundred years before, this now-major road was nothing more than a quiet country lane (formerly known as Tyburn Lane).

As we made our way further up Park Lane, we could see all the five-star hotels, such a far cry from all the quiet two-storey buildings we passed daily in Fuerteventura. The Park Lane Hotel, standing taller than all the rest with its twenty-eight floors, then just a little further up was The Dorchester, this was somewhere Nicky was dying to visit as she had not long before read how Elizabeth Taylor and Richard Burton spent many an evening there. And further up still was the iconic Grosvenor House Hotel, which has an incredible 494 rooms to choose from, making it one of the largest luxury hotels in all of London. The great ballroom has been a popular destination for some of London's most prestigious events, with it being large enough to comfortably sit over two thousand people for banquet dinners and award shows. The room was originally built as an ice rink.

Nicky and I were obviously tired but both of us were walking at pace trying our best to take in everything going on around us. We hardly spoke a word while making our way to the hotel. It wasn't till we got closer to Marble Arch that Nicky asked if I knew where I was going. As we got nearer the top, I began to take a left at the Marble Arch bus terminus. Just to our right we could see the iconic arch. This marble-faced structure was just beginning to gleam brightly under the morning sun. Again, just seeing these famous structures really lifted my heart. There was no two ways about it, we were certainly in London.

It wasn't long till we were heading a little way down Bayswater

Road. This seemed quite narrow after not long walking up the very expansive Park Lane. Just across the road we could see the entrance to Stanhope Place. Again, another little wave of excitement hit me as that was us finally getting to our hotel. Nicky was over the moon, realising how close we were to the West End and Central London. Yeah, we had gone through it all on the internet back in our apartment in Spain but I'm sure Nicky won't mind if I have a little dig at her navigational skills.

Walking up into Stanhope Place, things around us had become much quieter; the sound of the traffic had disappeared. Finally reaching the Parkwood, we could see 'No Vacancies' on the door. Nicky and I looked at each other and smiled. We were both thinking the same thing; imagine coming all this way to find our booking had somehow vanished.

Having our printed paperwork in hand we weren't too seriously worried, so I stepped forward and rang the bell. The door was answered quickly, and the lady was very welcoming as she brought us straight into their small but adequate reception. I apologised for being so early and guessed that our room wouldn't be ready yet. The lady kindly said that hopefully they could have a room ready for us around 11 o'clock. That was fine by us, as we were quite happy to do a bit of exploring for a couple of hours. Again, one of my main worries before we left Corralejo was that travelling through the evening and not getting much sleep would leave us feeling incredibly tired on our first day. Thankfully we both felt fine, although I'd certainly put that down to the excitement and rush of mixed emotions I'd had down at the bus station still flowing through my veins. I just couldn't wait to get back out onto the street.

CHAPTER 12

FOR WE HAVE DINED ON HONEYDEW

Our bags were safely tucked away in reception, so it wasn't long before we were back out on the street, full of excitement. Again I was being driven by some emotional high, desperate to get out and somehow hoover up my past. Luckily just outside the front door of the Parkwood was Connaught Place, which lay straight ahead of us, so we followed that out until it took us right onto Edgeware Road. This was much busier with traffic, and I was quick to point out to Nicky that this was the route the coach would take when I travelled back and forth between London and Edinburgh. These were not exactly happy times, but I was excited that the day had come many years later where I could revisit these streets and share the experience with someone who had become more than just my best friend. The memory of being so excited that I was finally leaving London had gone full circle. Here was me; I couldn't be happier that I had returned.

We turned slightly to the right, made our way across the road and headed for Oxford Street. Most of the shops were still closed; I'd almost forgotten how early we got into London. As I checked my watch, I realised it wasn't even 9 o'clock yet. Nicky and I were fast walkers at the best of times so I knew this would come in handy once the streets became busy. It wasn't long till we were passing Selfridges, then Bond Street Station, and heading for Oxford Circus. Nicky was astounded at everything around her. Spookily enough, it had been nearly twenty years since she last visited London and like me, she had spent a massive chunk of her life living in Fuerteventura so I could see she was enjoying herself already.

As we began to approach Regent Street, it was becoming slightly busier as more and more people were rushing up from Oxford Circus Tube Station. Suddenly I could feel everything becoming familiar; it was like I had seen some of those very same people before. Of course it wasn't that I recognised anyone, it was more the look on their faces. They all looked deep in thought, no one taking notice of anyone else as they spilled up from the underground, rushing in all directions. I thought to myself, *There's no way I'd be able to recognise anyone anyway. People who were in their thirties will now be in their fifties and people who were in their fifties will now been in their seventies.* Time had certainly moved on yet that look on everybody's faces had stayed the same. Okay, lots of the big stores had changed names, fashions were different, even the big red buses looked shiny and new, but that rush-hour traffic, that rat race, were still alive and well. Again, I was hit with a feeling of wellbeing. I was back but this time I was free to go where I wanted. I could stop, look at things, change direction, not tied to anything and on top of all that, I had money in my pocket to spend on whatever the hell I liked.

My mind wandered back to the time I felt envious of tourists who were no more than obstacles to be avoided, when you were rushing madly just to get to your next destination. This reaffirmed how much I was going to enjoy this holiday; I could feel myself smiling, which trust me, is not normal on the busy streets of London. Alive in the back of my mind, I knew I wasn't locked into their hustle and bustle.

As we headed all the way down Regent Street, I eventually saw the statue of Eros, which to me was the most central point in London. The only thing that left me a little disappointed was that Tower Records was gone. The whole place was empty, apart from a few signs saying that it was going to open up as another shop. Of course it was 2009, the world had changed; record shops had been disappearing for years. I remember pausing for a while and staring at that old building, wondering where everyone might have gone. Most of the people I had known in there found music to be the most important thing in their lives. Again, they would all be twenty years older; some of them may be on the other side of the world.

I did notice that Boots the chemists was still there operating in its usual place and of course up above it was the neon sign, brightly advertising a different range of high-end products, not that any of the people involved in the morning rush hour seemed to notice.

It wasn't long till we walked through Coventry Street and headed into Leicester Square. It was obvious that a lot of effort had been put into modernising the place. From there we passed the Leicester Square tube station, which I'd used so many times before. The more we walked, the more everything was becoming familiar as we crossed St Martin's Lane and headed for Covent Garden. It wasn't its usual busy self as it was still early and just beginning to open up. Needless to say there were still a few early-bird tourists like us trying to make the most of their day.

In the square just in front of St Paul's Church, the entertainers who could usually be seen juggling an assortment of items were not around either. These guys really help bring a sort of carnival atmosphere to the place and have been entertaining people at Covent Garden for many years. In fact we once had a guy entertaining at the Dunas Caleta who every year would make his way to London just to work in Covent Garden. He said after a few weeks working there you can actually earn some decent money.

As we walked past the London Transport Museum we headed down to the Strand and walked back along to Trafalgar Square. The Square itself was quiet, not a lot of people around, but the same could not be said of the traffic. The rush hour was now moving thick and fast, the usual mix of buses, taxis, cars, delivery vans, and some very official-looking vehicles taking people down into Westminster. Nicky and I turned in the direction of the Houses of Parliament and it wasn't long until we were passing the Scottish office and then the

Cenotaph, which had proudly stood there since 1920. Lots of previous prime ministers and important foreign dignitaries had lain wreaths there over the years in remembrance of the many brave people who lost their lives during the great wars.

Not long after this, we were passing 10 Downing Street. I told Nicky I could remember passing it almost 40 years earlier with my Uncle John, only back in those days you were able to walk right past the front door. Nicky and I could only peer through the large cast-iron gates, which were well protected by three well-armed policemen. Mind you, they seemed fairly happy as most of the time it's only tourists trying to grab some pictures. Just a little bit further along from 10 Downing Street there were some call boxes, so with it being just after 10 o'clock in the morning Nicky decided to phone her mum, who was out in Fuerteventura staying in our apartment, looking after Harry the dog.

It was then, listening to Nicky talking to her mum, that I realised she had been just as excited as me as we walked through London. Nicky told her mum that she couldn't believe she had seen so much already, given the fact we had only been in London a few hours, and we hadn't even moved into our hotel either.

After the phone call we made our way past St James' Park along the Mall, then up past Buckingham Palace, along by Green Park and then back into Hyde Park, eventually getting us back to the hotel for bang on 11 o'clock. It was perfect timing as our room was ready for us to move into. It was a double right on the top floor. With no lifts to be had, it was quite hard work dragging our large suitcase up all those narrow stairs. The room was lovely, a really comfortable bed with an ensuite bathroom. It was well lit with a nice big window so we could gaze down on the street below. Although still very excited, we were both understandably exhausted, so we just jumped straight into bed and managed to fall asleep very quickly.

The holiday not surprisingly went very quickly. Not once did we use the underground or any of the local buses, we just walked everywhere. I did try to get us on a bus on the Sunday morning. We were off to Camden Market and just as we were walking along Oxford Street I spotted a bus with Archway on the front. I thought, *Perfect, that'll take us directly past Camden.* As I climbed onto the bus the driver pointed out that they don't take cash and we would need an Oyster card, so rather disgruntledly I left the bus and decided to walk all the way up to the Market. Spookily enough, this became a tradition every Sunday when we spent a week in London. A breakfast at the hotel, walk to Camden Market, and walk all the way back again.

The holiday had gone by too quickly. Never again would we only book five days; from there on it would be seven days every time.

One very memorable evening of that holiday was obviously the Monday-night meal at Le Gavroche. Again, we booked this on the advice of my dad. Never before had I eaten in a two-Michelin-star restaurant and if I was to be honest, I felt like a fish out of water when we first got in there. Of course, before we went I had done quite a bit of research about not just the restaurant but the Roux dynasty in general. So even walking to the restaurant, which is in Upper Brooke Street, had me feeling nervously excited. And the other great point, it wasn't too far away from our hotel. It was the most dressed up Nicky and I had ever been together. Living in Fuerteventura, eating out is a much more relaxed affair. With it always being really hot, you try to dress appropriately, usually meaning more comfortably, and with Corralejo being a surfing town, the dress code is much more casual.

We crossed the busy Park Lane Road just where the monument representing all the poor animals that died during the war stands. It's one of the saddest monuments I've ever seen and leaves you feeling quite heartbroken. Saying that, it's so cleverly made; the sculptor rightly knew what he was doing giving the monument such a strong visual impact. For anyone that is an animal lover, you'll find it's something that's beautifully made but the images are so powerful you'll not forget it in a hurry. Just on one final note, a few years later I had the chance to get a few tickets to go to the theatre to watch War Horse, but with the image of the animals on the war monument in my mind, I had to decline.

Like a lot of the townhouses in London, you can never judge how big they are by focusing on the front doors. They can sometimes be conservatively small. As you enter they're akin to the Tardis in Dr Who. Looking from the outside, things can seem quite small but as soon as you enter it's like stepping into another world.

After a friendly welcome at the front door of the Gavroche you're taken down the stairs into the heart of the restaurant. The lighting is very soft and dimmed, which actually helps the pristine clean cutlery shine and the crystal glasses sparkle. The bright white tablecloths hang perfectly over the tables. The walls are dark green and adorned with an assortment of fine French art, all hand painted. The chairs are made from sturdy brown wood and covered in a lovely red velvet. Above all of that, there is the quiet chattering coming from the busy tables, while the many well-dressed staff move around effortlessly, making sure glasses are filled and the high standards are maintained to perfection.

Once sat at our table, Nicky and I couldn't help but sit and smile. We were probably slightly overwhelmed with the grandeur and professionalism around us. I remember looking over at Nicky and thinking I'd never seen her looking so beautiful. I was literally sitting in one of London's finest restaurants with my very own princess. There was no doubt about it, Nicky is and always has been a very attractive girl but seeing her sitting in Gavroche that evening really did place her as the Jewel in the Crown.

When we received our menus, that's where we became a bit unstuck. I was okay in Avenidas Restaurant in Corralejo, where I'd be guzzling my large gin and tonic, ordering my usual gambas al ajillo (hot sizzling garlic prawns), and then for a main course having lubina (sea bass). It was nearing the end of the holiday so just to add a special touch to this already fabulous evening, without hesitation I suggested we just order the Menu Exceptional, which included a matching glass of wine for each course. This was about seven to eight courses which also included a small amuse bouche. (Just on a further note, each year we would return to the Gavroche and Nicky would always have her favourite starter, which was a real classic, the 'Soufflé Suissesse'.)

It was an incredible evening, to say the least. The food was just out of this world; the different flavours and textures melted in your mouth. Even as each of the wines were poured the sommelier would tell us about each of them and where they came from, and even though we were nodding our heads like we had a clue what he was talking about, it just went in one ear and out the other.

We must have been there for just over two hours and would've loved to stay even longer, but all good things must come to an end. That whole experience hit me like a charge of electricity. I promised Nicky we were definitely doing that again. That feeling I got the moment I walked into the bus station at Victoria, and the similar feelings I had as we left the Gavroche, were the motivation for more, bigger and better holidays in London.

CHAPTER 13

LE MERIDIEN (NOW THE DILLY)

Once we got back to Corralejo I still had a few more days of my holiday to go, so Nicky booked us a few nights in the south of the island down by Jandia, in a hotel called the Occidental. The hotel is actually just below the island's highest volcano, Pico de la Zarza, but sits on a cliff looking out over the Atlantic. It was nice to get away again and this is a beautiful hotel, and you can easily go down the steps that take you down onto the long beaches. But I was oblivious to everything going on around me, as all I wanted to do was talk about London. Yes, that was it, I had the bug. We were going to have a week in London every year come hell or highwater. We even started a rota, so every day was planned out – our restaurants, shows, and even bike hire were all booked before we arrived back in London.

I used to love Friday nights where Nicky and I would spend hours checking out hotels, locations, and of course their prices. Eventually we would find the hotel of our choice and the location was just perfect for us. Now it maybe wasn't the greatest five-star hotel in London but if I was to be honest, I wouldn't want to stay anywhere else. Things could have been so different, though, for our second holiday in London. We booked a boutique hotel in Soho not too far away from Regent Street. We had not long watched a programme all about the ins and outs of this hotel being refurbished. It seemed quite Rock 'n' Roll and was exactly the sort of vibe the new owner was trying to promote, but just at the last minute I got cold feet. Nicky couldn't understand why I wanted to cancel it; it had taken us long enough to finally make a decision and get booked up.

But for me, something just didn't feel right. I just knew it wasn't the place for me.

I had a bad feeling about the place. So once Nicky cancelled it, I told her I really fancied the Le Meridien (now the Dilly) which was closer to Piccadilly and wedged right in between Regent Street and Green Park. One thing that really swung it for me was that it had a very big swimming pool and was really close to where I used to work at Tower Records. It turned out to be just perfect for us; the location was ideal. If we had booked a lunch somewhere it was never too far to quickly go back to the hotel and get changed if need be. It was so central and situated in my favourite place in Central London. Every time we walked into their reception, I felt like I was returning home.

Another special little touch was that I remembered the doorman from all those years back, when I worked at Tower Records. I remembered shouting cheerio to him the night I walked all the way down to Victoria Bus Station to buy my ticket so I could escape back to Scotland. I knew he didn't recognise me, but when we started spending a week there once a year, he began to welcome us each time we returned. It was nice to have that familiarity; I understood how our guests felt each time they returned to the Dunas. The guests loved it when they could see our regular staff each time they walked through the door. It would give them the feeling they were at their home from home.

Another thing I used to do was make sure we had a room facing onto Regent Street. I know some of the people on the front desk must have thought it a weird request, which I fully understand. But I always love having my bedroom window facing north wherever I stay, and I like to think to myself when walking down Regent Street, *Ahhh, this is where I'm staying for the week*, and still feel the same thing as I'm walking along Green Par. That's where the entrance to the Meridien was.

Even as we arrived at Victoria Station each time, after the half-hour journey on the Gatwick Express, I always left the station the same way. We would go back up that escalator through the arcade, take a right-hand turn and walk along Buckingham Palace Road, then a left, which would then lead down past the walled part of the garden at Buckingham Palace. Then we would take another left and pass the old hotel, the Rubens, eventually taking us right to the front entrance of Buckingham Palace. Say what you like about Buckingham Palace and the Mall, but it's an incredible sight, especially as you look down that long road adorned with trees on either side and right at the opposite end you can see Admiralty Arch. Although Roman by design it is actually classic Edwardian architecture.

This is something else that really tugs at my feelings of nostalgia. I can always remember my Grannie Smith having one of those old viewfinders. You would need to point it towards the window so you had sufficient light, then insert a round disc with fourteen little pictures inset around the outer edges. Once the disc was in place you would hold the viewfinder up to your eyes and click a little button on the right-hand side. This would allow those little pictures to pass by one at a time. In those days the quality of the pictures was just incredible; everything looked so lifelike. My grandmother had about four of these round discs and all were from Queen Elizabeth II's coronation. The pictures of the procession were so clear and looked like they had been taken from a camera high up in the trees somewhere in the middle of the Mall. It made the carriages look so splendorous and you felt like you could just reach out your hand and touch the leaves of the trees. When I was that young, I could never imagine being somewhere like that. It seemed like a different world, one that I would only sometimes catch a glimpse of on TV. So, a little part me wanted to go back in time and pat that little child on the head and tell him, "Listen, one day you'll walk down that very same road."

When you've spent most of the year on a hot, dusty island that has beautiful beaches with incredible waves, it's quite a dramatic change of circumstances and it's not just the contrasting views. It's all the noise as well – cars, lorries, buses, motorcycles, police sirens, the sound of horse's hooves that would often pass by.

About halfway along the Mall we would take another left, walking past the King George VI & Queen Elizabeth memorial. Then crossing the even busier Pall Mall, we would start heading up towards St James' Square. It was then just a little further up a small lane called Church Place and out onto Piccadilly. From there we could see Le Meridien in all its glory. Every time, I would excitedly stop and take a picture. For some reason it was always sunny, which would make the large panes of glass engulfing the terrace restaurant shine brightly. It's quite a spectacular building, which first opened its doors back in 1908 as one of London's most luxurious hotels, then named The Piccadilly. With so many more large and fabulous hotels having been built in and around London, it could be forgiven for possibly losing some of its past grandeur, but it is still a big player in its field, with over 255 rooms and 28 suites.

Again, the hotel was in the perfect location for us. As I've said before, for me Piccadilly is the most central place in the heart of London, and right next door to where 20 years earlier, I used to work.

After crossing the busy road, we eventually walked into the reception. As usual we were very early and our room wasn't quite ready, but it was never a problem as we would just leave our bags and head back out into Piccadilly. We would never bring any toiletries with us, and would always enjoy our little visits to Boots where we could get everything. Luckily it was only a stone's throw from the hotel. But before going to Boots to get the necessities we always ventured into Soho, our first port of call to walk through Golden Square with its lovely gardens in the middle. It is surrounded by 40 townhouses that historically were home to lords, ladies, dukes, viscounts and other opulent dignitaries. As the lords and ladies eventually moved out it became a bit more cosmopolitan, a place for the aspiring bourgeois, writers, dancers, and musicians. With these types of people being a bit flightier, it wasn't long before the buildings slowly but surely became more commercially used, for business and by professional types. In the present day Golden Square is synonymous with people and businesses from the film and music industry. Some of the offices are used by agents; production companies within the advertising world also.

One place we had to visit as we passed through Golden Square was a Gregg's, which is on your left-hand side just before you enter Beak Street. Again, after living in the warm climate of Fuerteventura for all those years, you do miss some of the popular choices available to people living in the UK, so we just had to grab a couple of Steak Bakes. This, too, would become a tradition every time we booked in at the Meridien early. We would eat our Steak Bakes while browsing through the shop windows as we slowly walked through Carnaby Street.

Once famous for being the birthplace of the swinging sixties, it may have lost a little of its previous swagger but it's still very popular with the many visitors to London, and still holds quite a few very influential independent boutiques alongside the very popular and fashionable brand stores. On the whole Soho is still massively popular with young and old alike, and although the first thing I talked about was Steak Bakes, please remember it was just an early-morning snack until we eventually got the key to our room. When it comes to choices of food, Soho has it all. It doesn't matter what day of the week it is, it's always packed. Okay, maybe Sundays are an exception to the rule, but in general they literally have everything to suit, whether it be Italian, sushi, tapas, Mexican, fish and chips, burger bars, or some of Europe's best finest cuisine, it's all there. The choice of bars, coffee shops, and pubs are much the same, whether it be jazz, rock, disco, or any of the latest trends, you'll most certainly find your musical fix in the very colourful streets of Soho.

Talking of colourful, there's a notable amount of sex shops dotted around the Berwick and Brewer Street area. It's all part of the very acceptable diversity that just adds to the very fabric of its bohemian atmosphere.

After visiting Boots and getting all the little bits and pieces we needed for the week's stay we would make our way back to the hotel. This was always another exciting little moment for me as it was time to find out what room we were getting. I knew the room would face Regent Street, but didn't know if it would be a Classic room with a king-size bed or a Deluxe room with a queen-size. It was always just the luck of the draw, to be honest. It certainly didn't make many odds at the end of the day; either way the beds were always comfortable, it was just a real bonus if you were lucky enough to get a Deluxe room. I'd fallen in love with this hotel so they couldn't put a foot wrong in my eyes. I even enjoyed the lifts; they were always very dark and mirrored with new-world music playing softly in the background.

Once we eventually got to our room we would quickly get changed and into our swimming gear. Since we always stayed in the same part of the hotel, we made the same journey to the pool every time. We would take a left after leaving our room, a short distance along the corridor then a right-hand turn down a few steps, just past the staff lift, then up a few stairs and left again to the guest lifts. There were three lifts in total so you never had to wait too long. With my request for a particular room type, we were always on the third or fourth floor, so we had to travel four or five floors down to the lower ground floor to the Health Club, which is somewhat impressive to say the least. At first you walk into a nice reception area, which is spacious and parked quite close to a well-equipped gym with strong but subtle lighting. Not far from that are the two squash courts, and just beyond those is the swimming pool. In fact from certain parts of the gym you can look down into the pool area.

Once Nicky and I received our towels from reception we would then head to our separate changing room, then meet up again poolside. The pool area is fantastic; it has a large pillar near the middle of the pool, the ceiling is very high and all around the outside walls they have these wonderful arches. Some of them are like windows to another part of the hotel but it's just that the glass panes in the arches are mirrored, which gives that wonderful effect. A lot of the surface is covered in lovely small blue tiles with small fountains in set places, making it look very much like an ancient Roman spa. I've been in lots of wonderful scenic swimming pools in my life, outside and in, but there was something wonderfully luxurious about Le Meridien's swimming pool, and as if that's not enough we still had the use of the sauna, which is to the right-hand side of the pool, and tucked into the corner is the ample Jacuzzi. It was always such a brilliant feeling swimming in the pool of your favourite hotel right below the busy streets of Piccadilly. I'm sure if you tried really hard you might just be able to hear some noise coming from the underground as the tubes passed below.

CHAPTER 14

BIG THURSDAY

After our first holiday in London together I promised Nicky that not a minute of our time would be wasted. Every day would be something special, so our holiday rota was meticulously planned out. Our first night in London was always a Wednesday, so we would either book a show, which would then be followed by an after-show meal, or if not that, we would book a table in another of London's finest restaurants. As much as that was always a great start to the holiday, the main thing in the back of my mind was excitedly thinking about the day after, the big cycle from Gabriel's Wharf all the way up to Hampstead Heath and back again. This was very prominent in my mind before we even started our first holiday in London. It excited me, thinking of Nicky and I getting up to Hampstead then possibly through Highgate and on to Archway, where I once lived so many years before. This fire was re-lit the moment I walked back into that bus station in 2009, with that explosion of emotions rushing through every nerve ending in my body. That was the very moment all my plans seemed to come together. I knew exactly what I wanted to do and where I wanted to revisit. I had left little emotional markers all over London and I was here to pick them all up again. These little markers were places I knew my past memories would shine through clear as day.

You can't imagine the disappointment I felt when we got down to the London Bicycle Company on the Saturday morning, that first holiday, to find there were no bikes available to rent. I had been clever enough to source the company and the location on the internet but hadn't been smart enough to book the bikes online. I was so looking forward to it. I had it all planned out. It was going to be a real challenge after being away for so long but I was desperate to do this; it was a mission I just had to complete.

We got down to the London Bicycle Company early enough, but there were quite a lot of people who turned up behind us and of course they had all pre-booked their bikes for hire. The guy at the shop was polite enough but he just had no other bikes he could give us. It wasn't all lost as we were able to book two bikes for the Monday, a few days later, but walking away from Gabriel's Wharf I was almost inconsolable.

As we walked along the side of the Thames I was gutted. I had just done that same walk full of hope and great expectations, so looking forward to this great adventure. All the worry about the busy roads had gone; I was ready to visit my past and recapture these old memories and answer that question I had in my head so many years earlier. Will I ever come back and be able to share this experience with someone close? Even as Nicky dragged me into the Sea World Centre to pick up my mood, this might in fact have made it a little worse, considering some of the fish they had in the tanks we would see on a daily basis while out swimming just off the harbour at Corralejo.

The one thing that did cheer me up was when we eventually got back up to Piccadilly, we noticed there was a matinee on in the Criterion Theatre for The 39 Steps. This was an adaptation of a Hitchcock classic turned into a comical yarn, with only a cast of four and a collection of brilliantly used lo-fi props. It was just what the doctor ordered. The energy and jokes were coming thick and fast as the four cast members sped through their costume changes with precision and hilarity in equal measure. It wasn't what I was expecting that afternoon but at the end of the show we clapped and cheered for a fantastic performance. We appreciated the hard work – 139 costume changes had to be made in only an hour and a half by our sweat-drenched performers.

Learning from our mistakes, we made sure we booked our bikes before travelling and to be honest, I think it's better to travel through the streets and parks while London's working so from there on in, we would book the bikes for Thursday.

I would definitely say the Thursday was my favourite day of the holiday. It wasn't just the humongous cycle all the way through London, but we would without fail book a show for that evening, finishing off with an after-show meal. We would always start the day nice and early, up, showered, and ready well before 9 o'clock. We would then make our way down to the second floor, to the Terrace Restaurant, always using the lift that specifically opened right in front of the restaurant. It must be one of the nicest places to have breakfast in all of London. It was consistently very peaceful, beautifully set out, and always very comfortable with a very relaxed atmosphere. It's almost like having breakfast in a botanical garden, with lots of natural light streaming in through the large glass ceiling and windows which look out over Piccadilly. It's not only a great view down over the busy road to Green Park, but nice to admire the structure and architecture of the building itself.

Another nice touch was that a few ladies seemed to work there every year we stayed at the hotel, which not only gives you that nice feeling of welcome familiarity, but leaves you feeling confident that the food and service will always be to that same high standard. With us heading out for a big cycle there were no excuses needed for taking advantage of a hearty breakfast before we left. There was always a nice fruity shot to welcome you into the restaurant each morning, so I'd always follow that up with a large glass of fresh orange juice, then a bowl of cereal or muesli. Then I would fill my plate with fried eggs, hash browns, bacon, a little sausage, mushrooms and beans. If you think that makes me sound a little greedy, I won't bother talking about my cup of coffee and toast that went with it. If I really wanted to go mad there was a great selection of different breads and fresh meats, with the extra little choice of cakes for some of the guests who have more of a sweet tooth in the mornings.

Now in honesty it was only on the Thursday and possibly the Sunday mornings that I really pushed the boat out and ate a heavier breakfast. But it's important to point out that there were lots of really appetising, healthy options for breakfast available. There was a choice of four different fruit juices, an assortment of yoghurts, and a whole range of fruits from all over the world to satisfy their very international client base. Many times, while having my breakfast in Le Meridien, I would see lots of people deep in thought as the conversations were obviously very much about business deals and transactions. Nicky was forever telling me to stop being nosey. I didn't mean to be, I was just fascinated by the all the people from different walks of life. Again, a far cry from the hotel I was working in back in Fuerteventura.

Once I'd demolished my rather large breakfast it'll come as no surprise that I would then have to make one last visit to the toilet before we hit the busy streets of London. Inconspicuously dressed, meaning not wishing to look too much like we were tourists, we would ready ourselves for the walk all the way down Gabriel's Wharf. We always travelled light and made sure we were adequately dressed, with very little in our pockets except, say, my wallet with a little money in it and our then camera phones. I also carried a little stone I'd brought all the way from Fuerteventura, but I'll talk about that later.

I always felt excited as we made our way out of reception and out into the busy street. First I'd make a point of grabbing Vasco, the old doorman's attention just so I could say good morning and briefly tell him of our day's plans. I always felt he was a big part of the hotel, and I wanted him to know. Obviously I didn't want to make too much of a fuss or come over as being patronising, I just subtly wanted him to know I was always grateful for his friendly and welcoming smile.

Stepping out of the hotel, we would always take a left in the direction of Eros, the historic statue that stood proudly right in the centre of Piccadilly Circus. First, we would pass Cordings which was a very high-end outfitters of quality country-styled clothing. Most certainly not the sort of fashion or lifestyle that I would ever aspire to, but I couldn't help admiring the longevity of the shop as it had been there even longer than the hotel itself. The shop has now been in that location since the late 1800s and is co-owned by none other than the legendary guitarist, Eric Clapton.

We then crossed a small street, which I was all too familiar with, called Air Street. I could still see the large sliding door used to unload all the music that would eventually reach the shop floor of the iconic Tower Records. Although at the time I was glad to leave and make my way back to Scotland, I still got that warm nostalgic feeling tugging at my heartstrings. I couldn't help but wonder what had become of all the people I knew had worked there.

It's funny, as you first come out of the hotel with the sun shining brightly, you're hit with a cascade of bright colours and lots of noise coming from the busy streets. It happens so quickly. One minute you're in the calming elegance of a dimly lit reception and the second you walk out of the door you're right into the clamour of life in the centre of Piccadilly. I would imagine for some people it must be quite overwhelming at first. My mind was always too distracted looking up Air Street, part of me thinking about Tower Records and the rest of me excitedly thinking about the day ahead and our fabulous cycle all the way up to the north of London.

Just before Piccadilly Circus and the statue more commonly known as Eros, whose real name is Anteros (the Greek god of requited love), we took a left and crossed the busy street which took us in the direction of Lower Regent Street. First, we passed the stairs going down to Piccadilly Tube Station, which is right on the corner. The building we passed was once used by the Clydesdale Bank. Many a time I've stood in front of where the cash machine was, almost praying that this time when I put my card in there will be cash for me to draw out. There was no doubt about it, this whole area was littered with lots of little memories for me, and not all of them great, but still they managed to leave me with a feeling of melancholy.

There was one time while I was working for the now defunct PC Business World selling advertising space, I had needed a new briefcase. Thinking on my feet, *If I can get down to Piccadilly there's bound to be a shop in the vicinity that'll sell briefcases.* My plan was to hopefully pick up a new briefcase somewhere in Piccadilly, then down into the tube station, get myself onto the District Line and from there head straight along to Turnham Green as my appointment was with an agency in nearby Chiswick. Everything seemed to be going to plan as I got myself into a well-known department store and luckily came across a cracking case, which even came with its own Filofax (thankfully the advancement of technology rid us of these very silly things). I couldn't believe it was only 14 pounds, so I quickly scooped it up and hurriedly made my way to the cash desk, which didn't seem to be too busy; there were only two nice ladies in front of me. Unfortunately for me these two ladies didn't seem to be in a hurry and were struggling to make up their minds regarding a few items they were planning on buying. Worse than that, there was now a bit of a queue building behind me. All I could do was turn to the other people and shrug my shoulders, doing my best to keep a lid on my impatience.

Eventually the two ladies managed to decide and left happily with their purchase. I could tell by the look on face of the girl serving them, that they had been hard work. I smiled at her, knowing she certainly wasn't going to have that trouble with me. The girl kindly asked if I would like a bag and I told her not to bother as it was being called into action straight away. As I was standing trying to be that cool customer she wished she could have every day, she said, "Right, that'll be 214 pounds please, sir?"

My head jutted forward with my eyes obviously looking like they couldn't believe their ears. "Wot!?" I said, rather sharply.

Even she looked startled at my lightning-quick response. In my shock I paused for a few seconds, beginning to realise that what I thought was a pound sign, was a badly printed '2'. Not only that but as I looked at the briefcase properly, I began to realise that this was all leather, made to the finest standards, and had a very high-end Italian maker's name on it. I could only look back at the girl, hold my hands up and say, "Look, I'm really sorry," turn and get out of their as quickly as possible.

As I hurriedly made my way out the shop, I'm sure everyone left behind me in the queue must have been having a great laugh at my expense. That thought didn't stay with me for long as I quickly made my way to Covent Garden where I managed to pick up a bog-standard briefcase for the princely sum of 25 pounds. Again, rushing all the way back through the maddening crowds to Piccadilly Tube Station I managed to catch a train that got me to Turnham Station, and luckily found the small agency in Chiswick fairly quickly. The meeting itself turned out to be a complete waste of time, as I just babbled my way through some information that seemed of no interest to them at all. Thankfully now I can just look back and laugh, at my own stupidity of course.

Nicky and I would then begin to make our way down Lower Regent Street, where the heavy traffic would dissipate and when the sun was shining you would always get a clear view of Big Ben. I apologise if I tend to repeat myself, but the views were almost surreal. It was hard trying to take it all in, especially when only a few mornings before our views were rocks, sea, sand, and seagulls. Most of the noise would come from the waves crashing in on the rocky shoreline, but as we walked down Regent Street we would still hear the rumblings of the traffic; every now and again that high-pitched sound from police sirens.

Walking downhill always helped us move a little faster as we speedily went past Jermyn Street. It never took us too long and before we knew it, we would nearly be at the bottom of Regent Street. To the left of us would be two very prominent statues – the Guards Crimean War memorial and in front of that, a little smaller but no less important, the Florence Nightingale statue. Although standing proudly, these statues are a reminder of past darker times, as the Ottoman empire propped up by the British and French fought a bloody war with the Russians. Just to our right-hand side we would always pass the Embassy of Papua New Guinea just before we crossed the road on Pall Mall.

Pall Mall is very well known to have some of the most high-end gentlemen's clubs, and most of the streets around here are still lit on an evening by the old Victorian gas lamps. On another note it makes sense that the Suffragettes would choose this very street when protesting in the cause of women's rights, while at the same time trying to convince men to allow women the vote. The protest, when first started was ignored and more insultingly, scoffed at. This soon changed and women managed to get them all to pay more attention as they changed tact, smashing windows as they made their way along this most celebrious of streets.

We would then pass the Royal Society of London attached to Carlton House, which is still a place of great importance to this day, and to think it all started in the mid-1600s as the 'invisible college' of natural philosophers and physicians. Still functioning as the UK's national science academy and a fellowship of some 1,600 of the world's most eminent scientists, I would just love to get in there. I mean, obviously not on an academic front, in fact to join that gang you need to have made some great contributions in the world of sciences, mathematics, engineering, medical science, or added to the improvement of natural knowledge. But wouldn't it be a great idea if we could just get our elected leaders to go in there and ask them, "Right, just tell us your ideas on making this a better and safer planet to live on!?"

It wasn't long till we were heading down the Duke of York steps, which was another view I had first glimpsed way back in 1974, when I had my photograph taken standing right next to the Duke of York column at the top of the steps. Heading down, we could now see the Mall, the trees of St James' Park and of course, Horse Guards Road. Again, the views are just stunning. As we crossed the very wide road, our eyes trying to take everything in, in one direction is the spectacular Admiralty Arch while in the other, just off in the distance down this magnificently tree-lined road, is Buckingham Palace.

Walking down the side of St James' Garden on a sunny morning you can see the police memorial, which is completely covered in ivy. I couldn't help thinking that if they took away all the bricks and mortar you'd still be left with a green, leafy montage of the original building. Nicky would always be drawn to the ponds in St James' Park. You can smell the birds as they noisily frolicked around in the calm waters of the pond. I'd always had to patiently wait as Nicky tried to take as many pictures as possible. With so many different birds swimming in the pond there would always be an assortment of loose feathers floating around on top of the water. Pink pelicans, ducks, swans, and even parrakeets would help bring colour and life to this beautifully laid-out park. As mesmerising as it all was, Nicky could tell I was on a mission and would catch me checking my watch, knowing that my only goal was to get down to the bicycle shop as soon as possible. I would remind her not to worry as we always cycled past the pond twice each time we made our epic journey to the north of London.

From there we would cross the road and make our way across the expansive Horse Guards Parade Ground. It must be at least the size of four full football pitches. Our feet made that light crunching sound as we walked across the gravelled surface, till we eventually reached the narrow-arched tunnel at the household cavalry museum. This would briefly shelter us from the bright sunlight, which was obviously amplified by the light-coloured gravel.

It was just a short walk under cover till we came out onto the busier Whitehall. This entrance is always flanked by two horsed guards who stand so quietly that if you hadn't seen them, you wouldn't have noticed they were there. Turning to our right, we headed past the Scottish office and onto the entrance at 10 Downing Street which even at that early time of the morning still has tourists staring in to see if there's any sign of life. We don't ever stop to pay it too much attention, simply because I'm always in a hurry to get down to the London Bicycle Company shop at Gabriel's Wharf.

Ironically there were a few quicker ways to get down to Gabriel's Wharf; we could've turned left and gone down Whitehall Place, or even before that just taken a left at the Duke of York stairs and headed directly for the Hungerford Bridge crossing. But force of habit and probably a lot to do with my ADHD, we always had to go the same scenic route, adding an extra mile to the morning's journey. Saying all that, with the sun shining everything around us was very impressive, especially close to the Cenotaph where the road must be at its widest. This, all surrounded by government buildings that seem to double up as monuments of power, was magnified tenfold as we approached Parliament Square. As you look across the green you can see Westminster Abbey, which has been the location for great coronations and royal weddings since 1066. To the left of that stands the possibly even more iconic Houses of Parliament, once regarded as the mother of all Parliaments, although some rightly or not would argue that these are accolades probably more suited to its past.

Before, it might have been a place where ideologues would dogmatically argue their case until they arrived pragmatically at their conclusions. Now, it's more regarded as a hollow talking shop where both its main parties' candidates are only sitting in these constituencies because they have been facilitated by their sponsors. This might be a slightly cynical point of view as I'm sure there are many Parliamentarians that were very proud to be elected to the house democratically by their constituents. Whatever anyone's point of view, it's still a very impressive building and a focal point for the many tourists' cameras, and I must admit that even in Fuerteventura it was always to the sound of Big Ben that we would start off our New Year celebrations, although it was a taped recording.

Eventually Nicky and I would take a left turn past the very busy Westminster tube station. Every now and again we would catch a glimpse of some of the well-known faces hurriedly making their way towards Parliament. Eventually we would then have to cross another busy junction, which would take some of the traffic down and along the Embankment and allow us onto Westminster Bridge. This incredible view is slightly deceptive as it doesn't give any idea of the twist and turns that the Thames has. In fact, there's no indication that would let you know it's over 215 miles long. It's hard to imagine how it all must have looked to the Romans when they first sailed up the river in 43AD, with nothing but the smallest of settlements until they themselves created Londinium just a little further up the Thames, where the city is now.

With so much to see from Westminster Bridge we would always stop to take pictures. With Parliament at my back I would always take a picture of Nicky with the London Eye in the background and of course, next to that is the very impressive county hall, which was once the headquarters of local government. After a lot of political shenanigans, it was eventually shut down and turned in a high-end, five-star hotel. On the bridge and looking down to your left, you can see the busy Westminster Pier, constantly ferrying tourists on the river boats up and down the Thames, stopping at Tower Bridge and going further down to Greenwich. We couldn't hang about too long taking pictures as we still had a bit further to go before we got to Gabriels's Wharf.

Westminster Bridge was always usually busy, with people rushing into London for work. This old bridge was originally built in 1862 and seemed to be wearing well when you considered the amount of traffic and people that came this way every day. Making our way down the stairs on the south side of the bridge, we would begin to head along the Queen's Walk. From here you begin to realise how big the London Eye really is. Not once in all the seven holidays did we ever get on. The views must be amazing but if I'm totally honest, I was probably worried about my irrational fear of heights. I just didn't fancy myself being curled up on the floor of one of these large pods crying like a baby.

As we passed the Jubilee Gardens we couldn't help noticing the Shell building towering high up into the sky, a timely reminder of how London is an important player in international oil markets. It's also very noticeable that both sides of the Thames are very much lined with trees. As we looked over to our left, we could see the Horse Guard's Hotel, which looks like a palace surrounded by all the greenery of the trees. As we approached the Hungerford Bridge, we could sometimes hear the noise coming from some of the early-bird skateboarders frantically rushing and jumping about in the undercroft of the South Bank Centre. If you pass this place later in the day, it can be busy, with many more skateboarders and members of the public who like to just hang out and watch. It's impressive that urban culture has managed to find a foothold right in the heart of a very celebrious part of London.

Ever since the early 70s, the undercroft at the South Bank has become a sort of Mecca for legions of past and present skateboarders. Incredibly the skateboarders managed to successfully convince city planners to overturn a decision to redevelop the whole area into another transient home for new restaurants and bars.

Interestingly, either side of the Hungerford Bridge are the Golden Jubilee footbridges, which were only completed after 2002 and were aptly named after Queen Elizabeth II's Jubilee. These two bridges are quite complicated in their design but at the end of the day, the four-metre-wide walkways would certainly be called suspension bridges. On the easterly side closest to the south bank, one of the supporting pillars has become a skateboard graveyard and is covered in lots of well-designed broken boards.

As we walked further on things began to quieten down to a more serene atmosphere approaching the Waterloo Bridge. We could see people putting up trestle tables and stacking them with second-hand books. Some of the stalls were more carefully positioned, as some of the books were classics and the more valuable ones were collectable antiques. Even though we were out in the open the air it still had that smell, like we were in an old library. The Waterloo or South Bank Book Market as it's better known, started in the very early 80s and has gone from strength to strength over the years. Come wind, rain, or shine it manages to stay open every day.

Just to our right was the BFI South Bank, formerly known as the National Film Theatre. It's not just the latest releases, they do tend to show a lot of old classics. A little closer to the path we walked along each time is the Laurence Olivier Statue. This would then lead us on to the actual National Theatre. This whole area was just alive when it came to the world of arts, with its film theatres and of course the television studios, which were always in high demand. It wouldn't be the first time we passed this area while one of the popular breakfast shows were running an event on the pier, asking lots of passers-by if they would like to join in. Obviously, we wouldn't have the time or the inclination on the few times they approached us. Our cycle was way too important, so time was never on our side.

From there, it was only about twenty yards away, so it wasn't long till we were actually walking into Gabriel's Wharf. The wharf itself is lovely, it's full of little shops selling bric-a-brac and bohemian little fashion outlets, and of course quite a few quaint little cafés with views towards the River Thames. Further back into the wharf we could see all the bikes chained together under a large tarpaulin. It was always best to get down a little sharpish as this allowed you to get first choice of the bikes. Nicky and I would then stand close to the small booking office, while at the same time watching out for the guys walking in to open up. After the disappointment of our very first visit, when we didn't manage to get bikes at all, I always made sure I had a printout of our booking held firmly in my hand. As soon as the lads from the bike shop walked into the wharf, I could feel my excitement build up inside me and I was already checking out the bikes.

Once all the paperwork was handed over, it didn't take them long to peel back the large tarpaulin and undo the many locks and chains. I would select what I thought were two suitable bikes, then the lads would check the gears, tyres and brakes, then off we would go. All wired up and full of go, I would try to calmly tell the lads to expect us back around 4 o'clock. They would usually shout back, "No problem, just be careful!"

It was always such a great moment pushing our bikes out of Gabriel's Wharf. The only way I could explain my excitement, would be to say it felt like someone had just handed me a million pounds, when in fact I was only pushing a bike that worth about two hundred. The bike itself was shamrock green with 'londonbicyclecompanyhire.com' written in yellow across the middle bar. It wasn't really that noticeable while you were cycling, but I didn't mind that, as I always preferred not to look like a tourist as we travelled through London.

CHAPTER 15

HAMPSTEAD, HERE WE COME

As soon as we were back out onto the Queen's Walk, we would climb onto the bikes and head in the direction of Blackfriars Bridge. The first five or 10 minutes were spent getting used to the feel of the bike. Nicky and I cycled every day back in Fuerteventura. I had a 26-inch-wheel carbon fibre Trek 9.8, whereas Nicky's was a 29-inch-wheel aluminium Scott, so we were adept when it came to cycling. But the challenges of being on a bike you're not used to, and the extremely busy roads of a fast and furious London, are something you never treat lightly.

As we travelled along the rest of the Queen's Walk the path began to narrow, especially as we get closer to Blackfriars Bridge. Passing a few other boutiques and al fresco dining establishments, the path began to narrow as we are all herded a little closer together. We would dismount our bikes till we eventually reached a small set of stairs that would take us up onto the bridge. My attention was always drawn to the pub right on the corner of the stairs called the Doggetts Coat and Badge.

As it was usually only just after 10 o'clock in the morning, it was always empty, but I remember saying to Nicky, "I really like the look of that place."

To which she would normally reply, "Yeah you said that the last time we passed here."

Once up onto the bridge the path widened again, so we didn't feel we were infringing on any pedestrian's rights as we cycled by. I know cycling on pavements is frowned upon, with good reason especially on the busy streets of London, but Nicky's safety was paramount, and we only did it where the paths were obviously not busy. Being up higher on the bridge, the views again were fantastic as we looked west in the direction we always headed. Nearing the end of Blackfriars Bridge there's a nice long ramp that takes you right down onto the Embankment. This was always a great start to the cycle as this part of the Embankment was usually quiet, so we could pick up a little bit of pace heading down that ramp. Moving fast was great for giving us more confidence but it was important we stayed focused, so we made sure we didn't allow our eyes to stray too far from the path.

Again, being relatively early there were never too many pedestrians to worry about, but the traffic was always busy and there were always a lot of parked buses along the way. To our left we would see the HQS *Wellington* and then just a little further along, the Temple Pier Bar & Co, which is an old boat that has been moored up for a good number of years. Back in the day, probably the early nineties, my friend Ian Myles and myself found ourselves down on this very boat having a drink. As I looked across from where we were sitting, I could've sworn a guy I saw was Nigel Benn. So, being my usual impulsive self I just couldn't help myself and shouted over. Nowadays I would never do anything like that, even less so if it was Nigel Benn. I mean, he wasn't called the Dark Destroyer for nothing. Sadly, it wasn't him, but it was his brother who turned out to be a lovely guy called Mark. I always do my best to be polite and respectful and I think he appreciated me being a massive fan of his brother, and was quite happy to chat with me for a while. Being young and very impressionable, I was over the moon, and it certainly isn't an afternoon I'm ever likely to forget. Unfortunately Ian, not being too keen regarding boxing, seemed rather disinterested and was surprised at my knowledge of boxing.

Nicky and I would always head along the Embankment at a steady pace, and it wasn't too long before we passed under Waterloo Bridge.

Over to our right just through the trees we would be able to see the Savoy in all its grandeur, but our eyes would be quickly drawn back to Cleopatra's Needle. This very prominent obelisk sat in Alexandria for almost 2,000 years until it was offered to London as a gesture of good will from the ruler of Egypt and Sudan in 1819. The obelisk was eventually erected where it is today on the Embankment, in 1878.

We always enjoyed this early part of the cycle as everything around us looked spectacular, especially as we passed Northumberland Avenue as, again, we would see the Royal Horse Guard's Hotel, only this time passing a lot closer. With its many towers and arched windows, I always imagined how nice it must be to get one of the top-floor rooms, with their balconies big enough to sit two people comfortably. I thought it would be great on a nice summer's evening, just ordering room service and sitting enjoying a meal with a bottle of fine wine and taking in the wonderful views across the Thames, especially with it all being lit up on an evening.

On this part of the journey, we would be heading back towards Westminster Bridge, only by this time it was always even busier, with an increased amount of people swelled by tourists that liked to frequent this area. This was probably much to the annoyance of the civil servants and parliamentarians rushing back and forth from Portcullis House to the Houses of Parliament. At this point Nicky and I would again dismount our bikes until we reached the other side of the road at Great George Street, just at the side of the HM Revenue and Customs building. Thankfully on this part of the street, things would begin to quieten down again, so we could remount our bikes and start heading along Birdcage Walk in the direction of Horse Guards Road.

Cycling back along St James' Park was always a joy. There wouldn't ever be too many people and on a few occasions, we were lucky enough to pass the Household Cavalry Mounted Regiment. While respectably keeping a safe distance, I would do my best to cycle alongside them so I could grab a photograph or two. The sound of their hooves on the road certainly drew the attention away from the noise of all the birds squawking and singing in the nearby pond. Like I mentioned earlier, there wasn't a week's holiday that the sun didn't shine during our cycle, which really made the Guardsmen on horseback look spectacular, with their shiny silver helmets and metal chest armour gleaming in the bright sunshine.

As we turned off from Horse Guards Road, we would then head left in the direction of Buckingham Palace, cycling along the Mall which has tall trees either side of the road. Again, with the beautiful St James' Park to our left and only a little distance across the road, stately homes, gardens and townhouses, most of them residencies with Royal connections. It's an easy cycle travelling along the Mall, with its paths and roads being so expansive, so it was never long till we were crossing the road and heading towards the Memorial Garden, our view of Buckingham Palace slightly obscured by the Victoria Memorial. You could always tell if the Queen was in residence as the Royal standard flag flew above Buckingham Palace.

Once over the road we would pass Canada Gate and head up the path at the slightly steeper Constitution Hill, till we finally reached the ever-busy roundabout at the top of the road. Carefully and patiently, we would wait for the lights to change so we could cross and pass through the Wellington Arch, but always had to be extremely wary as traffic would shoot around at incredible speeds. Once that was completed, we would pass Apsley House, then make our way safely into Hyde Park. Once into the park we would take a left and head along Serpentine Road till we came to the public toilets, where we would take turns guarding the bikes while going in one at a time. We never took a bike lock with us. We were always offered locks at the bike shop, but we preferred to travel as light as possible.

Directly up from the toilets you can see the Band Stand, which meant a great deal to me for a few reasons. Of course no one old enough could ever forget that tragic bombing incident back in 1982, but I had another special memory of this place. In fact, it was just a little further left from the Band Stand where myself and three other friends – Ian Myles, Iain Fisher, and Eric Pattie – had slept under a tree in our sleeping bags on deck chairs, one night back in 1979. To be more specific it was the 12th of August, the night after we saw Led Zeppelin at Knebworth Park with just over 180,000 other people. I think it was Iain Fisher's idea originally, knowing that we weren't travelling back to Scotland until the Monday morning from Victoria Coach Station. He worked out that Hyde Park wasn't too far away from the station and August being the height of summer in London, and knowing we would already have our sleeping bags with us, it just seemed like a great idea.

Sadly in 1990, while I was still living in London, I received a dreadful phone call from Iain Fisher. I couldn't believe what I heard. Eric had died of a massive heart attack on his way to Hong Kong, travelling from Manila. It was hard to take in as he was only 26 years of age. As close as we all were, Eric was the one I spent most of my formative years growing up with, from Primary school to Balwearie High School, and eventually even working together at Marconi's at Hillend industrial estate in Fife. Death is terrible at the best of times but is something you get used to as you get older, yet for someone so young and one of my best friends, it was just devastating. In remembrance of Eric, every time we did the cycle we visited the very spot where we slept around that tree. Sadly, that old tree has gone and there's only a stump to show where it once stood. But very close by is a new tree, which looks like it has been growing there for a while. So right at the bottom of the tree, I would bury a small stone brought all the way from Fuerteventura. A few days before flying to London, we would swim out at a place at the back of harbour wall in Corralejo, dive down and retrieve the stone. So, there are seven of those small stones buried there, which I'm hoping might confuse some archaeologist at some future date.

Something that always struck a chord with me was the familiarity of the sounds while we were stopped next to that tree with our bikes. It was that strange sound of traffic being muffled by the trees that lined the road at Park Lane. It always took me back to the very first time we stopped there, August 12th, 1979, our heads just poking out of our sleeping bags very early in the morning. Those exact same sounds I could hear every time we stopped there, and of course let's not forget, it was something Nicky would start to become familiar with also.

Again, I would always get hit with that warm feeling of hyper-focus euphoria, some sort of nostalgic pathway back to my past. This rejuvenated me as I excitedly looked forward to passing through more of these little memory beacons of light.

After burying the stone, Nicky and I would climb back onto our bikes and start making our way along the path called Louisa Duckworth Walk, which eventually led us onto the wider path heading north towards Marble Arch. This park road lies under the cover of the trees, so we would always see lots of squirrels, which were like small dogs to us as we were used to seeing the much smaller chipmunks that lived close to our apartment in Corralejo. As we cycled on again, we had the spacious green park to our left and the ever-busy Park Lane to our right, still with that familiar muffled sound, although always just a little louder as ran parallel to the road. Even though we were still in the park we had to stay quite focused on the road ahead as there were always other cyclists rushing backwards and forwards in each direction, and of course the many runners that make good use of this sizeable park right in the heart of London.

Once under the shelter of the trees' leaves and out of the bright sunlight, it seemed a bit cooler, but that all changed once everything opened up as we reached Speaker's Corner. Again, to our right we would see the bus park and just a little beyond that, Marble Arch itself. This part of the park always seemed much busier, probably with it being close to Oxford Street. Following the path all the way round, we would eventually take a turn to our left and prepare to cross the busy but narrow Bayswater Road. Once we crossed the road, we headed over into Stanhope Place to do our usual, which was to have a picture outside the first hotel we stayed at in 2009, the Parkwood.

Now the next part of the journey was always very precarious, as we would usually travel down Connaught Place and battle our way through the heavy traffic on the Edgware Road. This was one of the main arteries for buses and heavy goods vehicles heading in and out of London, especially northbound traffic. Even once we crossed Edgware Road things still didn't get any easier, as we were sucked into the slipstream of London's fast-moving transport system. There would certainly be no casual chatting between us as I could only just every now and again turn my head to check Nicky was okay and not being swallowed up the frantic fast flow of traffic. A sort of relaxed, touristy cycle, jauntily making our way round the sights of London, had turned into a mad dash till we could find safer routes to travel on.

We would take a left at Portman Square then head towards Manchester Square, moving up Wimpole Street, then heading across Harley Street. Thankfully things always quietened down a bit as we slowly cycled through this very prestigious part of London. This is where all the rich and famous people come; it's a hub for private healthcare where doctors who specialise in almost everything offer their services at a price. It was a welcome break, hitting this part of London, as the traffic really thins out.

It was that previous heavy traffic that would eventually inspire us to try to find an easier way through the city. Of course with us planning on getting to the north of London, this was always going to prove difficult. From day one of planning these long cycle journeys I obviously had not looked for the quickest route, I just wanted the most scenic and if possible, the safest. So just before the 2015 holiday

I tried to see if it was possible to find a quieter route, not being too fussed if it got a little bit longer. We were never in a mad rush, we always had all day, so time was on our side. After a little bit of research and checking out some videos on YouTube, I found that if we could get ourselves to Paddington Basin, we could make our way around to Little Venice and from there on to Regent's Canal. This was a brilliant idea, or so I thought.

Halfway along, we would leave the canal just at the bottom of Primrose Hill, which was directly across from the zoo. My only real concern was getting lost while making our way to Paddington Basin. I knew once we got there everything else should just fall into place, and let's not forget this would be even more scenic.

On the day of this cycle, I was even more excited than usual knowing there was a little more adventure added to this great day out. One other added bonus was that the route around the canals kept us on the left-hand side of the path all the way, so even if we had to pass other oncoming cyclists, we wouldn't be too close to the water and there was even less chance of us falling into the canal. Yup, I had thought of everything, so on this occasion once we got to the Parkwood at Stanhope Place, instead of going along Connaught Place and heading towards the Edgeware Road, we would just carry on to Connaught Square. Little did we know, we would stumble upon an ex-prime minister's house with three heavily armed police guarding his front door. If you're wondering how I knew this, I couldn't help myself and stopped to ask. I must admit they were really friendly, and I made the upmost effort to be as polite as possible. But more importantly, I had to really focus on getting us to Paddington Basin. I knew if I took a left at Connaught Square, I could get onto another road facing north and start heading towards Norfolk Crescent.

Things seemed to be going to plan. Thankfully the roads weren't too busy as we eventually passed through the Crescent; all we had to do was pass through some traffic lights and on to another street called Sale Place. This was an easy, straight road to follow, and I was over the moon when we reached Paddington Post Office. There I could see a small entrance which would lead us right into Paddington Basin. I was overjoyed. I even got off my bike and raised both my arms in celebratory fashion. Maybe it was a bit of relief that I'd managed to find it without getting us lost. Either way I knew that we only had to head into the Basin area and follow the canal round to Little Venice, then on to Regent's Canal. No more heavy traffic, just a scenic cycle until we got close to Primrose Hill.

As we entered the Basin everything looked very modern, in fact some of it looked very much like a business park with a few statuettes to help reinforce that post-modern feel. We hadn't cycled too far along when we spotted a duck with all its little ducklings huddled around in a little enclave. It was then we realised that one of the ducklings had become trapped and the mother wasn't able to rescue it. Without any fuss, Nicky was off her bike like a flash. She was down on her hands and knees, stretching down into the drain cover where the little duckling had become stuck. Once Nicky freed the poor little thing it joined the rest of the group, and we watched them happily paddle off together with Mum leading the way.

As we made our way into Little Venice, we were blown away by how nice it was. When you think of London you always think of the city, or Big Ben, the West End, Buckingham Palace just to mention a few of the iconic sights. But Little Venice is like being somewhere out in the country, especially when you reach Browning's Pool. The boats, or barges as they're called, are all decoratively painted. Some are ladened with plant pots full of colourful flowers. But it's all very relaxed as the calm waters shimmer with the sunlight, all surrounded by trees and greenery. This is, again, not what you would think of when you imagine London, as it's so serene and laid back. Even out in the middle of the pond there's a small island frequented by happy little birds nestled in the bushes, all singing away to themselves.

This was where I became slightly discombobulated, but in a nice way. I'd stopped thinking, basically. We just kept cycling on, letting the canal path lead the way. We passed under a small bridge still following the canal and on the opposite side of the path we began to see large houses with beautiful gardens leading all the way down to the water's edge. I was feeling quite confident as I was sure I recognised a lot of these wonderful views from the many videos I watched back in the apartment in Fuerte. As far as I was concerned, my many hours of research had paid off handsomely. This had definitely been one of my better ideas. But as we cycled on and on, the views were beginning to change somewhat.

On the other side of the canal I could see what looked like an industrial estate. Not too concerned, we cycled on. Then just a little further we seemed to be heading past an underpass to our left. The idea that something wasn't quite right began to enter my mind. But for some reason it was also in my mind just to keep plodding on. *It'll come right eventually,* I told myself. Now across from the canal on the other side I could see a rather extensive cemetery, but still something inside told me to keep cycling on. Something would jump out at me to indicate we were okay and going in the right direction, or so I kept telling myself. In the back of my mind I was thinking of what Nicky was going to say if I told her, "Er, I'm not sure but I think we are lost."

We even crossed the busy A406 North Circular. Why didn't I stop even to just check the compass on my phone? It was 2015 at the time; I had what is supposed to be a smartphone. I was obviously too dumb for that. We eventually cycled alongside another canal boat where I could see a guy sitting peacefully, hand rolling a cigarette. "Hi there," I said. "You couldn't tell us where we join the Regent's Canal, please?"

I could see by the look on his face he was going to tell me something I didn't really want to hear.

"Oooh, you've come about ten miles in the wrong direction.

You'll need to head back closer to Little Venice, if you want to get on that."

Straight away I lifted my hand to rub my forehead. I couldn't believe what I'd just heard. I was looking at Nicky and just waiting on her calling me all the names under the sun.

"Okay, no problem, thanks for that," I sheepishly replied.

At the time it was the end of the world. Cycling all the way to Kenwood House from Gabriel's Wharf is challenging enough, especially with the route we took, but here I was, needlessly adding literally an extra 20 miles onto the journey. I quickly realised that just to make things that little bit more difficult, we would have to cycle closer to the water all the way back.

Thankfully Nicky hadn't grasped the magnitude of my humongous cock-up and about turned her bike without a word of complaint. I thought she might just be saving her reaction to give me both barrels once we got a little further away from that guy sitting on his canal boat. But no, it was just a case of getting our heads down and heading back to Little Venice tout de suite!

Obviously once I got to Paddington Basin earlier, I had let my guard down. Foolishly I should've remembered that we were supposed to cycle along Blomfield Road then across Aberdeen Place, then down onto Regent's Canal. But I remembered back at the Westbourne Terrace Road bridge, I was too busy trying to be clever, pointing out to Nicky what the rope marks on the off side of the canal bridge walls were. These, I cleverly pointed out, were caused by the towing lines, when boats were being pulled by horses many years before. I was even able to point out that the ropes when wet could pick up grit, making them even more abrasive. As I had been telling her this, my eyes were drawn down the canal. I was sure I recognised everything I was seeing and foolishly believed that all we had to do was keep travelling along this canal. My concentration had obviously been too drowned in my overstated feelings of wellbeing to realise the error of my ways. Thankfully, the canal path was relatively quiet, and we managed to get back down to Little Venice in under an hour and quickly realised that the bridge with the rope marks was the one we should've crossed, rather than gone under. It was, again, ironic, me trying to be clever while I was actually being very stupid.

Blomfield Road was quite narrow but steadily busy, and we then had to cross the even busier A5 to eventually get us onto the quieter Aberdeen Place. It didn't take us long to find a small path that led us right down onto Regent's Canal. We should've been feeling tired but in honesty it was more a feeling of relief, knowing that we were back on the right track. Just to repeat, the canals are lovely at any time of the year, but this was May and everything around the canal was blossoming brightly. This part was much busier with other cyclists, walkers, runners, and a few people with their rods out, seated and fishing by the water's edge.

Heading in the direction of Camden, we were on the left-hand side of the canal, and it wasn't long till we could see the large Regent's Park Mosque, which was something we should've witnessed over an hour earlier. My spirits were lifted even further as I heard all the squawks coming from the tropical birds housed in the large aviary within Regent's Park Zoo. It was just a case of keeping our eyes open for the little turning that would take us up from the canal and onto the road just below Primrose Hill.

We were soon cycling alongside Primrose Hill Park and dismounting again as we headed along Regent's Park Road. There was no real need to get off our bikes, we just loved to soak up the atmosphere while we walked through this very fashionable part of London. It was nice passing lots of busy little cafés and restaurants; most people sitting there seemed to know each other, most of them appearing to be very well-to-do and possibly dressed a little eccentrically. It always felt like we were walking through another of

London's little quaint villages as we slowly made our way towards the bridge that would take us over the main rail line, carrying all the busy trains coming in and out of King's Cross. Just over the bridge we would always pass an antique shop that had a West Highland Terrier sitting outside. In all seven years passing this shop, that little dog was always there, and every time we would stop and take a picture.

Once over the bridge it was just a small journey down and across the busier Adelaide Road and a slower cycle up Eton College Road. The first few cycles Nicky enquired, "Is this where Eton College is?"

Both times id reply, "No!! It's in Berkshire."

In Nicky's defence I'm sure she wasn't the only person to ask the same question over the years.

Once we reached the top of the road it was a quick left turn, then a right, which took us onto Haverstock Hill. Incredibly, we could've been on this road hours earlier if we had taken a more direct route from Waterloo Bridge. But of course, this would've been far more hazardous due to the heavier traffic and far less scenic. This cycle was a lot more about enjoying and experiencing the journey than it was about getting from A to B in the shortest time. A great excuse for me when it came to discussing my foolish 20-mile detour at Little Venice, but I think Nicky and I were on the same page and both agree that the routes we took were very memorable and allowed us to enjoy arguably some of the nicest parts of London.

Haverstock Hill was another challenge. With this being a lot steeper, it would see us out of the saddle and having to really dig in to get up this hill. Thankfully, it levelled off slightly once we got to Belize Park. This was another area within London like a small, self-sufficient little town, with a collection of shops that served everything needed so as not to have to travel too far. It had several nice pubs and restaurants and of course a busy tube station, so people could easily commute in and out of central London. Again, looking around at all the large houses, you could see this was another very wealthy area. As we travelled through this part my spirits were lifted; this was us now starting to head into Hampstead. Every time we reached this point we would dismount from our bikes and slowly walk up the hill. It was all about taking in the atmosphere of this lovely area of London.

Nicky's eyes would always light up as we did this walk and many times she would say, "Wow, if I could afford it, I'd love to live here." This always brought a smile to my face as it made me think back to all those years previous, wondering if I'd ever be back here one day with someone I loved so I could share the experience of how lovely Hampstead was.

As soon as we got into the main part of Hampstead, I'd be in that hyper-focused euphoric state of mind, almost bursting with happiness and energy, my senses electrified by everything going on around me. I suppose to the people walking around us, this was just another day, but for me these were some of the greatest days of my life. I had to agree with Nicky; if I had to live in London, I couldn't think of anywhere better than Hampstead and in honesty, I was very familiar with the place. It was somewhere I knew very well, the only reality being affordability. Most of the houses we passed must have been worth millions of pounds.

Like I said earlier, every time we did this cycle, we were very fortunate that it was always a sunny day. Once we arrived in Hampstead it was always around lunchtime. All the delicatessens and cafés were full of people very happy, relaxed, and chatting away with each other, all very close to the small street, Flask Walk. Of course, there's all your usual well-known commercial retail outlets but what really grabbed Nicky's attention were the fantastically modern fashion boutiques up and down the high street.

On reaching Hampstead Heath Tube Station we'd then take a right-hand turn and head up Heath Street again. Although quite steep it wasn't too much of a concern as I knew we were getting that little bit closer to our destination, Kenwood House. Eventually reaching the top of the hill, you can see Jack Straw's Castle. I was always reminded of the time I walked up from West Heath Street from Golder's Green, lost, trying to find my way back to Archway. I suppose I could've been forgiven as I'd only been in London a few days when I mapped my way home following the tube stations, only to find I had stuck more than 10 miles extra on my journey.

Jack Straw's Castle itself is a grade II listed building named after the leader of the peasants' revolt in 1381. Jack Straw had taken refuge there but was sadly caught and hung for his troubles. Mind you, even to this day his efforts have not been forgotten, although this certainly wouldn't have been much comfort to him as they were hurriedly tying that rope around his neck.

Right in the middle of all this is Whitestone Pond. At one time it was a popular bathing spot for a lot of the locals but earlier, the pond was called Horse Pond as it was a watering hole for the military horses. Now it's been relegated to being a nice feature stuck in the middle of a very busy roundabout.

Our journey always took us onto Spaniard's Road, where we could cycle along the path with ease. It was mostly level and never too busy with walkers, in fact both sides of the road were very green, nicely covered in trees, it was almost like being back in the countryside. We would pass a few inlets which would've taken us down into the Heath, but we always preferred to carry on, going alongside the busy road all the way to the Spaniard's Inn. On reaching the tollgate the road bottlenecks as it's choked between the Spaniard's Inn and the 18th-century toll gate. This could never be rectified, as both buildings are listed as heritage sites, much to the annoyance of the many motorists that pass this way.

The Spaniard's Inn itself has an incredible history. Built in 1585, it eventually became an inn named after the Spanish Ambassador to James I of England, or James the 6th of Scotland. But more interestingly, Dick Turpin's father was the innkeeper there in the 1700s and it is reputed that Dick Turpin was born there. It's difficult to pinpoint any truth as to where Turpin really hung out, as his lifestyle had him cavorting all over the southeast. But one thing is for sure, the Spaniard's Inn was a favourite place for the likes of John Keats, Lord Byron, and even Bram Stoker of *Dracula* fame. Sadly, we never did enter that place but plan to visit it one day. Most likely a Sunday, for us.

Once we had cycled round the toll house it was just a little further down the road that we would eventually reach the Kenwood House car park. It was a strange feeling every time we turned in; it was like coming home. There'd always be the odd car parked just letting their dogs from out of the back as they prepared to go for a walk around the Heath. Or we would pass a few people who had just left Kenwood House, heading back to their cars. Either way, I was always filled with excitement returning to one of my favourite places in London and of course, my head was filled with many memories of the times I had enjoyed cycling through the Heath many years before.

As we made our way down behind Kenwood House the path eventually opened up to a massive green expanse. It's very picturesque especially on a sunny day, as the view from the front of the house looks down the grassy slopes all the way to the pond, and the rest of the area is full of tall trees with thick foliage, certainly a sight to behold in the height of summer. Even though Kenwood House stands on one of the highest points in the Heath, it's still impossible to see all of this beautiful park as it's around 320 hectares in size.

If you take a right and keep going you eventually enter the quieter part of the Heath where there's more forest and wildlife. Whereas heading down to your left takes you to the beautiful ponds, where people can fish for the likes of carp, bream, roach, tench, gudgeon, perch, and pike. But probably more important is that these ponds are some of the best outdoor swimming spots in London. There's a ladies' pond, one for the men, and a mixed pond, all of them open all year round. And when I say all year round, yes, some hardy people swim those icy waters in the middle of winter.

Eventually getting to the front of the house, we would take our time to just stand and gaze at this beautiful sight, which never seems to change. Like I said earlier, in all seven holidays we had in London, which comprised of five in September and two in May, we had a clear blue, cloudless sky with the sun shining, and it was nice to eventually get off our bikes, relax and enjoy this wonderful, picturesque, postcard views.

The house itself was a stately home first built in the early part of the 17th century, then remodelled by the architect Robert Adam. Although it was originally built in red brick the whole façade is painted white, which gives its prominence amongst all the browns and lush greens of the Heath. The house obviously had its fair share of aristocratic owners and residents but is now in the capable hands of English Heritage and still houses some illustrious interiors, sculptures, and jewellery. Most notable are the house's internationally renowned paintings, which include works by Reynolds, Van Dyck, Vermeer, Gainsborough, and Rembrandt no less. Although we did peer through the window a few times, not once did we ever enter that great house. We were more fascinated by the surrounding beauty of the Heath.

A nice realisation for me was that I could tell I hadn't oversold the place to Nicky. She, too, was lovestruck with its idyllic setting. It was a long way off from the dry desert conditions we were used to, so this magnificent explosion of colour, sight, and sound of birds singing high up amongst the trees was somewhat mesmerising for us both. And of course, there was the satisfaction that I'd fulfilled a dream from so many years earlier. I would be out on my bike, stop and ponder about life, wondering if I'd ever come back in the future and share a moment with someone who would enjoy the serenity and beauty of the place. It was so nice to know that Nicky shared that same excitement as I took her around all the spots where I'd often be hit with that melancholy feeling as I people watched. Only now, these places had taken on a different meaning; these were timeless little moments sentimentally cemented into both our hearts.

Once we had scoured most of the Heath and enjoyed taking in some of the incredible expansive views from specific locations, it was time to head into the Brewhouse. This lovely restaurant is within a beautiful walled garden and is a perfect place to sit down and fill your faces with freshly cooked, wholesome food. This timeless sanctuary has become a haven for some of London's most celebrated writers, actors, and academics, where they can sit, relax, and enjoy the peaceful setting. Somewhere you can for once escape the maddening rush of London's fast lifestyle. Even as you enter the Brewhouse, it has this farmhouse feel with its high ceilings and 18th-century architecture. The warm smells of sumptuous food permeate the large room.

Always after a long cycle, you want to sample everything you see before you, so I had to consciously make the effort not to overdo it. Every time we went, we'd always get ourselves a large piece of cream-filled sponge cake, which would just melt in your mouth. Nicky, not being as greedy as me, could never manage to finish all of hers so we would feed it to the small birds who cheekily landed right at our table. Even at busier times, everyone is quietly spoken so there's this lo-fi hum of voices softly chattering away. Every now and again either myself or Nicky would say to each other, "Do you see who that is?" More often than not we'd spot another well-known face.

Thinking back to the first time we went down to Gabriel's Wharf that Saturday morning only to find out there weren't any bikes left for hire, it had turned out to be a blessing in disguise. It's much nicer to cycle and visit all these lovely places when the main populace of London's hard at work. This was especially helpful when travelling around the Heath and probably added to the peace and quiet of the Brewhouse.

The worst part was leaving Kenwood House. It was always a massive tug on my heart strings. I think I can speak for both myself and Nicky when I say we never wanted to leave. Whether it was that euphoric mix of emotions, the memories, the feeling of belonging somewhere, maybe it just came down to delusions of grandeur; either way that feeling of melancholy always returned as I left that hallowed place.

CHAPTER 16

QUICKLY TRAVELLING THE LONG ROAD HOME

The second time we visited Hampstead, we didn't leave the usual way, which was back through the Kenwood carpark. This time as soon as we left the Brewhouse, we took a left.

Just before you leave the Kenwood there's a lovely viewpoint that lets you see all the way down to St Paul's Cathedral. This spot became a regular visit each time we cycled to the Heath. But as you take another left there's a narrow road that takes you out onto Heath Lane. This was another road I had cycled along many times before, all those years ago. Another little part of our long journey I was really excited about; it was another important mission that had to be completed. Yes, I was heading for Archway to see the house on Gladsmuir Road and just a little further along, Dresden Avenue, where I had stayed in that small bedsit. The last time I was there I was clamouring out of the door in the early hours of the morning, heavily laden with what I had left of my worldly goods. The mission then was to get to the bus station in Victoria and get myself on the road home with as little fuss as possible. It was incredible to think here I was, heading back to that same place, full of excitement exactly twenty years later.

Heath Lane was lovely. It's lined with lots of large, beautiful houses with gardens to match. Then we passed another large green field, which was part of the very well-to-do Highgate School. It wasn't long before we hit the busy junction that takes you right into

Highgate Village. Once again the memories came flooding back. This was another beautiful spot I would regularly cycle through; it also reminded me of Sigrun. She loved this place dearly and always wanted to live there. She loved all the little shops and cafés and would always find some excuse to go there.

Spookily enough, Highgate is a hilltop village that is an enclave for quite a few well-known celebrities who also have a soft spot for this most expensive London suburb. Highgate is also home to London's most historical graveyard, which receives thousands of visitors every year. Although any time we have visited it's always been deathly quiet, with most of it very natural and overgrown. I think I would be right in saying that a lot of people go there just to visit the grave of Carl Marx, who was first and foremost a German philosopher who wrote many great theories on social cohesion, but I'm sure many would argue that he has fallen into the trap of becoming an icon used in rather shallow arguments divided between Socialism and Capitalism. Ironically both outdated and not fit for purpose. Personally I'm more for progressive politics and hope social justice will one day prevail.

Once we had completed the short journey through Highgate High Street, we would quickly make our way down Highgate Hill, eventually taking us off that steep slope and left onto Hornsey Lane. This really picked up the momentum as I was back in familiar territory. I always had to keep myself in check and make sure I wasn't taking off and leaving Nicky to frantically try and catch up behind me.

Next, we crossed the Hornsey Lane bridge, which is high up above the busy A1 leading up from Archway. This old bridge was built in 1897 and has infamously picked up the nickname 'suicide bridge'. Sadly, there were a few times back in the day while covering the short distance over that old bridge, you'd see flowers and small messages attached to the railings where some broken soul had decided to jump and take their own life. I never did mention that to Nicky as I was too caught up in the mission I had set before me. I remember it did cross my mind but with us travelling at pace, the moment seemed to pass and it's only a short distance after the bridge that you take a right turn and begin to head down Fitzwarren Gardens. It's all downhill and so close. I remember being so excited that it was hard to keep my hands on the brakes. I could feel myself comfortably leaning round the corners as we sped down Whitehall Park Road. Thankfully the brakes did come on as we got to the bottom of the road and again turned left onto Gladsmuir Road.

My heart was racing excitedly as I recognised the place. Nothing much had changed apart from, say, the cars parked around the streets were brighter and obviously a bit more modern. The place looked exactly as I had imagined it would. The old three-storey red-brick buildings, slightly sheltered from the tall leafy trees. The paths were in need of attention as the thick trunks of the trees had pushed up and dislodged a few of the old paving stones. Suddenly, I realised I was outside the house I had first lived in; I was taken aback at first but began to recognise the old place. Something very noticeable was the small chequered tiles on the footpath leading to the front door steps. I remember having a terrible urge to knock on the door just to ask whoever was staying there if I could have a look around.

My mind began to wander again. I started thinking of all the people I could remember that stayed there. Of course, there was Ian Myles, my childhood friend who I still kept in touch with. Ian would Skype me from Singapore, or even California.

Then there was Estella; she was always the consummate professional. She worked in the head office of Saatchi & Saatchi in London. She was always well spoken, perfectly groomed and as sharp as a pin.

Then there was Mark. Very similar to Ian, he was an ambitious designer. He even left the popular band Black to focus on his career, although he did keep his drum kit set up in his room. I liked Mark; he had this natural talent of just being a really cool guy.

Then there was Judy. She used to make her own jewellery but did spend a bit of time working for Phillips, the auctioneers. She had fabulous books all about antiques. Judy had the special talent that she could talk to me, and I would shut up and listen. That's a trick many people who have been around me would've loved to learn. Judy and I would always talk about the idea of going around the specialised markets to hunt down valuable antiques. Although I personally didn't have much in the way of knowledge, it was still something that really interested me. I just wish we had done it. Even to this day I still really enjoy watching programmes like Bargain Hunt and Antiques Road Trip and often think of Judy.

Then there was Martin. Yet again, another designer but also a massive mountain biking enthusiast. I remember Martin and I were sitting watching the TV on the eve of the Gulf War and the news cameras were covering the area around Westminster. It seemed there were thousands of people down there, peacefully protesting. In fact it almost looked like a carnival atmosphere, when all of sudden Martin suggested, "Hey, do you fancy going down there?" in his soft, laid-back Newcastle accent.

"Yeah, okay," I replied excitedly.

So we quickly grabbed our jackets and jumped into the car. Once we got down to Trafalgar Square, we noticed the police had blocked off Whitehall, so it took us a bit of time to get parked. But once we got closer to Parliament the scenes were unbelievable. There were thousands of people everywhere; weird and wonderful, different groups of people, different religious sects, lots of hippy types handing out candles, people crying and generally upset at the outbreak of war. It was then that Martin and I began realising the severity of the situation. Our faces dropped very solemnly. The banners and handwritten posters, the anti-war chants ringing loudly in our ears. I'll always remember that car journey back to Gladsmuir Road. Yes, it was very different from the one we first took driving down there. We were both very quiet and thoughtful, realising war was way more serious than something you sometimes manage to catch a glimpse of on your TV. It was real. Lots of poor, helpless human beings were going to die and none of it their making. These were very powerful forces at work and there was nothing we the people could do to stop it.

Then I remembered two other people who were very connected to that old house. First off, there was Brooke. This guy was a freelance photographer; he would always be doing pictures for up-and-coming young models. I remember helping him out a few times. To me, these girls were incredible. I was always really nice and polite, whereas Brooke would order them around and treat it like it was some sort of job he wasn't really enjoying. Looking back, I realise I was just being naïve; this was obviously Brooke trying to be cool. In fact later I heard Brooke had left under a bit of a cloud.

Then finally there was Sigrun. She always got on well with Judy. Like me, Sigrun was quite a strong personality and always a real force of energy once she got going.

As I stared at that old door I couldn't help wondering where they had all gone and how they were getting on. The last time I'd heard from Sigrun was when I first moved back to Kinghorn, when she called me on the phone at my parents' house, but that was the last I heard from her. It was then I said to Nicky, "We must go and see Sigrun's old house." But first, we cycled to the end of Gladsmuir Road. At Dresden Avenue, I could see the door through which I'd hurriedly left that early morning twenty years previous. Disappointingly the grocer's shop next door had gone. I could see it had been converted into what looked like a lawyer's office. Directly across the road the laundrette was still there. Nothing much seemed to have changed from what I could make out.

Again, I just wanted to go through that door and take one last look around the old room. As we were standing outside looking up, I saw my old bedroom window again. It left me with a feeling of nostalgic melancholy. So much had happened in my life since I'd last slept up there.

We didn't hang about there too long as we still had to try and find Sigrun's old house. Without too much thought I realised I was just following my nose. With all the memories that had come flooding back I was relying on my intuition to get me there. We cycled up Cressida Road, then on to Whitehall Park, which then eventually led us back onto Hornsey Lane. We only had to travel around 100 metres until we found the turning to Stanhope Road. It was great; everything was falling into place.

I remembered that Sigrun's house hadn't really been so far away, and it wasn't long until we again turned onto Claremont Road, which took us right onto Stanhope Gardens. It had only taken us about ten minutes to find ourselves right outside that old house. It was very obvious that both houses had gone through quite a bit of renovation. A lot of the trees and bushes that filled the garden around the entrances had been cut back. It all looked very open and modern.

First, I thought of old Mike Leonard. I met him on quite a few occasions all those years ago; I'd even helped store some old stuff in one of the old sheds in his back garden. How I wished I'd quizzed him more at the time, but he was quite clever in that respect; he always managed to keep me talking, which I suppose wasn't too difficult a task. And to think, Pink Floyd could've retained their original name, which was Leonard's Lodgers. Waters, Mason, were first to move into that house then a year later. Syd Barrett would join them, and I think it was Syd who eventually came up with the now worldly famous name, Pink Floyd.

Now a lot of people may be wondering what all my excitement is about. I mean, okay, it's just another rock band. But Pink Floyd were a cultural phenomenon, and let's not forget that Mike Leonard was pivotal in creating all those weird light displays, which became synonymous with the whole psychedelic movement. I even mentioned to Nicky as we were looking up at both the houses that maybe one day, they'll eventually put up one of those blue plaques to commemorate the part they played in that time and place in history.

Another thing we used to do as we were emotionally struggling to pull ourselves out of Hampstead Heath, was take another slight detour by crossing the road at the Kenwood House car park and head done Winnington Road. Just a little further on we would take a left and head down Ingram Avenue. This, we would follow all the way till it took us to what is known as the Heath Extension. It was just lovely, cycling through this extremely affluent area with houses the size of mansions and gardens to match. Nicky and I joked that once we were rich this would probably be our preferred place to buy a second home in London.

All of this eventually had to come to an end. There was no more putting it off; we would always reluctantly have to make our way back down into central London. Without fail, though, we would always get off our bikes and walk the short distance through Hampstead and similarly when we approached Primrose Hill. It was all about soaking up every last bit of that idyllic atmosphere these two lovely parts of London instilled in us.

The journey back was always so much faster, helped by the fact that a great deal of it was downhill. It only became a bit more precarious as we got as far down as Portland Place, where we would turn right at New Cavendish Street. Tired after a long cycle, our minds were never as sharp and it felt like we were being sucked along with the busy late afternoon traffic. It was always a great relief once we got back to Hyde Park. From there, we would start to take our time and focus on completing the last leg of the journey.

Again we would head down Constitution Hill and back along the quieter and more spacious Mall. We would have to dismount our bike once we got closer to Westminster Bridge, but once we crossed that and headed down the steps not far from the London Eye, we knew it was a nice easy run all the way back to Gabriel's Wharf.

It was usually just after 4 o'clock as we pushed our bikes into Gabriel's Wharf with the late afternoon sun still warm on our backs. As we returned the bikes safely into the hands of the lads who worked at the London Bicycle Company, we always told them we had enjoyed our day and looked forward to seeing them again the following year.

Although still excited from a long day's cycle, we would walk out of Gabriel's Wharf with tiredness slowly beginning to climb over us, and of course that little tinge of sadness knowing that deep down, this was the end of my favourite day of the year. *Oh well, not to worry, we will just have to plan to do it all again someday,* I'd always tell myself.

CHAPTER 17

THEATRE NIGHTS

One great thing after we finished the cycle was that we knew the excitement wasn't finished there. We still had a cracking evening to enjoy. But first we had to walk all the way back to our hotel. Thankfully we always took the more direct way back. We crossed over the Golden Jubilee Bridge again, past the skateboard graveyard, and once we reached the north side we crossed through really old tiled alleyways. They were always badly lit and slightly dank, until we eventually came out and into the train station at Charing Cross.

From there we would cross the Strand, head across the top of Trafalgar Square, and then on up till we reached our hotel, Le Meridien. We knew after a long day the best thing we could do was keep moving so traditionally, once we got back to the hotel, we would quickly get changed and head down to that fabulous swimming pool. For some reason we were always really lucky and after the end of every cycle had that whole pool to ourselves. This included the sauna and Jacuzzi, which were fantastic for your legs after a long day.

Thursdays were a very special night of our holidays in London, as we always booked a show for that evening followed by a meal. The planning of the shows was something we always prepared well in advance. Many nights, months before we arrived in London, we would sit up late working out which shows to book. It wasn't just the shows themselves; we always made a point of trying to book the best seats possible. Of course this comes at a price but as far as we were concerned, each of our visits to London was regarded as a holiday of a lifetime, so there was no expense spared. Even as we got ready, we would raid our small minibar and open a bottle of Moët Chandon.

That was the fantastic thing about staying in a hotel right in the heart of Piccadilly. We were right in the heart of Theatre Land, only five minutes away from our shows. It's not just the shows, it's the theatres themselves that give you that special feeling. Always while getting seated, you can't help but look around and marvel at the very dated architecture and more importantly, its history.

With a lot of these theatres being more than a hundred years old, it's incredible to think of how many different shows have been performed in these iconic buildings, and add to that the famous actors who have been household names over the years. Like Wembley's place in football or Wimbledon's place in tennis, these theatres are all collective spiritual homes to the world of acting. Okay, Nicky and I could never claim to be the most prolific, or most ardent of theatre goers, but we were definitely taking in two to three shows every time we spent a week in London. Again, Thursday was a must after every cycle, but we did do a few Wednesdays and a good number of Saturday matinees. I can't really talk about every theatre or show we had seen over the years, as this would turn this writing into 'The Book of Reviews', but I will list the shows I can remember, for anyone reading who may be able to relate or might have seen the same shows themselves.

Our shows were chosen either because we were interested in the subject matter, or it might even have been because of the actors performing. And of course, sometimes we would just take a chance, as it was as much about the whole theatre experience, a little bit like that acquired taste you get for whisky. There's no bad shows, just some are better than others.

As I wrote earlier, one of the first shows we saw was The 39 Steps at the Criterion Theatre. This was another one of those Saturday afternoon walk-ins. It really cheered me up after the disappointment of not being able to hire bikes that day. All done in an early 19th-century fashion, the four cast members gave an energetic, hilarious performance that had me laughing openly. Sadly, the second time going to see it, the whole show seemed a bit tired, which was surprising.

Then there was the very entertaining Yes Prime Minster at the Gielgud Theatre on Shaftsbury Avenue. We were lucky enough to book premium seats on the opening night. It was great; we were surrounded by journalists and well-known theatre critics, which just added to the whole experience. Even at a young age I was a massive fan of the original TV serious, watching Jim Hacker (Paul Edington) rise to fame. But as great as the cast were in this fabulous hit TV series, the real star was Nigel Hawthorne, who played the very devilish and Machiavellian Sir Humprey Appleby, so I was really excited about going to see this one. There was a feeling of nostalgia and anticipation. I'm glad to report that it did live up to its high expectations, with a few modern twists thrown in.

Another show in a similar vein was Hand Bagged which we saw in the Vaudeville Theatre on the Strand. When we first booked this from our apartment in Fuerteventura months earlier, I sensed that this wasn't one Nicky was really looking forward to. It was a very comedic look at the relationship between a young Queen Elizabeth and a young Margaret Thatcher, also an older Queen Elizabeth and an older Margaret Thatcher. I wouldn't say Nicky was dreading it, but it might be fair to say she was a little apprehensive before we got there. Luckily, to her surprise she really enjoyed and it was nice to see her openly laughing enthusiastically. There was no surprise that this play would eventually be rerun, with rave reviews across the board.

Another play that caught me unawares was Carmen Disruption, which was performed at the very specially developed Almedia Theatre in Islington. I had no prior knowledge of what I was walking into; the whole reason for me being there was that my longtime but distant friend Sharon Small was performing. I had been in contact with Sharon not long before visiting London and she offered me tickets as a kind gesture. Not having done any research, and with Nicky and I just turning up on the day, we didn't have a clue what to expect. One thing is for sure, if Sharon's in it you can bet your bottom dollar it's going to be good. Sharon has been a very hard-working actor for many years and deserves all the accolades and success that she's received. I may be biased here but I don't think Sharon has ever worked on anything that has had the misfortune to pick up bad reviews. I think most directors are happy to give Sharon the part knowing she brings a Midas Touch to every part she plays.

Again, I was caught very unawares by this thought-provoking Carmen Disruption. The intrigue begins as you look down into the centre of the round stage, only to see a bull's carcass. The show moves at a whirlwind pace and you're bombarded with a cacophony of thoughts spoken from a cast playing parts of people, lost and lonely, hanging on to an empty shadow of their lives through a reliance on social media. At the same time the whole feel and atmosphere is electrified by the haunting and beautiful sounds of the very alluring Carmen. I was completely blown away, to say the least.

We met up with Sharon at her house the following day with her husband, kids, brother Ryan and his wife, but for some reason I still feel I didn't convey to her how brilliant that show was or what it meant to me.

Another Saturday matinee we just happened to choose on the spur of the moment was Noël Coward's Private Lives. This play kind of takes on a new meaning as it is very much associated with the very explosive relationship between Elizabeth Taylor and Richard Burton. These very powerful soulmates had a tumultuous partnership as they struggled to live together, but couldn't bear to be apart. Although this show has had many famous faces playing these parts over the years, the two very troubled characters take it to another level, giving a new meaning to 'life imitates art far more than art imitates life'. This was definitely one of Nicky's choices.

As we wandered into the Gielgud Theatre, once again the main attraction here for Nicky was that Toby Stephens and Anna Chancellor were playing the main parts. It was great fun; another classic performed with artistic precision. I'm sure they had to really concentrate on delivering their lines as they cavorted around the stage with great energy.

Earlier in the day we had been at the Portobello Market, which was sadly not a great deal of fun as both Nicky and I were suffering after drinking far too much red wine the night before. So, Nicky's quickfire decision to walk into the Gielgud Theatre and watch Private Lives transformed the whole day.

Another great show we booked well in advance was American Buffalo at the Wyndham Theatre, which is right next to Leicester Square Tube Station. Starring Damien Lewis, John Goodman, and Tom Sturridge, we knew the tickets would go like hotcakes, so there could be no hanging about. Over the years Nicky had become an internet maestro, very adept at securing our preferred tickets, but it was most certainly a case of the early bird catches the worm. So as soon as they became available online, Nicky was on it.

The show itself was an acting masterclass, which in its entirety was performed in one location, that being Don's Junk Shop in Chicago.

Something similar that we saw, although not as powerful, was The Prisoner of Second Avenue at the Vaudeville Theatre starring Jeff Goldblum. The similarity lay in the fact that they were both Broadway reproductions from the 70s. There's quite an obvious difference in style when it comes to British and American plays, or maybe it's the difference between London and New York productions as they both vie for the same theatrical crowns.

On our first visit to London one Friday night, we decided at the last minute to walk into the Dominion Theatre on Tottenham Road and watch We Will Rock You. As an early experience it was quite a lot of fun. Other shows we saw that I would class as fun and comedic would be The Play That Goes Wrong, which has become a firm favourite, at the Duchess Theatre, and The Lady Killers, again at the Vaudeville Theatre, with John Gordon Sinclair playing the main part. I had great memories of John Gordon Sinclair from back in my younger days, when he played the hapless hero in Gregory's Girl, which to me was an 80s classic.

Then another very good show we both found really funny was Jumpy, which was on at Duke of York starring Tamsin Gregg, and we felt a really good performance coming from Doon Mackichan. This was a very contemporary piece looking at the struggles for modern-day parents trying to bargain with even more modern-thinking kids. Poor Mum played by Tamsin Gregg struggles as she succumbs to accusations from her kids that she and her opinions are proving she's getting old.

One other play we enjoyed greatly was The Kitchen, at the National Theatre on the South Bank. This was a remake of a play from 1959 about a very large, busy kitchen in a swanky hotel in London. It cleverly starts at a hectic pace. A large cast move with fire in their bellies as a busy lunchtime rush confines all hands to the deck. As the rush hour dissipates the characters slow down to reveal more about themselves and their dreams. This is all done in a very virtuosic fashion, going along nicely with the original play.

Just as some of the characters prepare to make changes in their mundane lives so they can follow their dreams, their present reality kicks in and the demands of the evening meal quash their hopes as they're drawn back into dehumanising cogs of the kitchen machinery. But it all becomes too much for the German fish chef, who declares he's had enough and runs amok having a mental breakdown, while the others fall back into line. Something that started so lively and jolly, giving off a very feel-good vibe, slowly turns into something a little darker and more sinister, but all said and done, it was a thoroughly enjoyable show.

Without fail after every Thursday show we made our way to Joe Allen's in Exeter Street. No, it wasn't the greatest diner in the world, it was just the perfect place to go after a show. Even your entrance to this theatrical haunt had the perfect start. After making your way down quiet, unassuming steps you would open the door to this lively, vibrant restaurant. As you walked in the place seemed a little dark apart from small neon lights advertising Budweiser and other strangely styled New York delicacies. The other sensory highlight is the sound of the piano being gently played along with the happy buzz of voices that help make the atmosphere. On closer inspection you can see the walls are adorned with posters from shows that have run over the previous years. Some are of actors grouped together for that last end-of-night picture. You can see the beads of sweat still freshly dripping down their faces.

The walls are all darkly painted and the tables are made of a dark, shiny, brown wood. The experience becomes even better as you're led to your table. For some reason we were lucky enough to always be seated around the same place every time. It was always a table that ran down a dividing wall with small glassless arches, allowing us to look through to the bar area. This gave us a better view into the room, which was always full of the great and good from the acting world. So, for the first five visits we passed the ever-smiling pianist, who always spoke to us like he had known us all our lives. This was just the nicest welcome, as we settled into one of London's great theatre institutions.

Sadly, early in January of 2014, that revered pianist, Jimmy Hardwick, passed away, which must have left a great chasm in the hearts of his many friends.

CHAPTER 18
SHOPAHOLICS' PARADISE

Nothing was ever written in stone regarding plans for Fridays but one thing we would definitely do is have a lunch planned in another of London's great restaurants. Similarly, it was much the same on a Friday evening; we would pull out all the stops to make sure we had another meal to remember, but the in-between time on Friday was usually spent shopping, and I'm not embarrassed to say I enjoyed it. Personally, when I go shopping for something in particular, I can be in and out in a matter of minutes. Nicky, on the other hand, can take weeks deciding on whether she likes a certain item. In fact, there have been many times, after weeks of indecision, she returns to the shop and said item is gone.

I would say, "Look, you should've have bought it when you had the chance."

Nicky would defiantly reply, "Oh, it just wasn't meant to be."

Another one of Nicky's traits when she looks at something she likes, is to go straight to the price tag and quickly say, "Oh, I'm not paying that, I'll wait till the sales start."

Even when I'd say, "Look, I'll pay for it," still, she'd have none of it.

But now we were hitting Oxford Street, which has been called London's 'jugular vein of consumerism'. Yes, nearly a mile and a half long and home to the UK's finest names in high-street fashion. This is a shopper's paradise. The famous stretch of road first started out under the name of Tyburn Road, until in the early part of the 17th

century, when it became the worldly famous Oxford Street. In honesty it didn't really start becoming recognised for what it is today until the very early 19th century, when John Lewis, Harry Gordon Selfridge and latterly Marks and Spencer's moved in, and of course there were the smaller outlets such as booksellers, shoemakers, and goldsmiths.

As Oxford Street has developed over the years, the amount of people visiting has grown to nearly 100 million a year. That's nearly 280 thousand people walking those pavements every day. A lot of the big-name stores have now cleverly opened shops either side of Oxford Street, to try and capitalise on the 8 billion pounds spent yearly. Something I began to pick up on over the years was that every time they were doing any redevelopment for new stores, they tried to build a little further back, allowing them to make the pavements a bit wider. This obviously helped create more space for the busy and congested Oxford Street. The only time they can't do this is when it's a listed building.

Like I said before, I didn't mind shopping with Nicky and always suggested to her that if something makes you look a million dollars, then there's no need to get too het up about the price tag; within reason, of course. Nicky is very good looking so I will also admit to enjoying watching her trying on all these lovely clothes and asking me every time, "What do you think?"

I'd always reply, "Lovely." The next step was to convince her to buy it.

I always find these large stores incredibly interesting and find myself people watching. Whether it's the lighting or the particular music they play, you'll find everyone transcends into that same mindset. Their faces drop and become expressionless; their partners are given the job of holding on to the bags while the ladies shuffle through the coat hangers trying to find their size. Sometimes tensions do rise if there are younger children with them. The kids become bored and irritable and begin to play up, which invariably is his fault for not controlling the situation. A lot of people don't realise how exhausting it can be as you're walking in and out of these busy stores laden with bags and wearing heavy coats, and of course there's all the temperature changes you go through. To add on top of that, if you've been forced to do these rounds and you really don't enjoy shopping, slowly but surely you lose the will to live.

Thankfully it wasn't like that for Nicky and myself, especially if it was a Friday. Normally we'd be looking for something to wear that evening so, again, I found it quite fun. I even found myself chatting with the store assistants as Nicky tried something on. The girls were mostly pleasant and I think it made a change from having to deal with irate or rude customers.

For Nicky and I this was never a problem; we always travelled light. As we moved along Oxford Street, we made sure we walked in the fast lane, happily nipping in and out of all our preferred shops.

One of Nicky's favourite places to go was definitely Selfridges, and if I must be honest, it was mine as well. From the minute you walk in the door you get the feeling you're a little underdressed, as the shop floor is so busy with lots of very glamourous assistants, all smartly dressed with not a hair out of place. Their faces are a great advert for the products they sell, as their make-up is Photoshop perfect. It obviously all works really well as lots of ladies, especially at weekends, book appointments to have their makeup put on in Selfridges before they go out for the evening.

As we made our way through this very busy store, it wasn't long till we were on the escalators. If you look around, all you see are very high-end designer names in premium spots. It's not just the expensive items, the investment in shopfitting itself has been taken to another level. Anyone thinking about making a career in shopfitting need look no further than Selfridges; this is a masterclass and it never stops as things change dramatically through the seasons. The pressures on the people working within that fast-moving industry must be phenomenal and remember, it's a fine balancing act, keeping the store owners and product makers happy. Of course, I had spent a little time in advertising in a previous life, so I still had strange fascination with marketing and all the project management that went along with it.

Making our way to the third floor, Nicky would always like to look through some of the luxurious clothes on offer. It was incredible to think that some of the most expensive items were more likely to be worn only once and then hung up in a wardrobe, never to see the light of day again. It's definitely another reason I personally couldn't warm to the fashion industry, although saying that, I was always happy to inspire Nicky to purchase whatever she saw fit. Again, I would repeat my mantra, "If it makes you look a million dollars, it's worth every penny." This was probably just another way of me masking my ADHD impulsive spending habits, whereas Nicky was much more sensible and a damn sight more frugal. Yes, it's incredible to think Nicky and I have fallen out with each other just because she's not spent a fortune on herself.

The real reason I enjoyed visiting Selfridges so much was that after Nicky had finished browsing through all the fabulous clothes, we would make our way back down to the ground floor to grab some food at YO! Sushi. This was a dream come true for me. You pull up a seat and eat as much as you can handle as beautifully prepared sushi literally passes along a conveyor belt. The small dishes the food is kept in are colour coded as to how expensive each dish is. This didn't deter me from eating whatever I wanted. After we were finished, there was usually quite a collection of these small plates stacked up beside me. My mouth still waters every time I think back to that brightly lit conveyor belt.

Although not on Oxford Street, Harrods was another place we happily visited. Like Selfridges they employ thousands of staff, and have a special concierge service where someone can walk around and help you shop and carry your bags for you. Although, again, we would make our way to the ladies' floor so Nicky could browse the very expensive designer fashions on offer, her favourite department was undoubtably the pet shop. It was fantastic, going in to see all the lovely small puppies and kittens. The staff always assured us they were never there too long; they were quickly bought then whisked off to some of London's more affluent residential areas.

Sadly, in the earlier part of the 19th century, believe it or not Harrods sold wild animals such as lions and panthers. Thankfully those days are behind them. The pet shop eventually closed in early 2014 as it had to make way for a multi-million-pound refurb. It turned into another women's fashion floor. As sad as we were to find out that the Harrods pet store was closed, we fully understood that a lot of other people probably found it a very unethical business practice. We always felt those animals were going to nice homes with large gardens.

Another place we visited was the original purpose-built shopping location, Regent's Street. Unlike Oxford Street most of the prestigious flagship stores have remained much the same. These iconic 200-year-old buildings always felt like home anyway, as every time we stayed at the Le Meridien our rooms looked down onto Regent's Street. Walking up and down was always much easier, as the footpaths have always been a lot wider, whereas Oxford Street tends to bottleneck in places.

There were quite a few times Nicky did eventually buy some beautiful clothes from Guess and a few of the other well-known outlets, and remember, it was just as much fun for me watching her trying on these lovely clothes as this only enhanced Nicky's beauty even more.

Of course, I can't mention Regent's Street without mentioning Hamleys, the world's largest toy store, which has been in the same location since 1881. The shop had its ups and downs way back in the early 1920s, but that, as they say, is all in the past. Hamleys can now boast something like five million visitors every year with its seven wonderous floors. I remember one year in particular; I had gone in to get myself a box of magic tricks. It was really only the one trick I was after, but it cost thirty pounds to buy the whole box. The specific trick was one that I would do just before I introduced one of our regular magic shows onto the stage at the Dunas Caleta in Fuerteventura. I would make a small piece of bright red cloth disappear into the palm of my hand with the aid of a small fake thumbpiece. When I performed the trick, I'd notice a few faces quite surprised at my newfound talent, so smiling proudly, would about turn and walk off the stage feeling very pleased with myself.

So, once we returned to our hotel room, I couldn't wait to open my box of tricks and quickly peeled away the cellophane wrapping. I tipped the contents of the magic box out onto the bed. You can imagine my disappointment when I realised the only trick missing was the very one I was after. Nicky found this highly amusing, as my childish torment was in full swing. I couldn't believe it; out of all twelve tricks the only one I really wanted was missing.

Nicky suggested, "Not to worry. We still have the receipt, we can take it back tomorrow," but I was having none of it. As soon as we were changed and ready, I had to go back and get it sorted as soon as possible. Again, another symptom of my ADHD impulsiveness; I just couldn't sensibly wait until the next day, which was a Saturday.

It must have been around 18:45 when we went rushing back into Hamleys. The restaurant we had booked was still quite a walk away and I didn't want to be late. When I eventually got to the counter where I had first purchased the box of tricks, I could see the very guy I bought it from. This lifted my spirits, hoping he would still remember me. The only problem being, he was actually demonstrating some of the very same tricks in front of 15 to 20 young children. Knowing I was in a bit of a rush, I stood closely behind all the children impetuously waving my magic box, trying to get his attention. I could see by the look on Nicky's face she wasn't too pleased by my actions, but I carried on regardless.

Eventually when he finished the trick he was doing he sternly said to me, "Can I help you?"

I quickly babbled out my displeasure at not having the trick I wanted in my magic box and asked if I could change it straight away as we had a table booked. I even pointed at Nicky, all dressed up for our meal, to back myself up. Again she shook her head at me dragging her into the situation. I could see he wasn't happy with my rude intervention but grabbed one of the magic boxes and asked me to step forward so we could swap over the boxes. "Ahh, brilliant."

Still smiling, I pushed my way through the kids and handed over the box. As he passed me a new one, I thanked him again and apologised for my rash behaviour, but started to tear off the cellophane as quickly as I could. Once I got the box opened. I could see the trick I was really after and without thinking. I passed the rest of the box. with all the other tricks in it. to a small child who standing nearby. "There you go, that's an early Christmas present for you." I said. still smiling. The child seemed quite startled at my generosity. But as I looked back up at the shop assistant, I saw he was once again not very happy with my actions. I raised my hands and apologetically explained that we were off to a nice restaurant and I couldn't really take the magic box with me. I could understand his displeasure and realised he was doing his best to sell as many of these magic boxes as possible, and I had just given one away for free.

With one last, "Sorry," I turned and smiled at the kids and left as quickly as possible. Anyway, it was mission completed. I had that trick I wanted in my pocket.

Bond Street and New Bond Street were other places Nicky and I often walked through over the years, but a lot of the shops were very prestigious, upmarket jewellers and fashion retailers that were just a little out of our price range, to say the least. Again, a lot of the shopfronts were very decoratively designed, and you could see there was no expense spared when it came to fitting these shops out. The one thing that did grab our attention was that they never seemed to be very busy with customers. Some of the doors would even have a couple of burly security men standing guard. We could only imagine that because their products were so expensive, they'd only have to sell a few per day to make a substantial profit at the end of the month.

Years earlier, Bond Street was the place the Mayfair elite would go to socialise and became a well-known district for the bourgeoisie to live in the houses just above the shops.

Just at the bottom of Bond Street there's the lovely Burlington Arcade. No doubt about it, this is the original shopping centre, dating back nearly two hundred years. All the shopfronts have dramatically stayed the same throughout the years, so it definitely feels like you step back in time as you slowly browse past the shops. Again, most of the things on offer are an eclectic mix of prestigious jewellery, macarons, old-fashioned chocolate shops, leather goods, and high-end footwear. Although back in the day it was a place for the rich and wealthy to go shopping, that also attracted pickpockets and their partners in crime, prostitutes. Now just before anyone thinks I'm being sexist here or having a go at the ladies working in that age-old profession, I'm not. But still to this day, whistling is banned in the arcades because this was how prostitutes would warn pickpockets if the police were on the way. The girls would literally hang out of the windows above the shops, not only plying for their own trade but working as lookouts for some of the more illicit traders on the street.

Similar to the Burlington Arcade is Covent Garden. This area started off as a walled garden owned by Benedictine Monks of the Abbey of St Peter, Westminster. It stayed a lovely green area until the

1650s when the powers that be at the time allowed houses to be built around the actual area known as Covent Garden. At first it managed to lure all the rich and wealthy to these fine houses, but once they started a marketplace and opened a few taverns, things began to change. By the 18th century, Covent Garden was a renowned red light district, attracting notable prostitutes such as Betty Careless and Jane (mother) Douglas, whose customers were mostly from the higher echelons of society. But in 1830 things would change again when they built a more permanent market hall. This was the beginning of what became the supplying hub of most of London's fruit and vegetables.

But by the mid-19th century things were becoming impractical, what with the lack of space and even worse than that was the congestion and traffic jams building up on a daily basis. So in 1974 the market was closed and moved to a more practical location at Nine Elms, Battersea. But six years later the old Covent Garden was cleaned up and redeveloped and would reopen as a shopping arcade.

It didn't take long for it to become what it is today, a magnet for tourists and Londoners alike, who like to hang out in the beautiful piazza-styled setting. What really helps give this place that special buzz, has to be the entertainers who perform in front of St Paul's Church. As you walk around Covent Garden, it doesn't matter which part you're in, you can always hear their enthusiastic shouts as they cajole the crowds into a frenzy of fun and laughter. Even though you're right in the heart of central London, Covent Garden is protected from the rush of busy traffic and it's that laid back, happy atmosphere that had us drifting in and out of here daily. They, too, have a collection of eclectic shops and stalls, which are probably more aimed at tourists but we certainly didn't mind, as we bought a few special keepsakes there over the years.

CHAPTER 19

WELCOME TO THE BBC

Obviously, working at the same hotel for many years, you become very friendly with lots of the repeat guests who visit every year. In fact, sometimes these people would come back two or three times a year. It became quite the norm for some of these lovely guests to say such things as, "Hey, if you are back in the UK and you need somewhere to stay just give us a shout." These were certainly heartfelt offers, which we very much appreciated, but realistically just couldn't take up. Again, we would always have a week visiting family, which left us another week to kick back and spend some time away together.

I always had lots of holiday days left over at the end of the year, but for one reason or another I never seemed to get round to taking them. One offer we couldn't refuse was from Joe Willis and his lovely partner Penny, who would visit once or twice a year from London. Joe and Penny both worked at the BBC in Portland Place, which is now very much the headquarters after a very extensive renovation in 2005. Joe has worked for the BBC for almost forty years. He started there as a young, fresh-faced apprentice. Joe's hunger for knowledge would see him cover all sorts of important roles within the organisation, which included starting as a broadcast engineer, then becoming a technology project manager, and then eventually the senior technology manager for BBC Portland Road. That must have been an incredibly daunting job considering the size and massive responsibility such a position holds. But Joe himself was always a happy-go-lucky kind of guy who didn't ever seem to show signs of stress. Obviously, his love of technological advances made him relish every challenge that came his way.

Penny, who had also put many years in with the BBC, used to organise the petty cash for a lot of the smaller outside broadcasting operations.

So, when Joe said to Nicky and I, "Look, next time you're in London, send me an email and I'll give you a tour of the BBC," I jumped at the chance.

Now people have a lot of differing opinions on the BBC, especially where I come from in Scotland. Whether those are towards a lack of funding regarding Scottish programming, or even more serious concerns regarding political bias, even in England there's similar accusations of London/political intransigence. But after all is said and done the BBC historically was regarded as one of the world's finest broadcasting companies. Even as far back as the 30s, when all forms of technology were very basic, the BBC were still able to keep everyone connected as they broadcasted around the globe. As a child I remember hearing my grandparents telling me there was no such thing as television; they would all have to sit around listening to the radio. This, I must admit never impressed me. In fact, it only confirmed what I believed, that these must have been terrible times and my grandparents were obviously really old. Although in their defence, when I was that young, I could never envisage the idea that my grandparents were ever young themselves, and I was sure they were born this way. And in the same breath I could never imagine looking that old. These thoughts were not worth entertaining as this was too far off into the future and beyond my imagination.

For me personally, like many others it was something we grew up with, from children's programmes when we were really young, to the test card when there was nothing on, that iconic picture of the little girl, the blackboard with the unfinished noughts and crosses game. With her little friend, the clown, all very reminiscent of that classic film, The Wizard of Oz.

Programmes such as Jackanory and the all-important Blue Peter, whose presenters seemed to be born into the programme, as if they existed nowhere else in the world. Presenters such as Peter Purves, Valerie Singleton, latterly Leslie Judd, but possibly the most popular of them all, John Noakes and his inseparable partner, Shep the black and white border collie. Of course, there were lots of other Blue Peter presenters, it's just the forementioned names were the ones that influenced me the most.

Even some of the cartoon programmes commissioned from America, especially Tom and Jerry, and a personal favourite was the unbeatable Bugs Bunny. This one in particular saved me from the indignation of insults that would come my way because of my buck teeth. Getting called Bugs was a badge of honour.

The Goodies, Fawlty Towers, Dad's Army, It Ain't Half Hot Mum, The Two Ronnies, and of course the unforgettable Morecambe and Wise Christmas Show. Then into the eighties we had Only Fools and Horses, Yes Minister, Are You Being Served, amongst many others. Not the Nine O'Clock News, The Kenny Everett Show, The Young Ones, The Comic Strip, and of course the much-missed Top of the Pops. The great sporting events that happened yearly on in the calendar, the football cup finals, Wimbledon, and then just as summer was coming to an end, the golf open, which my dad would have on religiously.

Saturday mornings were much the same. I'd be glued to the telly watching things like Swap Shop, the football review programmes and then eventually chased out of the house as soon as the horse racing came on. I know I could've mentioned so much more. David Attenborough's legendary nature programmes, award-winning TV series Plays For Today, and another favourite of mine, Ricky Gervais and The Office.

From the late 70s to the late 80s I spent a lot of time working for a company called Marconi's. Every day Radio 1 would play non-stop above our heads, so we were all very familiar with the DJs from the morning shows through to the late afternoon, and if we ever did overtime, we'd get even more obscure evening shows. You didn't have to be an ardent fan of the BBC, with only three channels on the TV to choose from and it blaring out all day on the radio, it was just there, all around you.

So, when Joe made this fantastic offer, I jumped at the chance to visit this (and it's hard not to overuse this word) iconic building. It was great timing as well, as we arranged to visit around 5 o'clock on a Monday evening, just before another pre-arranged meal across the road at the Langham Hotel.

As we walked up Regent Street towards Portland Place, our eyes caught sight of that historic grade II listed building, with its famous art deco façade. But it's not till you get closer that you begin to realise the scale of the renovation carried out. This bright, new, shiny extension eventually begins to dwarf the original building as you make your way to the new reception encased behind large glass doors. Our growing excitement was lifted a little further as we spotted a few of the more famous faces passing us in both directions.

It wasn't long before we attached our visitor passes and were eventually greeted by the ever-smiling Joe as he casually walked us past security and into the heart of the building. Although full of people, it's all very quiet and calm. Most faces are firmly focused on their own specific roles. Even as we travelled in the lifts, the conversations sounded very technical, with many of their projects very abbreviated so obviously Nicky and I didn't have a clue what they were talking about most of the time. Everything is quietly spoken between colleagues, without much in the way of social interaction. Maybe it was just our timing, because it was slightly later in the day, but certainly on first observations things seemed very solemn.

Joe managed to get permission allowing us into the main newsroom, which understandably had very strict rules and regulations. The thing that struck me right away was the near silence in the place. I always thought newsrooms were electrifying places, people rushing around, shouting, hurriedly trying to get confirmation of stories over the phone. Middle-aged men with their ties loosened, sweating profusely as they desperately tried to meet life-or-death deadline situations. Okay, maybe that sounds rather old fashioned. It makes me sound like I've been watching far too much TV myself. Anyway, the reality couldn't have been more different. You could've heard a pin drop.

Again, everyone was mentally locked into their computers. The outer reaches of the office seemed to be where a lot of the editing news stories were happening. Once finished it all made its way towards the middle and like a well-run kitchen it all came together at the pass. This was the central part of the large newsroom. Again the flurry, hurry, and stress were being filtered through one massive network of communications systems, almost unnoticeable from a distance. Everything is planned and timed to perfection; there's even extra stories with well-edited video to run just in case for some reason or another, any of the headlining stories have to be pulled at the drop of a hat. They have a well backed-up collection of news, pictures and video they can access if they need to announce world-leading personalities' obituaries.

Then there's the actual news desks themselves, where the end product is finally delivered. All very modern and uncluttered, like something from a vast space station with all the latest technology. Cameras carefully set up in such a way that the news readers hardly notice them. I must admit I was really impressed with everything I saw. This was an environment I would never have a chance of working in, well beyond my capabilities. I just felt lucky to be in there as a visitor. At worst I could maybe say some of these people were nerds, but in honesty they were extremely clever individuals and very professional, very much unsung heroes of the whole organisation.

Even the oldest part of the building was refurbished and still, to this day, houses some of the BBC's more established and traditional radio channels and has been renamed the John Peel Wing. Radio 1 and some of the more up-to-date shows are all produced in the newly built part, which was actually completed in 2005, but again, it was so impressive to walk around and see it all. With nine floors above ground and three below, there was plenty to keep me fascinated. Even the past has been cleverly galvanised into the newer side of the building, with quotes from the great and good from the past inscribed into the walls for all to see.

We eventually went to meet Penny up on one of the higher floors. She sat very close to a certain Andrew Marr and just across from Hard Talks' Stephen Sackur. The temptation to go over and start quizzing him was very real. My ADHD impulsivity had me champing at the bit, but luckily Nicky squeezed my arm with a look that said, "Don't bother."

The evening's tour of the BBC at Portland Place finished with a few photographs taken from the very top floor, looking back down towards Regent Street. Then it was off down for a few drinks at the BBC bar. It was great; we could've stayed there much longer than we did as we really enjoyed Penny and Joe's company, but luckily for them we had a table booked in a restaurant.

One evening, while sitting in our apartment in Corralejo, Fuerteventura, we were watching a programme about the BBC and in particular the Television Centre at White City. At one stage they showed an excerpt of Ronnie Corbett telling a funny story from his big chair. I told Nicky that I always remembered watching the Two Ronnies when I was much younger, still living with my family in Kinghorn. I felt quite sad as this was all about to end, meaning that they planned to close down the old Television Centre in Sheperd's

Bush. Again, my feelings of nostalgia had me thinking back to more innocent days where I'd be lying on the floor, gazing up at our standard 21-inch colour TV set. I was reminded of all the programmes we would sit and watch, so it wasn't just about the TV Centre ending, it was a lot to do with my past and memories disappearing as well.

It suddenly struck me that maybe the Television Centre did tours, where guides might take you around to look at old studios. So as usual, I pestered Nicky to check it out on the internet. To our surprise they did, and unbelievably it was only £10 each for their troubles. I remember once Nicky booked it, I was really excited. As I've pointed out before, a lot of my memories growing up were of things like Blue Peter. So, the idea of walking through that same studio I'd watched a TV programme from over forty years earlier, really tugged at my very nostalgic heart strings. Everything was so believable back in those days; being able to make presents from plastic cups, old cereal boxes, string, Sellotape, leftover bits of wallpaper, oh, and remember to get permission from your mums and dads before using the scissors. Christmases were always special too. Okay, we knew Santa didn't really exist, but were still hanging on to that little bit of Christmas magic Blue Peter managed to reignite. Especially when it came to the Christmas appeals. One year they asked people to send in old metal cutlery with a target they hoped to reach before Christmas. Of course, this was always achieved come the last Blue Peter programme before Christmas Day.

Another important part of the last show before Christmas was the opening of all of the Blue Peter pets and presenters' presents. But just before the programme finished, it was time to call in a brass band with lots of children following suit, holding up little lanterns while singing along to classic Christmas hymns. Once the conjured feelings of nostalgia began to fade, I realised this would still be an incredible part of another great London holiday.

To save messing about with tubes and buying tickets, we just opted for the easiest option. As soon as we had finished our breakfast at the Terrace Restaurant at Le Meridien, we went straight to reception and organised a taxi. I can even remember the driver adjusting his mirror when we asked to go to the Television Centre. We were fairly smartly dressed and of course we had that well lived-in tan you get from living lots of years abroad. Yes, it's quite a deceptive look, to be honest. People think you're somebody you're not, which was certainly not a problem for us as it always seemed to work in our favour.

In honesty, we were not in the Television Centre for long. We did manage see all the important stuff. It was great seeing all the old studios, especially Studio 8, which was home to nearly all the comedies ever made. The only problem being, our visit was in 2013 and it was very visible that they were running things down. It was sad to see it all ending, but with it being a world run on money, I don't suppose there could've been anything done to save it.

Nicky made a cracking suggestion to me. She said, "They should've turned it into a BBC TV Museum, a mixture of old stage settings and waxwork characters similar to Madame Tussaud's." Obviously, I'm no expert but maybe Nicky had hit on something there. The opportunities were endless; it might have grown more important over the years, as it became one of London's star attractions, bringing in visitors from all over the world. Like all those things, no doubt there could've been restaurants and souvenir shops, all helping to preserve the memories of a once great place.

After our visit to the BBC TV studios, we made our way into Westfield Shopping Centre. As Nicky browsed the shops my mind was still buzzing with ideas of who to contact about renovating BBC Television Centre into a museum. Yup, that's the paradox of my ADHD – a mixture of great ideas and free-flowing nonsense.

CHAPTER 20

DILLY-DALLYING ON A SUNNY DAY

For some reason we never really planned too much for a Saturday morning, although I must admit we aways made sure we had a really busy holiday rota, making sure we had lots of fantastic things to do during our week's stay. But a Saturday was a nice day to just dilly-dally around hidden gems of London. With Oxford Street being a little too busy, it was always nice to walk further into Mayfair as it was a lot quieter there during the weekends, as opposed to the busier weekdays.

Once past Berkeley Square, heading west you come across Charles Street. Just a little further along we would head down Queen's Street, which would eventually lead us on to Curzon Street. Again, on a weekday this place would be busy as it has lots of large international companies and many smaller offices are based there, so on a Saturday morning the place had a completely different feel to it. The small cafés and coffee shops were a bit more laid back and the people sitting around tables were visibly in a far more relaxed frame of mind.

Just a little further on we would get to where we were really headed, and that was Shepherd Market. This is a lovely place, and is where Mayfair got its name from. Back in the 17th century they would have a fair with circus-style acts, singers, musicians, and the more gruesome bare-knuckle fighting. Shepherd Market is, again, like a quiet little village right in the heart of London and even has its own little pond. It's hard to imagine with all the surrounding established buildings looking like they've been around for ever, that this little place was once set amongst green fields. Again, similarly to Covent

Garden there are no sounds from heavy traffic, just the humdrum of voices coming from the cafés and restaurants, all mostly set up with outside tables.

Although very much like a small piazza, this place is less touristy and seems to bring out a lot of people who live in the lovely small houses in and around Shepherd Market. It'll come as no surprise to hear this is where renowned writers such as Noel Coward, Anthony Powell, Michael Arlen, and Sophie Fedorovich chose to live, in this quaint little corner in London. Weirdly there's a small flat once owned by Harry Neilson where both Mama Cass and Keith Moon died, which is only a stone's throw away from Shepherd Market. It's probably important to mention that Mama Cass died of a heart attack in 1974, whereas Keith Moon died of an overdose in 1978. Both tragic events especially to their family, friends, and many fans.

From there we would make our way up to the even more tranquil Mount Street Gardens. It's very green, surrounded by large, leafy trees and quite a few red-brick grade II listed buildings. You can choose to sit, relax and dream away your day as there are a few benches to sit on. It wasn't always like that; in fact on that very site was a real-life workhouse, probably even worse than the ones you've read about in some Charles Dickens classic. Thankfully it was razed to the ground and eventually replaced with these lovely gardens in 1889. It even has the original water fountain that still works to this day. Mount Street Gardens are quite well hidden away even with three different entrances. They would be very easy to miss if sitting in a moving vehicle. In fact, I'm sure you could walk past two of them and not notice the 'Enter' signs. The people that live there are probably quite happy with these unobtrusive, almost secretive entrances.

Sometimes on a Saturday morning we would take a more easterly direction and head back along in the direction of Covent Garden. Again this walk was less businesslike, and the streets were mostly busy with tourists. Everything felt laid back as we made our way through the spacious Leicester Square, across Charing Cross Road, on past St Martin's Lane, and then on to Covent Garden. It was nice just to stand and watch some of the entertainers. We understood how hard they were working; we knew how much effort and enthusiasm it took to warm up and excite a crowd. It's very much like plate spinning, especially for these guys performing on the street; there's no time for pauses as they make sure they dart in and out and chat to different parts of the crowd to keep them lively. You can see their eyes always scanning to make sure everyone's on board, while at the same time trying to stay focused on the more difficult parts of their act.

It wouldn't be the first time Nicky and I said, "Wow, that guy would be great for my hotel." I'd even go as far as to say that some of these great performers could've shown a few of our acts a thing or two. Again, we would slowly walk around the Market Hall, which was full of stalls selling knickknacks and keepsakes, and shops selling more expensive gifts. Eventually we would leave Covent Garden on the north side, heading to James Street and past the Covent Garden Tube Station, then across Long Acre, on to Neal Street, until we headed left again to the Seven Dials. This is another very special place right in the heart of London. Built in the late 1600s, it has seven roads coming from it, all heading in different directions. But it really got its name from an architect who actually carved a sundial pillar right in the centre of the development, hence the name Seven Dials.

From there it was on to Denmark Street, which is famous for its many shops selling musical instruments. Now I've never been a musician at any time in my life, but I have been a massive fan of music. It would be fair to say that all the musicians from the wide and varied bands I have liked, bought instruments from this very famous street in London at one time or another. The street itself is nothing to write home about and that's probably putting it politely, but the shop windows are a sight to behold as the instruments gleam like glittering prizes.

One Saturday morning, just as we were walking up St James' Street coming out of Covent Garden, instead of doing our usual and crossing Long Acre, I decided to turn right. Nicky didn't question my decision and at the time I wasn't sure why I decided to go that way. Anyway, as we kept walking, we decided to take a left down Drury Lane and down onto the Strand. Being a Saturday, this area was much quieter, with a lot less traffic on the roads than usual. It was another beautiful day and Nicky and I were travelling light, meaning we were not carrying any bags. We were dressed in jeans and t-shirts, had a little bit of money in our pockets, and of course our phones. It's such a great feeling of freedom travelling around London like that on a sunny day. We go where we want, when we want, and the sky's the limit when it comes to stopping for eats.

Heading round Aldwych, we then passed the Royal Courts of Justice, which have been sending people bang to rights since 1882. It's an incredible-looking building with wonderfully Victorian-style architecture. It was obviously very quiet as we walked past, but looking at the entrance, you're reminded of the many trade and industry disputes and accusations of personal negligence on the news and splashed as headlines across the press.

Then passing the old Bank of England, we made our way onto Fleet Street. First of all, it's an impressive place. As you pass the Temple Bar you are surrounded by old church buildings with old gothic designs. There's even a few dragon statuettes in places. Australia House is another building you can't miss as it sits in the middle of the road, dividing Fleet Street into two. The building itself was believed to be built over a 900-year-old sacred well, where the water is drawn from a subterranean London river, spookily enough called the River Fleet.

Something else that surprised us both was that when passing St Clement's Church (we had timed it only through good fortune, I must say), the bells rang out 'Oranges and Lemons' which got Nicky singing along.

Interestingly, Fleet Street is one of the oldest streets in London, hence the mixture of very old and new, but what makes it so significant is that it was the main route for the Royal Processions from the Tower of London to Westminster. Eventually, though, it would become home to most of the well-known National Press. These powerhouses of the media world would become the unchallenged kings of their own jungle. It's said that when all the printing presses were working in concert you could feel the ground under your very feet shudder. It wasn't just the major broad sheets that were based in Fleet Street, but a whole collection of different publications and writers had made this their home over the many years. People like Charles Dickens, Samuel Johnson, Mark Twain, and even the reluctant revolutionary Bejamin Franklin before he fled to America.

Having spent a little time in this world, and I'll admit it was only on the advertising side, I do wish I'd been a little better academically, as I still have a fascination with journalism and the fun it must be trying to hunt down a story. I can only imagine that all the famous little taverns and pubs in the area must have been great places to be as worldly news stories were breaking.

Things changed drastically in the 80s, though, as modern printing technology was coming to the fore and decimating lots of jobs in the industry. These giants of the newspaper world began to downsize and move out of Fleet Street altogether. Then along came the internet, which was a further blow to the industry. As distribution and readership figures plummeted, advertisers left in their droves as there were new avenues opening up to take advantage of. Websites and social media were growing at an incredible rate. These once-kings of the newspaper jungle were fast beginning to resemble the poor dinosaurs suffering after the tsunami created by the meteoric rise of the internet. A lot of the old printing presses still remain asleep deep under Fleet Street. Maybe one day they'll be dug up by some archaeologist only to be persevered in a museum.

As we drew closer to the financial centre of the city of London, things were even quieter. We had passed this way once before during the week. Usually as you get close to the City Thameslink station, the place is heaving with suited and booted banking professionals charging up and down the streets like they own them. Most of these people have a steely eyed look of confidence as they check their watches while simultaneously talking business down their phones.

The last time we travelled this way was when we were headed towards the Tower of London. I remember Nicky not really enjoying it as she found it a cold and unfriendly place. But this day was different. It was sunny, the busy streets were quiet, and the place seemed very relaxed. It was only then I decided to let Nicky know what I was hoping to see this day. Yes, I knew we weren't too far from Smithfield Market, and I'd always wanted to visit the William Wallace memorial which is placed on the outer wall of St Bartholomew the Great Church. The only problem was, I wasn't exactly sure where we were supposed to be going, but as we passed through Ludgate Hill we luckily turned up towards the Old Bailey. I was obstinately desperate not to ask the few passers-by for directions, I just had to find it on willpower alone.

It wasn't long till we were actually passing the Old Bailey itself. This wasn't exactly home to London's criminal fraternity, but it was certainly a halfway house, the first stop-off point before they must start their 'stretch' in jail. With 19 separate courts and over 70 cells, this was obviously a very busy place during the week, and I believe the streets can get busy with friends and family there to help protest their innocence. Some of the big names that have passed through those doors were the almost celebrity gangsters the Krays, the very evil killer Peter Sutcliffe, and someone who seems really out of sorts when you think of the word 'criminality', a certain Oscar Wilde, the outrageous poetic dandy.

Walking a little further, I remember my confidence lifting as we passed St Bartholomew's Hospital. This is not just an incredibly large building, the whole place fills quite a sizeable area with an array of different departments. Not only is it renowned as one of London's greatest teaching hospitals, but they have always done a great deal of work researching heart disease and worked extremely hard trying to find a cure for cancer. It was established on its present site as far back as 1123 and grew so much over the centuries that it now employs a workforce of nearly 17,000 people. Interestingly, I'm sure St Bartholomew's Hospital must be the only one in the UK that contains not just a library, but a museum as well.

With all that said and done, it was just slightly ironic that this place of hope and health was so close to an area where poor people were hung, drawn, and quartered. Although it must be said that in the early 17th century, because there were still so many executions dead bodies were plentiful. The surgeons of St Bartholomew's started to use these for anatomical research. So, one day you could be caught stealing an apple and the next you're hung and ending up having your body laid out on a slab as young doctors undignifiedly pull you to pieces. It has been claimed monies were exchanging hands between the executioners and the surgeons as they handed over the bodies. To think, people believe crime doesn't pay.

Even though we were close to where we wanted to be, I made the decision to take a left-hand turn. Although this was taking us away from Smithfield, I knew we would come across Postman's Park. Again, being a Saturday morning, we easily crossed the normally busy King Edward Street and entered the gates of the park. It's almost like a secret garden wedged in between the great St Paul's Cathedral, the old General Post Office, and of course St Bartholomew's Hospital. Once in there, it's beautifully set out with places to just sit back and enjoy the tranquillity, but the most striking thing here must be the Watt Memorial, dedicated to lots of people who gave their own lives trying to save others.

Without realising it, Nicky and I spent quite a bit of time slowly reading the plaques commemorating some of the kind acts of bravery of these poor people, who had ultimately paid with their lives. It was very sad and very humbling, but at the same time reassuring that there were good people in this world who could act so unselfishly in trying to help others.

This certainly had changed the tone as we entered Smithfield from the western entrance. All around were a collection of cafés and restaurants that were normally busy with the high flyers from the city, but on this bright, sunny, windless day it was very quiet. It almost felt like a Sunday.

We found one little café open where we bought ourselves a coffee and a sandwich each, to take with us as we slowly made our way around a very quiet Smithfield. Eventually we came across the William Wallace memorial plaque. The first thing Nicky said to me was, "Look, it says 'Sir'," which was rather a good starting point for me to talk about it. I then went on to explain to Nicky that being knighted by Robert the Bruce should have been enough to stop him being savagely killed in the brutal fashion that he was. But him being a knight was completely ignored; he hadn't even sworn allegiance to Edward the First, like most of the other Scottish nobility had in Berwick years earlier, so he shouldn't really have been charged with treason. But Edward the First was having none of it; he was going to make an example of him to show the people of Scotland that the dream was over. He hoped hearts and minds would be broken and his rule over Scotland would go unchallenged. Little did he realise it would have the complete opposite effect. There was rioting in all the towns and cities of Scotland and the masses swore their revenge for the murder of Scotland's favourite son.

Just as I was telling Nicky more about William Wallace, we were visited upon by a large squirrel. I think what made it seem so big, was that we were used to the smaller chipmunks we always saw back in Fuerteventura. As I fed him a little bit of my sandwich my eyes were drawn to looking around the surrounding area. It was incredible that this place, so quiet and tranquil, was the scene of so much horror and barbarism. I tried to imagine what it must have been like for William Wallace as he spent his last hours being pelted by a screaming crowd that had come to watch him being unceremoniously destroyed for their entertainment. Not only had he been dragged by horses all the way from the Tower of London, he was hung up on the gallows. This huge six-foot-seven man must have looked like a wild animal, all cut and bruised. Everywhere he looked he would see people screaming at him, the executioners parading around like heroes and getting cheers for every little cruel thing they did. As far as they were concerned, they had the best job in London, feeding their bloodlust by meting out their so-called justice in brutal fashion.

Then with a blunted cleaver, they would have torn at William Wallace's stomach till his intestines spewed out onto the ground, although still attached to his body. He would've still been awake as he watched the blood-covered executioner pick up his innards and throw them onto a burning stove. Only the cheers of the rampant crowd would've drowned out his screams of pain. His body was eventually chopped into four bits and hung around different parts of Scotland, and his tar-covered head was put on a spike high above the Tower of London. The smells, the atmosphere and the noise must have been hellish as hate-filled voices screamed for more.

Of course, it wasn't just the 35-year-old Wallace who died in this most horrendous fashion. Many, before and after, received the same brutal punishment. A lot of them would die because of trumped-up charges. Yes, if I was ever to find a time machine, the Middle Ages would certainly not be a time I would like to travel back to. Medieval seems to be a very appropriate word as it conjures up thoughts of squalor and barbarism.

Although still a beautiful sunny day with not a cloud in the sky, some of the old buildings around me seemed a little more sinister. An inexplicable feeling uneasiness had come over me. I wasn't sure if it was a little anger at the spiteful way William Wallace had been cruelly treated all those centuries before, or just the realisation that the whole place was steeped in unthinkable horror.

Just to the left of us was the west door entrance to St Bartholomew's Chapel, which Nicky and I decided to visit. On entering it was very dark inside and so much cooler. I'm not a religious person and wouldn't claim to believe in ghosts, but there was something very eerie about the place, especially after everything Nicky and I had been discussing before we walked into this stone-cold building. Then as I started to read a leaflet we picked up on the way in, I realised that this very old church had actually been here about two hundred years before William Wallace was hung, drawn, and quartered. If we hadn't had enough of discussing horror stories of the Middle Ages, we then discovered that St Bartholomew himself also died a very brutal death in Armenia, because he had convinced their king to convert to Christianity, so he was mercilessly flayed alive.

For anyone who doesn't understand what that means, it's when somebody's skin is torn from their bodies while they're still alive; possibly even more painful than being disembowelled. Nicky and I began to laugh as these stories of Medieval London were relentlessly cast up before us. Nothing pleasant at all could be spoken of these times. Although it had to be said, the architecture for these days was incredible. As we looked around the dark and unforgiving bleakness, I realised that probably nothing much in this ancient chapel had changed over the centuries. No matter what had gone on outside over the many years, none of it seemed to have affected the space we were in. The murderous squalor, the civil wars, even as the bombs dropped over London during the Second World War, this most ancient of places had managed to stay untouched by time or history.

I thought of HG Wells and his story of *The Time Machine*, which was made into a film in 1960. The book itself was actually written in 1895, an early science-fiction classic. I imagined Nicky and I being able to walk in and out of that chapel, crossing through all the different time zones, knowing that if we could make it back into the chapel, we would be safe.

Just as my imagination was running riot, I happened to look down at the bottom of a pillar and could see there had been some damage. On the floor beside it I saw some broken masonry. Without hesitating, I went over, bent down, picked up a few pieces of the crumbling stonework and quickly put them into my pocket. Straight away I had a feeling of guilt but reassured myself that the piece of broken masonry could never be used again, so I felt no harm done.

As we left that old church, I had a feeling of real excitement that I'd managed to get myself a brilliant souvenir to take back home to Fuerteventura. I even considered getting the little pieces of stone placed onto a nice piece of varnished wood. It would be something I could show people and tell them of our visit to William Wallace's memorial. Yes, my mood had certainly lifted. The bright sunshine once again had cleared the sinister feeling of gloom and doom that rose within me as we looked around the old church.

We now decided to head back in a different direction, so we walked past the quiet Smithfield Market and in the direction of St John's Gate. This was an area I was quite familiar with; I had worked near the bottom of Gray's Inn Road at the now defunct PC Business World, and had travelled around this place extensively. Obviously, the 15th-century St John's Gate hadn't changed. You could tell there had been little bits of restoration work done, and I could see the museum part had changed, but apart from that it was still just as impressive as ever. But as we headed along Clerkenwell Road there was a lot I didn't recognise; it was very noticeable that there had been a lot of construction work over the years. Even as we headed further on to Theobalds Road, the place still seemed relatively quiet and there were a few places I remembered. I would point them out to Nicky but I found my hand always made its way to my back pocket, where my little pieces of stone were.

My mind kept wandering back to some of the horror stories we had back at Smithfield. I was beginning to feel these little stones in my back pocket were a representation of that horror. Even worse, part of the horror. I tried to put it out of my mind as Nicky and I then discussed what we might do for lunch, very much looking forward to a swim in the pool at Le Meridien. I remember then that we had become quite excited, knowing that in the evening we had booked a table at another of London's best restaurants, the three-Michelin-starred Alain Ducasse restaurant at the Dorchester, no less. But still these little stones were playing on my mind. I thought, *What if they're cursed? What if something bad happens?* But why was I even thinking like that? I didn't believe in any of that hocus-pocus nonsense. I started to question what I knew and what I didn't. I couldn't really be one hundred percent on anything. This was my ADHD mind manifesting a state of overthinking. These thoughts can be really helpful when you're trying to be creative, but when it fuels needless worry and panic, it's just a complete hassle.

Due to my fantastic masking techniques, Nicky was completely unaware my mind was going through moments of nonsense factor infinity. It was certainly too ridiculous to bring up in conversation. But as we made our way back to the hotel, I was still trying to reason with myself. I mean, I wasn't a spiritual person and I certainly wasn't religious. Not that I was against the whole thing, it just wasn't something I felt was conducive with Einstein's theories regarding time, space, and relativity. Both my grannies were very religious and even had their favourite hymns. They were the sort of people who went to church every Sunday, so I wasn't ever going to be offensive about their beliefs or anyone else's for that matter; very much in their defence, as they could tell stories of wine being turned into water, or a certain person being able to walk on water. Why would they want to believe me when I said the whole known universe, which is 93 billion light-years in diameter and contains something like two trillion galaxies, all started from something more than a million times smaller than the thickness of a single hair.

These wide and varied thoughts were becoming so confusing that thankfully my mind decided to shut them off. Anyway, the smell of food had entered my nostrils, which opened up a whole new train of thought. Nicky asked me to be patient as she wanted to go back into the hotel before we grabbed some food. That was okay with me as my oh-so-white t-shirt had managed to pick up a coffee stain way back at Smithfield Market.

As we entered the hotel, we briefly said hello to the senior porter, Vasco, and quickly headed for the lift. It didn't take us long to get back to the room for a quick change and freshen up. I was actually glad to get the pieces of stone out of my back pocket. I was just fed up with them playing on my mind, so I placed them on the bedside table and put on a fresh pair of jeans.

As we headed out to grab some late Saturday lunch, I soon forgot about the silly thoughts. I was more interested in satisfying my ever-hungry stomach. We had been fortunate and managed to grab one of the outside tables at one of our favourite restaurants in Mount Street, called Scott's. Again, it's such a far cry from what we are used to. It's not just the high-end fashionable shops surrounding us, but some of the cars parked arounds were Bentleys, Porsches, and there was even a James-Bond-style Aston Martin close by.

The two hours we sat at that table seemed to flash by, and even although the street was unusually quiet a few well-known celebrities did pass us while we were eating.

After a really satisfying meal, we intentionally took a slow stroll back to the hotel, as we had promised each other we would go for a swim, so it was best not to do it on a full stomach.

It wasn't too long before we were walking back into the lift and making our way back to the room. Just as Nicky opened the door, it was obvious the cleaners had been in; the room was so much tidier and the bed had been freshly made. It was then, as I looked to my side of the bed, I shouted to Nicky, "They're gone!!"

Nicky, slightly startled at the ferocity of my shout, said, "What's gone?"

Still rather excited, I said, "The stones, the cleaner must have got rid of them."

Yup, right enough, my bedside table was nice and tidy and free of these wretched little stones. I was actually quite relieved that the situation had been taken out of my hands, by a cleaner no less. She must have looked down at them, thought, *Messy bugger,* and just swept them away into a dustpan. Nine hundred years of history gone, just like that. Nicky still couldn't understand my excitement; in fact she obviously didn't realise why I was so happy to lose them. Well I certainly wasn't going try and explain it to her.

CHAPTER 21

CAMDEN MARKET REVISITED

Yes, our first holiday to London certainly set a precedent when it came to going to Camden Market, all because the bus driver didn't take cash and I didn't have an Oyster Card. I didn't have a clue, to be totally honest. I was so pleased I had spotted that bus, and having Archway on the front of it, I knew this would take us exactly where we needed to go. Alas, it wasn't to be, as my lack of understanding of the modern London transport system would see us every Sunday, while holidaying in London, walking to Camden Market. In fairness it was only roughly about two and a half miles and after a hearty breakfast, just what the doctor ordered.

Again, the normally busy streets were always much quieter on a Sunday, so it was a steady but relaxed walk to get there. In later years we would come out of Le Meridien, take a sharp left at Air Street, then up Regent Street all the way to Oxford Circus. Once across the road it was then on to the upper part of Regent Street till we eventually got to the BBC. We would then walk up Portland Place with its spacious pavements, till we walked around Park Crescent. It was then we would cross Marylebone Road, either going directly through Regent's Park, or walking up the outer circular road past the Royal College of Physicians. We didn't mind going up the outer circular as Nicky enjoyed looking at the houses on Chester Terrace. These are grade I listed buildings and mostly have a clear, uninterrupted view over to Regent's Park. The upstairs rooms even have lovely little balconies at each of their windows.

There's no doubt about it, the houses are stunning, all built in the early 18th century with beautiful arches and pillars, painted a brilliant white, made even brighter on a lovely sunny day. Nicky had really grown to love these old houses and we passed them every time we returned from our cycle to Kenwood House. She felt it would be an ideal place to live, especially for our loyal little Yorkshire Terrier, Harry. The only small problem being, I didn't know where I was going to find the 15 to 20 million pounds needed to buy one of those places. It might also be worth pointing out we don't even do the lottery, so again, narrowing our chances of raising the cash.

Once we had walked a little further there was a turning to the right which took us in the direction of Camden. We could see the Edinboro Castle, which is the very same pub myself and Ian Myles went into all those years before, after we played softball. Every corner we walked around I'd have another story I could tell Nicky. Obviously for me it was great to have all those memories come flooding back, I just hope it wasn't too boring for Nicky as I babbled on excitedly.

As we drew nearer to Camden things started to get really busy again, as lots of people were making their way to Camden Market, a mixture of Londoners and tourists. Even though there were lots of people, it was much more relaxed as they were in that Sunday mode. The only things that seemed rushed were the bodies spilling out from the tube station.

Looking around, everything was very familiar; the streets were very much the same, but there was a massive difference with the brightly coloured shop signage, all very pronounced, with elaborate murals painted on the walls to give it that urban feeling. There was a real carnival feel to the place, most of the shops blaring out lots of different types of music, and with me being older, everyone seemed to look so much younger. A lot of the old pubs were still in the same place, although some of them had obviously upped their game as you could see lots of advertising boards showing their extensive snack menus.

Yes, it was beginning to dawn on me that this wasn't the Camden of old. Things around me were very chic and professional, the streets were much cleaner, and a lot of the more commercial retailers had moved in.

Once into Camden Lock, again, it was all very familiar but in that same breath, it had changed to a more professional set-up. Not that it was a problem, in fact it was more organised and very aesthetically pleasing. One thing we never did but I'm sure it would be really enjoyable, is the canal boats that do trips all the way along to the very beautiful Little Venice. It was always something we promised ourselves, but never got round to it.

Straight away as we walked over the bridge and into the market, my eyes were always drawn to the street food stalls. There was so much, I just never knew what to have and with all the different smells, it was fantastic. I just wished I had a bigger stomach so I could try all of it. As usual, Nicky would remind me that we had not long had a hearty breakfast, and it would probably be best to walk around the market first and then choose something to eat. Every time, I turned into a spoilt brat who felt like someone was intentionally trying to ruin my holiday. I didn't mind, really. I knew walking around the market would give me more time to think about what I fancied to eat.

There was no doubt about it, the market had really grown in popularity, not just in size. Of course there was no way we could leave without at least buying something. It's incredible to think nearly 250 thousand people visit Camden every week, and let's not forget it was always a popular destination for evening entertainment as well, with four or five music venues.

Eventually everything led us back to the food stalls, but even as the different aromas hit my nose, it still took me ages to decide what I was going to eat. Looking back I realise Nicky's patience was incredible; she would quietly wait till I'd finally made up my mind, then end up ordering something even nicer than I had bought. This would have me turning into the nicest guy in the world as I did my level best to convince her we should just share everything. My ADHD would explode into overdrive with so much choice at hand, so we realised the best thing to do was let Nicky choose for both of us.

Making our way back into central London, we would always go through Regent's Park. Just like Hampstead Heath, it was filled with lots of nice memories; the noises coming from the zoo, lots of people running or doing other sporting activities, elderly people sitting on the many benches just enjoying the tranquillity. In fact, every time without fail, we would go and watch some of the many football matches being played there, and I just couldn't leave till I managed to get a kick of a ball. I would stand willing that ball to make its way in my direction. You would think the teams would be happy with me going to retrieve the ball whenever I got a chance, but that wasn't always the case. I would sometimes receive dirty looks from some of the players as they were hoping to let that ball run out of play to run down the clock, as they'd say.

That was another interesting point about our walks to Camden on a Sunday morning. We would come across so many different things – the market itself, football matches, charity events and even demonstrations. I remember one Sunday in particular we were walking up past the BBC on Portland Place when we came across a large demonstration not too far from the Chinese embassy. It wasn't an angry demonstration, far from it. They all seemed to be very happy and didn't mind Nicky and I taking photos of them.

Then only ten minutes later we were walking through Regent's Park where there were thousands of people, all in fancy dress at some charity event. After visiting a busy Camden market, we made our way back down into Mayfair and as we walked through Grosvenor Square there were thousands of people protesting outside the American embassy. Even though these protesters were many and obviously very excitable, heavily armed police kept their distance as they kept a watchful eye on the situation.

After walking down from Grosvenor Square, we again took a left-hand turn into Mount Street, where everything was so quiet and peaceful. The contrast was incredible. We had managed to take in all these events, where the atmosphere had been happy in places yet hostile and angry in others. Again we had managed to sample it all, whereas for all the people who had solely been at their chosen events, their perspective of that day was completely different.

One thing that's very noticeable about London on a Sunday evening, is that most of the busy places have a day off. At first, I wasn't sure about that, as we were only there for a week so we wanted to cram in as much as possible. But the more London holidays went by, we grew into it and planned our Sundays accordingly. One place we enjoyed on a Sunday evening was the Comedy Store just off Coventry Street. This was always a great finish to a lovely day.

CHAPTER 22
FINE DINING AND EPICUREANISM

This is what the London holidays were all about. This fire and passion was lit all because I'd asked my dad what his choice of restaurant would be if he had to pick one in London. Yes, we started right at the top as during that first holiday we found ourselves entering Le Gavroche. This wasn't just a dynasty; this was a restaurant founded by Albert and Michel Senior, the pioneers and big-part players in the world of classic French dining.

London has a great history when it comes to creative cooking by chefs with revolutionary ideas on how restaurants should operate, and none were more important than Georges Auguste Escoffier. You only have to visit Le Gavroche to see that Escoffier's Brigades system is very much alive and well and this is the key to making sure everything is maintained to the highest of standards. There's not a stone goes unturned as everyone working in the restaurant is trained and marshalled in following the route to perfection.

Historically restaurant kitchens were known to be loud places, slightly disorganised with head chefs who could be boisterous and sometimes under the influence of alcohol. But Escoffier would change all this as he regimentally reworked restaurants from top to bottom. First, the kitchens themselves had to be always kept clean; organisation and quality of food had to be as damn near perfect as humanly possible. Tables, cutlery, glasses, and even the waiters had to be spotlessly clean as they, too, were a representation of the high standards that any restaurant worth its salt had to meet.

Etiquette is such that even the customers are drawn into this ethical code of conduct. As the waiters approach your table you learn to sit back and keep your arms by your side while they masterfully serve the food and drinks in front of you. Everything flows seamlessly, as if choreographed by some magic power, but still making sure you're left feeling that you are the most important people in the restaurant. This, I must repeat, is all because of Escoffier's well tried and tested Brigade system that he first created at the Savoy, The Ritz hotel in Paris and the Carlton in London. The French press even referred to him as *roi des cuisinier et cuisinier des roi* (king of chefs and chef of kings).

Of course, our first visits to these restaurants were quite overwhelming, especially once we were handed the menus. Personally I would go into a weird panic, like a rabbit in the headlights. They could've been written in Chinese for all I knew. It got even more confusing once the sommelier approached and started talking about wines. I'd stare back at him while gently nodding my head like I was taking in every word. I would then look across the table and say, "Nicky?" This is a great trick I learned from my ADHD moments. As your brain zones out of the conversation you at first mask the situation by kidding on that you've taken everything in, then you must quickly use an avoidance tactic, creating a diversion to direct all the attention.

The other way we got around this in the beginning was rather expensive but most enjoyable, and that was to order the Menu Exceptionnel, or tasting menus as they were better known. This was usually a seven-course meal with matching wines. In honesty, it's a great introduction to fine dining and for a Hungry Horace like me, it was just perfect. But to repeat, it can be very costly.

We did something similar in September of 2010 at the Landau Restaurant in the Langham Hotel. Michel Roux had not long taken over and installed one of his up-and-coming chefs called Chris King. The waiter serving us was a lovely, enthusiastic Moroccan lad who was doubling up as a sommelier, and when we looked at the menu, they were offering something a little bit different. Not only did they have a tasting menu, and one that was seven courses, but it didn't say what you were getting. So just as a bit of fun, this was the one Nicky and I chose. Doing the same with the wine, we left the decision up to the waiter, to give us what he thought appropriate with each dish. This excited the young Moroccan waiter. He thought we were being extremely clever and we really knew our stuff.

I suppose it was all rather deceptive; I was very well dressed with my deep Fuerteventura tan, whereas Nicky was completely stunning in a silky silver body-sculpting dress. The truth of the matter was, we knew they would be better judges than us when it came to selecting the food. Every dish and glass of wine was a lovely surprise; we couldn't have asked for anything more.

Needless to say every dish was fantastic and the wine selection seemed to go down a treat, and if that wasn't enough, at the end of the meal the waiter actually brought the young Chef Chris King right to our table. We were gobsmacked to say the least. Nicky and I began to get the feeling they thought we were somebody special, but had the truth been known, if Chris King had come out and said, 'We need a hand to wash some dishes,' Nicky and I would've been right there at the drop of a hat.

It was a fantastic meal and a really wonderful evening; the staff left us feeling really special and it was much appreciated. There was no surprise when we ended back there come the following September, in 2011, although it was quite noticeable that the young Moroccan waiter wasn't there. I didn't ask about him; we only hoped he was okay and doing well. Hopefully he was working in another of Michel Roux's restaurants. This certainly wasn't a problem as we had the good fortune on this evening to be looked after by the head sommelier, Zack Saghir. We once again decided to have the tasting menu, only this time we knew what we were getting and allowed

Zack to choose our wine.

As the meal wore on, we managed to chat a great deal with Zack, who turned out be a fantastic guy. In fact I'd go as far as to say we now feel very honoured to have met him. Zack had worked in the hospitality industry for most of his adult life, spending 27 of those happy years working at the Savoy on the Strand. I couldn't help myself, so I kept asking him things about his past – who he had worked with and the famous people he had met. It'll come as no surprise that he met quite a few presidents, prime ministers, and a whole host of stars from the film and music industry. Zack told us that a lot of these stars would eat regularly at the Savoy, so over many years he had befriended quite a few. It was obvious Zack was a nice and humble guy, so you really got the feeling he was a bit of a legend.

As we talked more, he told us of the many members of the Royal Family he had met, and the one that impressed him most was the late queen mother. Being a bit of a history buff, I was able to chip in with what I knew and I just happened to mention that the queen mother had family connections to the Earl of Kinghorne and Strathmore. This also allowed me the chance to proudly bring up my hometown of Kinghorn. I was even more impressed when Zack mentioned that he knew this through the many conversations he had with the queen mother over the years while dining at the Savoy.

At the end of the evening, when we were in a restaurant in London, I would always finish the night off with a glass of 18-year-old Macallan's whisky. To be honest, I liked all the Speyside whiskies, but this was my favourite. So, I just had to ask Zack one more important question. At the end of the queen mother's meal, did she also like a night cap? And if she did, what was it?

I was expecting Macallan's or some other fine malt whisky but whatever it was, I would order one. Zack told me the queen mother did like a drink at the end of the evening, but I was completely surprised when he told me she enjoyed a small glass of Grouse whisky. Of course at first this didn't add up with me. Surely she could afford the most expensive malt in the house. But it made sense that she would choose The Famous Grouse. First, it was one of the nicest and sweetest of the blended whiskies, but more importantly it related back to the Earl of Kinghorne and Strathmore. I eventually found that Queen Elizabeth also had a liking for the sweet Famous Grouse whisky, which would receive a Royal Warrant in 1984. It was also said that the queen's sister, Princess Margaret, had a liking for blended whisky too, but I'm sure that won't come as too much of a surprise.

I could've spoken to Zack all night. It was just a pleasure listening to him and we understood how much he had loved his time at the Savoy. We could tell he really felt a part of that place. It was a sentiment I could really relate to; it was just a little sad to hear that he always tried to avoid driving up the Strand as he still missed the old place so much.

It wasn't just the Landau we returned to. As I mentioned earlier, The Gavroche was somewhere we revisited, every one of the seven holidays we had in London. We even had a few lunches there. It got to the point where I would contact them close to our booking to try and arrange our particular seat of choice. Again, the ambience of a restaurant is another very important factor, so getting seats close together, where we both see the same things, allowed us to share the same perspective. I mean, it was okay for me but not so much for Nicky. If I've got a seat with my back to a wall, I can still look over her and watch what's happening around the restaurant, whereas she's just got to stare back at me. Not that we spent all our time looking over each other's shoulder, it was just nice to have the option to see and sample all of the atmosphere and more importantly, share the exact same memories.

Another enjoyable experience of going to these highbrow restaurants, was the walk itself. It was wonderful making our way through Mayfair, heading to London's greatest restaurants full of excitement and great expectations. This was especially true each time we made our way to the Dorchester. We would leave nice and early so we had plenty time to stroll along Green Park. It was always such a fantastic feeling leaving Le Meridien and walking out into the busy streets of Piccadilly. This was increased tenfold when we excitedly made our way to a three-Michelin-star restaurant based in one of London's most celebrious hotels.

My mind would always wander back to that evening twenty or so years earlier as I had walked that same route to get my ticket at Victoria Bus Station; the excitement I felt that I was leaving London and travelling home. Don't get me wrong, even back in those days I always loved the walk from Piccadilly along to Hyde Park Corner. I still remember being tinged with a little sadness as it was such a beautiful evening, heading along Green Park for the final time as I prepared to return to Scotland. Then jump forward again twenty years and to think, here I was, making that same journey only feeling even happier as I walked with Nicky past all these iconic shops and buildings.

It's funny, the people and faces always seemed the same as all those years ago; the same expressions, even dressed similarly. With it being such an affluent area it attracted a real mixture of opulent characters. Sometimes I fell into that feeling of euphoria again. My mind was buzzing but very happy as we strolled round Hyde Park Corner to make that walk up the still-busy Park Lane and on to the Dorchester. This was made even more special with Nicky by my side. She was picture perfect; it was like London and Nicky were made for each other.

Although inside we probably felt like two kids in a sweety shop, we always managed to hold it together as we entered reception at the Dorchester. In front of us was a long foyer decorated perfectly, giving it a feeling of elegance and sophistication. At the very far end of the foyer we could see a distinguished-looking bar, and all around us was very comfortable seating with a few people dotted around quietly sipping on coffees.

As we began to walk through the foyer, on the right-hand side we could see the Scottish Themed Caledonian restaurant (this has been now renovated and renamed), then a little further on to our left was the entrance to the three-Michelin-starred Alain Ducasse. Without hesitation I'd always turn to the person waiting at the restaurant reception and announce we had a table booked for two. Another habit I got into was to jokingly apologise for my name being Smith. I always tried to strike a balance between trying to show respect and hoping they would relax, knowing that as guests we were going to make it easy for them. I'm sure they would've had to deal with quite a lot more demanding guests than ourselves. This was something we would try to do in all the restaurants we ate in. It allows the waiting staff to be comfortable in the knowledge they should have least a couple of easy hours during their shift. We understood that it was always in the restaurant's interest to make sure their staff acted with formal professionalism, as the food and service were the main focal points of their business. But we always preferred a more human interaction, knowing something drastic would have to happen for us not to enjoy our meal. So the relaxing or slight bending of rules and etiquette was okay with us.

Something that always catches your eye as you walk through this beautiful restaurant is the luminescent curtain of over 4,000 shimmering fibre optics, which has within it the Table Lumière. The three times we ate there, though, we always sat at the very end tables just below the windows that looked out over Hyde Park. We always booked this restaurant for a Saturday so each time there was some event or another happening in the park. The restaurant had even called us before our first time eating there in 2010, to pre-warn us that the Pope was holding a youth vigil that very evening, so as to make sure we wouldn't get caught up in any unexpected delays due to certain roads being cordoned off.

Again, Nicky had a real fascination with this restaurant as she knew Elizabeth Taylor had a great love of this place also. This world-famous actress had stayed there as a child and would then visit often over the years. Eventually the Dorchester took it upon themselves to have a room named after her – The Elizabeth Taylor Harlequin Suite. Important family occasions and many of her birthdays were celebrated there and of course, the media, frenzied by her relationship with husband Richard Burton, spent a lot of time hounding the poor couple as they stayed there many evenings during that period.

Another favourite of Nicky's, which I briefly mentioned earlier, was Scott's on Mount Street. I'll never forget the first time we walked up this street and past this incredible restaurant. We had not long been through Hyde Park and decided to cross over the busy Park Lane to walk through Mayfair. It was during our first holiday together back in 2009 so my memories of these streets were a little rusty to say the least. As we got onto South Audley Street a taxi happened to pull up just a little ahead of us. As we got closer the guy travelling in the taxi had obviously had just paid his fare and was just closing the black cab door. Something in the way he was dressed impressed me. He was a little younger than me, similarly tanned but had a dark blue jacket with a fresh white shirt on, jeans, and a pair of expensive-looking brown shoes. I, coming from Fuerteventura, had only a few different looks, scruffy or scruffier. This comprised of board shorts and t-shirt or mix it up a bit with jeans and t-shirt. As we watched the guy walk a little faster ahead of us, we saw him turn left and head along what we learned was to become one of our favourites, Mount Street.

We took the same direction and watched as the guy walked up to a restaurant door, where a well-dressed man wearing a bowler hat smiled and open it for him to enter. It was then as we drew closer, I could see it was the restaurant Scott's. To the right-hand side of the door there was a line of tables all partitioned off slightly, with large green plants to give each table a little privacy. Every table was taken, most of them drinking wine, and the food looked amazing. I was finding it difficult not to stare, not helped by the fact that I'd spotted a woman who had overdone it with the plastic surgery. This all seemed to go unnoticed by her three friends sitting around her. I got the feeling this obvious overindulgence was almost just another decadent sign of showing off her wealth.

The boutiques and shops surrounding this restaurant were just out of this world, with their lavishly decorated front windows. Even the cars parked on the street, Bentleys, Ferraris, and of course a Rolls-Royce. It was so noticeable for me because a while back in Fuerteventura I had been studying things like peak oil, looking at future transportation like maglev trains, the possibilities of living in a world where we don't need to use money. I had become interested in a guy called Jaques Fresco, who started an organisation called the Venus Project. I was sure this was the way forward in trying to save the planet. But as I looked around me back on that sunny day on Mount Street in London, I just knew that me trying to talk to any of these people on this subject would be a tough sale, to say the least. I imagined myself walking up and down that street with a big black plastic bag saying to passers-by, "Okay, folks, there's no need for all that money of yours, just throw it into the bag and I'll get rid of it for you."

Ironically there's a cigar shop on Mount Street that sells hand-rolled Havana cigars with a photograph of the great revolutionary leader Che Guevara, another great paradox if ever there was one. But all said and done, Scott's would eventually be one of our go-to places every time we visited London, always preferring to book a seat at the bar rather than a table, especially if it was an early afternoon booking. The food is obviously fantastic and there's always a real buzz to the place. We could tell they had lots of regular customers; a lot of people stopped to chat as they passed tables. It wasn't too far from our hotel either, just a short walk along Green Park and then up through Berkeley Square and then a left turn onto Mount Street.

Just to repeat, that was the great thing about Le Meridien. It wasn't just in one of my favourite places, it was also and central to most of the places we wanted to go.

Never once did we have a bad meal in London. We travelled as far as La Cage Imaginaire in Hampstead one Sunday evening, then not as far in Primrose Hill, we went to Odette's, which was lovely, and that afternoon, after our meal we went for a walk through a small street fair. It was mid-May and we never did find out what the fair was all about.

We had a few after-show meals in and around the West End. Once we ate at the Asia de Cuba Restaurant, which I actually picked because I liked the look of one of their desserts – profiteroles covered in a butterscotch sauce. Then there was Rules, which I'm sure is one of London's oldest restaurants, although we were slightly unlucky as they didn't have everything on the menu. The following day it was being used as part of a film set for one of the James Bond movies. The food and atmosphere were still lovely, though, and Spectre wasn't a bad film either.

The Savoy was another place we just had to try; we had lunch in the River restaurant, then a few London holidays down the line we eventually tried the Savoy grill. I think that was the most I'd ever paid for a bottle of wine. I would like to be able to say money was no object, but it was actually a case of my own stupidity. It's always safer to let Nicky take control of the wine list.

You'll notice here I'm just flying through the restaurants we have been to, but I'm doing this for good reason. As I pointed out already, we've never had a bad meal in London so I don't want this to turn into some restaurant review, I'm just hoping that some of you reading this will have a pretty good understanding of the places we have eaten.

Another, which in some circles has been called one of London's most romantic, was the Clos Maggiore in Covent Garden, which we did on a Sunday evening. Then there was the Nobu in Berkeley Square – this was one of Nicky's choices. I wasn't so sure, it just sounded a bit too trendy for me. What I probably meant was that I felt I would've been the oldest guy there, but in actual fact we got a great window seat and the food was lovely. It's an Asian fusion restaurant, so I ended up enjoying it more than Nicky.

One night after seeing Ricky Gervais' Foregone Conclusion we had booked a table at Cecconi's in Burlington Gardens, close to Le Meridien. Our only worry was getting all the way back from the Hammersmith Theatre in time. Luckily, I flagged a taxi minutes after getting out of the show. This was another warm, comfortable restaurant that left us with a lovely feeling of wellbeing. It had been a really long day, so it was also handy that it was close to our hotel.

Some of the lunches we had were spectacular. I've already mentioned the River restaurant in the Savoy, but another classic we just happened to walk in and take a chance on was the Lanesborough. It was a beautiful restaurant and the food was just perfect. This is one we always promised to go back to yet never managed to return.

Another fabulous walk-in was The Foyer at Claridge's. This was done on one of our earlier holidays so we were still going through that starstruck faze of being blown away by all the five-star hotels and their wonderful service, which we were obviously unaccustomed to, living on what some might call a desert island.

One place we just had to visit was The Ritz. This iconic, luxurious hotel right in the heart of London was conceived by the legendary César Ritz on the 25th of May in 1906. It's considered one of the greatest of hotels in the world and certainly didn't fail to impress, with its opulent interiors and lavish furnishings. From the minute we walked through the door we were awash with splendour and elegance. I felt my eyes being drawn down to my shoes and realised I was checking myself over. The dress code expects you to at least be smartly dressed, but once I was standing in The Ritz, I couldn't help feeling under dressed for the occasion. Nicky dispelled my concerns as she whispered to me, "You look fine."

We were approached by the concierge who courteously pointed us in the direction of the restaurant. I assuredly grabbed Nicky's hand as we made our way down the hallway. Just to our left there was an area called the Palm Court, which was also very charming. We could see quite a few people there enjoying their afternoon teas. But it wasn't till we were led into the restaurant itself that we fully realised what all the fuss was about. Now I'll be honest, this is not a lifestyle I profess to being accustomed to, and the people sitting around weren't exactly the sort of people we would hang out with on a daily basis, so there's still that little feeling that you are a fish out of water. But I must say, sitting with these people, you can't help smiling and showing more obsequiousness in your mannerisms. In our defence we were always just so happy to be there.

The Ritz especially blew us away, with its large sparkling chandeliers hanging from their high ceilings, long richly coloured curtain running the whole way down the floor-to-ceiling windows, and towering marble columns that wouldn't look amiss in a colosseum, ornaments in gold leaf, with soft pink furnishings and white tablecloths. The Ritz restaurant is such a huge room that you can easily imagine the pomp and circumstance that's been enjoyed over the many years. You just can't fail to be impressed with its grand history, as it has welcomed so many famous faces through its doors – kings and queens, prime ministers, presidents, and lots of great names from the world of film and theatre. Like the Gavroche, The Savoy, The Connaught, and The Dorchester, the service is seamless, swift, unobtrusive, and ultimately professional as even we the customers were swept along with its symphonic grandeur.

Although I've mentioned so many of these restaurants, I've hardly spoken about the food itself. I just didn't feel I had to. We were right in the beating heart of fine dining and as you can imagine, everything was sublime.

Although there are a few restaurants I might have forgotten to mention, this last one will always stick in my memory for a few reasons. Thankfully all good apart from one embarrassing situation.

On the top floor of the Hilton is the fabulous Galvin at Windows, which became a favourite, especially when we managed to book it for a Friday night. Again, the evening always started off with that lovely walk from Le Meridien, along Green Park and round by Hyde Park Corner. Walking round past the Intercontinental Hotel, you're not that far away from the Hilton as it pierces the early evening sky. Closer to the Hilton, you can't help but gaze up all the way to the top floor. There's always that little feeling of anticipation. First off, we were looking forward to the meal but secondly, I have never been great with heights and for some reason I always think back to that 1974 film, Towering Inferno. Thankfully I didn't dwell on these thoughts for long as we were too excited and hoping to get our favourite window seat facing south.

The Hilton was the first skyscraper hotel to be built in London in 1963, so it's not old compared to the likes of The Grosvenor or The Savoy to name but two. But describing the shape of the Hilton is a little more difficult. All I can say is that it is triangular in design, but each of the three protruding points has two sides, which can afford you views all over London.

As we entered through the large glass doors, we made our way through the spacious lobby. There we would pass the reception, a few in-house shops, and a large popular bar. It wasn't hard to find the lifts, which didn't seem to take any time at all getting all the way up to the 28th floor.

On our first visit to Galvin at Windows we were given a window seat facing Marble Arch. I couldn't help myself. One of the windows was slightly open, so I just had to stand up and move towards the window for a better view across Hyde Park. Quite quickly, a waiter came rushing forward to say they preferred customers to safely keep their distance from any open windows. I understood this and apologised for causing concern. I could see by his badge that he was the head waiter and I also picked up on his soft Aberdonian accent, and that like me he was of Scottish origin. I told him I was from a small town in Fife called Kinghorn and that our claim to fame was that the last of the Celtic kings had lived and died there in a tragic accident. After chatting for a brief spell, we settled down to a most enjoyable meal as our fabulous view disappeared into the night.

The bright headlamps travelled back and forth up and down Park Lane. It was hard to determine what all the other lights belonged to and we tried with great difficulty to work out what was what over the night sky.

As our meal was nearly at an end Nicky would always finish with an Irish coffee, and I would splash out and order myself a whisky, usually an 18-year-old Macallan malt. So, once we politely gave our last order another young waiter returned with this book opened on a particular page and he said, "You may wish to look at this, sir." I looked down to see it was a book all about whiskies. Not only that, but the opened page showed a Dalmore Alexander the Third. I was really impressed and being in such a good mood, I just had to order this whisky, which I hadn't ever tried before.

I think the most important thing was their attention to detail. The communication between staff members is so important and like all the other restaurants we had enjoyed, you really notice and appreciate their efficiency. I think in that particular case I was just overwhelmed that the head waiter had remembered our conversation, especially as it was at least two hours after I had spoken to him in such a busy environment.

Galvin at the Windows was another restaurant we returned to and for the next three visits we were lucky enough to get the same window seat on the south-facing side. Again, being 28 floors up the views are just incredible, only on the south side you're looking directly down into the Buckingham Palace gardens, then across the Houses of Parliament and of course the London Eye, which almost gives it that fairground look.

As usual there's a buzz about this busy restaurant as day turns into evening. The lights are soft and not too bright, which helps add to the ambience. The first time we actually sat at that window facing south, is one I won't forget in a hurry. It's something that still bothers my ADHD-wired mind to this day. It all started so well. Just after taking the lift to the 28th floor, the doors opened and we were greeted straight away by the French maître d', Fred Sirieix. The guy was great, really friendly and knew exactly how to make us feel welcome. The best bit was when he introduced us to our fabulous table. I could only briefly look down at it as my eyes were drawn to the stunning views over some of the most iconic buildings in London.

Once we were both seated Nicky and I decided to have a gin and tonic as an aperitif. I was over the moon with our seating arrangements; it was an incredible start to our Friday night. We had a lovely walk from our hotel all the way to the Hilton, and then had an almost perfect table with incredible views, and then to top it all off, were served by Fred Sirieix. Our next decision was to go ahead and order the tasting menu. This was never difficult for me; given half the chance this is what I would choose every time.

Once the meal got underway, we ordered some wine and Nicky decided to visit the ladies' room to power her nose. I was left to just look around and ponder how I got so lucky. Everything was going so swimmingly. Just at that, I looked up and saw someone moving towards me. They had just come from further within the restaurant. It hit me like a bolt of lightning – it was Ricky Gervais. All of a sudden, my mind was rushing. Where was Nicky? I couldn't believe she wasn't sat with me. We were both massive fans. In fact we would probably watch all his DVDs two or three times a year, especially the multi-award-winning Office series.

As he got closer, I could see him looking at me. No doubt I was staring at him. For a brief second, he might even have wondered if he knew me, as I was very smartly dressed this evening. But still racing through my mind was, *Where's Nicky? She can't possibly miss out on this moment.*

Nicky and I have a similar sense of humour, but she used to openly laugh when we watched The Office, so I knew how much of a fan of Ricky Gervais she was…

And then it happened… While staring directly at Ricky Gervais I loudly shouted out, "Nicky!!!"

What was I expecting? Nicky to come running back into the restaurant to ask me, "What is it?"

As I shouted, I kept staring at Ricky Gervais. I saw his face drop. The disappointed expression said it all. I didn't even make an attempt to explain myself as he hurried past me. He obviously thought I was one of those loutish city boys having a dig as I looked at him menacingly while shouting out, "Ricky!" Why didn't I put my arms up and quickly explain to him in my ADHD rapid-fire motion that I was here on holiday with Nicky, and we were two of his biggest fans, and apologise for my spur-of-the-moment reaction? But it was too late, he was gone. I've always thought back to that evening. What must he have thought of me? I can still see that look on his face. I've always hoped one day I might get the chance to apologise for my insanely abrupt behaviour.

When Nicky finally came back to the table, the first thing she said to me was, "You're not going to believe who just passed me in the lobby."

I just shook my head and sighed.

"What's wrong?" Nicky asked.

When I explained what happened she just laughed, but I was mortified by my actions. I couldn't believe how stupid I had been. Over seven years holidaying in London, we had passed and spoken briefly with a few famous faces. I always tried to stay courteous and polite at all times, but this one time had been a real clanger.

The most important thing was, we still had a lovely evening, as we did every Friday at Galvin at Windows. Ironically, I've never really spoken to anyone about my embarrassing encounter with Ricky Gervais and didn't expect to be writing about it in a book, but I suppose it was just one I had to get off my chest.

Even after finishing our meal at the Hilton, it was nice on a Friday night just to walk back through Mayfair, along Hereford Street, past the Park Lane Mews where we stopped off to buy a teddy bear one evening. Incredibly it only cost us ten pounds but it's a souvenir Nicky still cherishes to this day.

Eventually we would walk past the Curzon cinema, then along Curzon Street itself, passing the Washington Mayfair Hotel and further on till we reached Berkeley Square. From there it was back down onto Green Park and then the short distance back along to Le Meridien.

Usually after a nice meal we raided the minibar one last time before we went to our bed to chat about the night's experiences. We would hear the little noises coming up from Regent's Street as people headed to clubs, or maybe the last stragglers making their way home. It was always great climbing into the fantastically comfortable bed. There was always that little air of excitement having had another wonderful night, and slowly but surely, we would happily drift off to sleep.

CHAPTER 23
LEAVING ON A JET PLANE

I may repeat little things here. I've not long written in this book, but it's just to reiterate my feelings about London and my life in general. Let me just start by saying it wasn't till later in my life that through a friend, it was brought to my attention I very much had ADHD (attention deficit hyperactivity disorder). Had I known about it much earlier, you probably wouldn't be reading this right now. I'd probably be someone you'd never heard of living what would be regarded as a more normal lifestyle. I may have spent most of my life closer to Kinghorn, my home town in Fife, working close to where I live, but in honesty, we will never know.

I do know where I have been and now understand why I've stumbled through life in a very haphazard way, going from pillar to post in the most uncoordinated fashion. Again, I'll be honest and say I feel sorry for my previous self, as I now see the difficulties I had in not understanding and possibly worse, not being understood. I have clear memories of when I was younger, just desperately wanting to be normal, knowing something within me wasn't right, while at the same time thinking I was just really stupid. But there were times I understood things and felt stuff that other people around me seemed oblivious of, paradoxically, because I couldn't just focus on the one thing. There was so much else happening. To some I would seem disinterested, almost ignorant of other people's plight like I didn't have a care in the world, while the opposite was true. Inside, my mind would be exploding with a raft of different emotions, trying to piece things together. But it does happen that when someone is talking to you, your mind zones out, it begins to wander and starts going through other strange scenarios, then when you realise you've lost the conversation you just start nodding your head, doing your best not to appear ignorant. The other mistake you make is not facing up to your problems. Procrastination becomes the name of the game, you learn avoidance skills and hide your own personal damage by masking your emotions.

But as luck would have it, my life took another fateful twist where I would see myself land on the island of Fuerteventura. I started swimming every day, I was cycling and getting lots of fresh air, which seemed to be the best cure for my ills. I didn't fully realise what was happening but my subconscious mind had been awakened and my body demanded this daily routine of energy burning. My job on the bar had me talking to people of all walks of life. My ADHD people pleasing was benefiting the people served on the complex. It was then an obvious progression that I would (and I must admit reluctantly) step over into the entertainment side of things.

I found myself walking round the complex having multiple conversations on all different subjects all at once, playing football, tennis, water polo, and conducting weekly volcano walks. Each evening before work I was doing ten-mile cycles while listening to all my favourite music loudly through my earphones.

On the positive side of ADHD, your mind takes shortcuts. In certain cases it thinks faster than neurotypical people. Through the way an ADHD person's mind works, you can think outside of the box and become very creative. Weirdly, the self-doubt and sometimes lack of confidence that comes with ADHD was helping me to stay grounded and prevented me from taking myself too seriously. All these changes going on in my life while I was completely oblivious to having ADHD, I was self-medicating, and it seems like only my subconscious knew.

So eventually returning to London was probably made more fun all because of the way my ADHD mind worked. The nostalgia, the little memory beams of light I had left there when I was younger. All because I would stand and have moments of hyperfocus, where I took in everything around me and thought to myself, *Will I ever be back here again?* Only to visit these same places twenty years later and pick up those same thoughts like it was only yesterday. But it was also the real satisfaction that my earlier questions were answered. I did return and with someone I love, with a bit of money in our pockets that gave us the freedom to do almost whatever we wanted.

On a final note, it was only after writing my first book that I eventually learned of my ADHD. It has been a great relief for me. I still suffer and have my moments, but I now have a better understanding so it's much easier to manage it. One other thing that has come from my writing is through my many hours of research and hard work, I've managed to get in touch with so many people from my past. Like me, many of them have been scattered to the four corners of the earth.

I fully appreciate that London means many things to lots of different people, and that there are so many other places and experiences I've yet to try. It's only my version of London, which I'm hoping many people will still be able to relate to. Nicky and I have spoken to a lot of waiters and reception staff who came from other cities in Europe and further afield, but their opinion was always the same. Once you worked in London, it was difficult for other places to compete.

I knew when people left our hotel in Fuerteventura they would stare out of the coaches and watch other people walking in and out of the complex, wishing that was them. In their minds they were already desperately planning their next visit to their spiritual home, The Pleasure Dome. I had the very same feeling as the taxi drew away from the Le Meridien, looking at all the people walking around Piccadilly, knowing as soon as we got back to Fuerteventura, I'd start planning my next return. We spent most of our lives on what seemed a desert island that we missed what some people might call the real world, but more importantly, I had a lot of deep emotional ties to London and returning was made that little bit more special because it had been one of my life's personal achievements.

Samuel Johnson was famously quoted as saying, 'when a man is tired of London, he is tired of life, for there is in London all that life can afford.' Well, you certainly can't argue with that.

ABOUT THE AUTHOR

The author has had a varied life and ended up settling down on the island of Fuerteventura for a good number of years, working as an entertainer in a small but popular hotel. Now in his later years he has settled back in the UK and decided to put his creative energies into his writing.

Two of the author's other books also available on Amazon are:

The Pleasure Dome Right in the Heart of Paradise

and

My Diary Harry, Evie and Charlie's Great Adventure

Gary can also be followed on Facebook under: Gary Johnston Smith

On Instagram under: Garyjohnstonsmith

On TicTok: Gary Johnston Smith

Printed in Great Britain
by Amazon